THE VAMPIRE GENESIS

THE VAMPIRE GENESIS

BY

JON FRANKOW

DEDICATION

This book is dedicated to the survivors and heroes of Hurricane Katrina.

It is also dedicated to everyone who took a chance on Archer Sweet the first time...this book is possible because you believed. I hope his journey will exceed your expectations!

Finally, to my father Edward, who never got to see this book. Your pain is gone, the burden lifted. Go in peace.

ACKNOWLEDGEMENTS

None of this would be possible without the amazing support and, as she'll tell you, suffering of my wife Kelly. H. Christine Lindblom, Leslie "Klutzy" Christ and the band of happy campers at The Author's Press. A nod of appreciation goes to Robyn Franckowiak, Michele Mercer, Gavin Redden, Beth Ficarro, Kathy Price, and Steve Kruep, for their thoughts, suggestions, and reactions to this work.

Special thanks go to Christopher Knight and Robert Lomas for planting the initial seeds with their meticulous research found in The Hiram Key, Amber Morgaine for her extensive knowledge of herbs and Mimi Lansou the proprietress of *Esoterica* in New Orleans for allowing me to mention her fantastic occult goods shop in these pages. Thanks also to Rene Lazier of Haunted History Tours for giving me the idea that vampires could be invisible. Get well soon, *mon ami*. A special thanks to Rolena Horn. Thanks to Judith A. Krize, *The Flychick* who gave me an interest in the occult. I miss you. Thanks most of all to The Holy Roman Catholic Church for providing so much convenient fodder. I love you most of all.

This is a work of fiction. All characters live in the mind of the author and are not inspired by actual events or people, living or undead. As always, a word of apology to those devoted to The Craft and the Catholic Church, from which I have so deeply and cavalierly drawn. As often as possible, I tried to remain true to ritual and form, but as with any work of fiction, certain license needed to be taken to help it all come together. All errors are my own.

PROLOGUE

Turkey, 20 May AD 325

How weak these humans, how pathetic, *his thoughts acid, his serene mood blemished only by the deep contempt he felt every time his gaze fell upon the sniveling wretch before him.* How easily manipulated and cowed they are.

"*An accord is struck then, between thee and me? We will tend your pitiful flock. In return, thou shalt be permitted to leave this gathering with thy head upon thy shoulders and thy tongue in thy head. Should this pact be violated, thy tongue will be the least of thy worries.*"

The trembling petitioner knelt on the cold tile floor, his reed-thin frame shaking uncontrollably beneath his heavy ceremonial robes. The supplicant nodded his head, grateful he was not expected to stand and allow his body to betray his stark terror. "*Y-yes...my master. The bond is made, it will forever remain unbroken.*"

"*Very well. Thou and thy pathetic puppets may leave my sight comforted by the easing of your burden. These petty quibbles over stuff and nonsense shall be no more.*" *The words flowing honey sweet, but dripping scorn, came reverberating from the tongue of the conqueror. Smiling suddenly, the speaker's usually beatific face split into an ugly visage of exultation, greed and mirth,* "*We have a taste for other things.*"

Staggered by the evil reflected in that face, the supplicant summoned his rapidly shriveling nerve, frantically grabbing the hems of his robes and hastened from the room trying, but failing to retain a modicum of dignity. It is over, thought the man rushing back to his brothers waiting for final word of the bargaining. Shivering, he felt a warm breeze across his face. It's as if The Morning Star himself beats his wings in wicked triumph. It is over and all of mankind will suffer for our weakness, politics and pettiness. We have failed. Heavenly Father above, we have failed you and our charges this day.

CHAPTER 1

LIFE IS A patently unfair bitch. An awful, uncaring, frequently cruel, self-indulgent divinity that keeps us all near to hand if only to serve her sick and deluded flights of fancy. Case in point, the rotten day for two inquisitive, intelligent young people stuck indoors on a fine autumn day.

The two women, girls really, sat huddled amidst a large stack of books, leafing through them all, one by one, page by page, illuminated by an ancient, battered, Coleman camping lantern and some old, brittle, black-turned-to-green candles they had found in a kitchen drawer shortly before ascending to the forbidding, musty, attic to work.

Joella Rodsell and Cynthia Crow, freshmen rooming together at Tulane, had been best friends since preschool. Initially hesitant about the task of cleaning out Joella's recently deceased grandmother's home, the drudgery of the morning was quickly forgotten when Cynthia found a diary secreted away at the bottom of a dresser drawer. With it was a key that opened a large cedar-lined steamer trunk in the attic. It was filled top to bottom with books, rolls of parchment in languages they couldn't always read, and individual pieces of paper whose edges crumbled to dust when they tried to lift them from the box. "Jo, where do you think your Gran got all of this? I didn't see anything in her diary about these things, just a couple of short entries in

Italian, and this key taped to the page giving the location where your Gran stored the box."

"Ya got me, Cyndi. Gran was a real odd duck; you know that. She was the one that got us into Wicca. Remember how pissed your Mom was when she found the altar in your room?"

Cyndi cringed at the memory, then giggled. "Yeah, but neither of us ever got as into it as your Gran did. She was practically a Hoodoo, putting salt in doorways and windows, coffin nails in lines on the floor here, there, and yonder. Do you still have your *gris-gris* bag she made us last year? Mine stank like it had dead fish parts in it. And what was up with the way she was always on some fast and cleansing ritual every time I saw her?"

"It's not shit if you believe, you wannabe witch. Gran always believed you were more serious about Wicca than I was because you were smarter."

"Uh-uh," replied Cyndi defensively. "Just because I have Indian blood in me and speak a couple of languages, she thought I was more mystical. She never said smarter, honey." Picking up another tome, Cyndi carefully started leafing through it, ignoring Joella and her continuing rant about whom her grandmother liked better. Picking up the next scroll, her breath caught in her throat audibly as she scanned it.

"What," asked Joella sullenly. She hadn't been able to make heads or tails of very much of what they had looked at so far. "Did you find the mystery of eternal life?"

"Huh-uh, Jo, just something really freaky. Listen to this:
'Beware ye sinner, beware ye saint!
Who brings about the darkest taint,
will see their blood before they die.
Safe for none, when west sets the sun.
Darkness falls on thee who summon.
What can't be named, swift and sure it has begun,
do not tarry, thou must run!
Who reads this spell, shall sow true hell.
For the bane of man is now upon thee."

"Brr. Cree-py, Cyndi. Where on the Goddess' great world did you come up with that?" Standing and stretching, Jo made her way through the clutter to look over Cyndi's shoulder at the ancient looking page. "How did you read that?"

"It's right here in grey and yellow. The ink is so old and faded; it's almost disappeared from the page. I just read it to myself, then gave you a basic translation. I'm pretty sure I got it right, or very close at least. Anyway, I think it flows better in English."

Jo edged her way around the stacks crossing her legs beneath her as she sat on the dusty floor of the dormer facing Cyndi and the scroll still in her lap. Looking down, Jo squinted again at the page to make out the squiggly letters, as if reading upside down would help it make more sense. After another moment of trying to decipher it, said, "Okay brain bitch, what dead language is that?"

"Temper, temper, sweetheart, there are no dead languages, only dormant minds. It's an old dialect, almost a direct translation from Aramaic to Latin. Remember when my Dad was doing that summer semester abroad last year, and I got to tag along? Well, Dad earned some extra Euros translating some old Italian diaries and textbooks from their original Latin to English for a few of the smaller country churches. Most of it was worthless, unless you're a fan of individual church and familial history or just enjoy reading about life in a small hamlet or village from a local priest or Abbot's perspective. I secretly think Dad instilled my gift for language when I was learning to talk, because..."

"Yeah, yeah, I remember. That was the worst summer of my life, running plantation tours in that Goddess awful period piece dress. You came back from Italy all tan and relaxed, and I was pasty and uptight from lack of sunlight. I couldn't get the smell of sweaty wool from that costume off of me for weeks."

"Don't interrupt when I'm on a roll, girl, or I'll smite you with my wand. Just let me finish, okay?"

"Brain Bitch," muttered Joella.

"Bitch Goddess, Jo. Let's get it right, shall we?" Cyndi winked and Jo stuck out her tongue. "Long story short, I picked up about three dialects of Latin that summer, and this is sort of similar to one of them. It sounds much more ominous in English. Here, listen." Cyndi read it again in Latin, her cadence slower and somewhat clumsy as she pronounced words from a long forgotten and dormant tongue.

"You're right," Joella said when Cyndi was finished reading it the third time, "It does sound scarier in English, but after you finished the Latin version, I felt a cold chill, like an icicle was melting down my back, seeping through the skin, dancing on my nerves and sinking into the marrow of my bones. Yech!"

Cyndi shivered, physically agreeing with Joella's assessment, and as she exhaled, she noticed she could see her breath steaming from her mouth. "The temperature must have taken a real nosedive," she said, rubbing her goose fleshy arms with glacial palms.

"M- May- Maybe the f-f-furnace s-shut off," Joella replied, her teeth beginning to chatter, clacking like the rails of the streetcar that rumbled past about four blocks away.

"It's only October. Louisiana never gets this cold." Icy fingers danced up and down her spinal cord like a concert pianist tickling the ivories, "I don't like this, Joella. Something is really setting my warning bells off."

"Don't be silly. You frightened yourself with that stupid poem, that's all. Hell, it doesn't even rhyme, in either language. Let's pack the books away and get back to work. That'll warm us right up."

"I don't think that was a poem, Jo. The more I think about it, I think it sounded more like an incantation to me, or maybe a kind of warning about something dangerous."

Jo was about to tell her what she thought of that idea, when she heard the voices, dry as corn husks rattling in a light wind, whisper in her head, "I claim the ignorant one my brother. They're always so very satisfying when they're this vapid. You may take the sorceress, slightly less sweet, but a delicacy on a par with little else." Joella spun back to face Cyndi, and saw the horror etched on her face. She had heard it too!

Screaming, they turned to run for the folding ladder leading back down to the ground level of the house. The ladder creaked with their effort to push their way down simultaneously. Jo had her foot on the third stair heading to the ground floor, Cyndi one rung behind her, when they were both wrenched violently back into the attic by unseen arms of banded steel unrelenting as a pit bull locked onto the throat of its enemy.

Later none of the neighbors would remember hearing any noise coming from the house. It was as still as a crypt.

CHAPTER 2

ARCHER SWEET STROLLED contentedly down the Moon Walk, whistling tunelessly; heedless of the people who turned to gawk at such frivolity. Stopping briefly, he watched with wondering eyes the blaze of light cresting the horizon, creating a dazzling corona as the Mississippi River reflected the early morning sunlight. He enjoyed the moment, freezing the image as a mental watercolor, then crossed the streetcar tracks, taking the gray granite stairs down to street level on Decatur. The colors of the awakening city were awe inspiring as he passed Jackson Square and enjoyed the autumnal burst of hues and subtle shades displayed by the few hardwood trees as they began to shed their summer coat and begin their long winter's rest. This was Archer's favorite time of year no matter where he lived. The stroll, while slightly out of the way from where he was going, was worth the extra time and distance. He had only called New Orleans home for the past five months. It had taken nearly two years following the death of his wife, Liz, before he decided to sell their old house in Jefferson trading it in for a large, slightly dilapidated apartment over a vacant store front on the corner of Toulouse and Burgundy Streets. He had spent a lot of time and a fair amount of money to open a mystical supply shop. The fact that he owned the property made bearable every trial and tribulation he endured in the too-long neglected apartment as he slowly renovated it, room by room.

If only tourists knew that the only better time than early spring in New Orleans was autumn. Then again, he thought, too many out-of-towners might spoil the vibe. October was on average the driest month of the year, with sunny skies and temperatures that usually peaked in the upper seventies only dipping in to the mid-fifties some nights. All in all, who could ask for much more? The Audubon Zoo held their annual Louisiana Swamp Festival to start the month, and Boo at the Zoo to end it. In between, there was Oktoberfest on the weekends, but what was New Orleans on a weekend without a party? The Fresh Art Festival and Steel Pony Express didn't swell the city to bursting like Mardi Gras, Jazz Fest, Southern Decadence, or The Sugar Bowl always did, so Archer decided not to count them as weekend parties.

A brief pungent waft of dry hay and stagnant urine from the line of mule drawn carriages smacked Archer in the nose in one breath, and the heavenly aromas of Café Du Monde beckoned with the shifting of the breeze; such was the way of things in the French Quarter. Archer stifled a sudden compulsion to stop in for a beignet and café au lait until he was across the street past Jackson Square, upwind of the temptation. Crossing the street near the French Market, he turned his attention to the address scrawled on his delivery card. He pushed open the wire door between the shops, entering the small alley that led to a quiet, calm courtyard brimming with wisteria, ferns, and a single magnolia tree battling to stave off its winter slumber.

Archer rang the painted buzzer by the doorway and in moments, a young looking, attractive face peered out through the heavy glass in the top center of the door. The face vanished briefly and Archer heard the sound of locks disengaging and bolts thrown open. The thick door swung open to reveal the rest of the woman, all dimples and long thick legs disappearing under an extra large T-shirt and black panties.

"Good morning, I have a delivery for Claudette Brendel, from Blessed Be. Are you she," he asked, kicking himself mentally for the awkward, albeit correct, turn of phrase.

"Mm-hmm. Yup. No, she's not here," the girl replied as she nibbled distractedly at a frizzy lock from her full mane of burnt toast-colored hair, shot through with fading henna highlights. Her left hand, with its classically tapered fingers adorned with henna tattoos that coiled up and down her chubby arms, brushed absently through her unruly locks. She was cute, in an earthy sort of way that made Archer's hormones surge, but seemed mentally vacant, emotionally unavailable, or more likely stoned. Still, Archer found himself distracted, wondering how small her head would be without the leonine mane of wild tresses, and daydreaming about how luxurious the feel of them would be as he ran his fingers through them.

"Okay then." Archer shook himself mentally. "Could you let her know that I came by with her supplies, and tell her she can come pick them up at her convenience at the store, since she missed our appointment time? That is, unless you want to pay for it and let her reimburse you? It'd sure be a shame to lug all of this back over to Toulouse and then have her bring it all back here again."

"Yeah, that would be a drag. Oh, wait! Claude left some cash on her nightstand for a delivery, a grimoire, a book about spell work, and potion ingredients, I think. Where'd you say you were from again?"

"Blessed Be," Archer replied as cheerfully as he could. "The best specialty store in town for all of your magical needs. We deliver to your doorstep." Archer had wanted to call his store The Harry Pottery Barn, but his friend Trick Boulieux had convinced him it was too close to infringement on two dynasties. Besides, he had said, "Wha' kinda serious practitioner would go to a store with such a dumb-ass name? Think 'bout it. You'll be swallowed up in a sea of tourists an' lawsuits. What else ya got?" Archer settled for his second favorite, Blessed Be.

"Claudette didn't come home last night, ya know? So I guess I'll get the money and if it's not for you, she can deal with it later. Hold on." The girl flounced away, her untamed locks trailing behind like silken hydras, narrowly avoiding catching some of it in the door as it closed behind her. Shortly, she returned with a bank envelope marked, Blessed Be supply money. "I guess this would be it, huh," she asked, her voice still sounding sleepy or dopey; to Archer, he couldn't decide on which dwarf.

He took the envelope and peered briefly inside, handing the paper sack of individually weighed and wrapped items to the girl and smiled. "Looks like it's all here. Please thank her for me, and I hope she comes back to visit us again soon."

"I just hope she comes back," mumbled the girl, as she turned from Archer to walk back inside with the bag of supplies. "It's just such a reckless thing, spending the night out with someone you don't know, ya know?" Not waiting for a response, talking to herself she closed the door, cutting off her stream of verbal meandering.

Archer left shaking his head as he pocketed the money and began his walk back to his store, choosing to pass briskly along the flat, even slate of the pedestrian walk on St. Ann Street. He passed the early arriving fortune tellers and artists, vying for the best spot on the mall, their ennui toward another day of the tourist trade hung heavily, at least until they got their coffee.

Until he got his feet under him, as the owner, proprietor, and only employee of Blessed Be, he wanted to make sure the doors were open on time every morning for anyone who might need something.

Business was slowly picking up as word got around the Wicca and Neo-Pagan community that he was open for business. They could find good merchandise at fair prices, and he delivered. Pretty soon, he would have to hire someone to take over the deliveries and maybe man the shop part time so he could have some semblance of a social life again. He was almost as time strapped running his store solo as he and Trick had been running The Moonlight Mission, a homeless shelter on the edge of the French Quarter. Trick at least had wised up finally hiring a couple of administrators after Archer left to open Blessed Be.

Well, he thought, scurrying along the banquette of alternating brick, concrete, and broken, uneven, slate, dry leaves swirling all about him and crunching under foot. *If it's quiet today, maybe I can get some work done in the apartments and have a drink or two tonight.* It was amazing how such a simple thing as a night out to relax seemed like an extended vacation when he thought about it.

CHAPTER 3

To his disappointment but not surprise, there was no line of customers clamoring to get in as Archer fit the key into the padlock of the set of cypress doors, and gave the left one a nudge with his hip. It shimmied a bit as the bottom of the door brushed the bare concrete floor and Archer reached to release the two slide bolts that freed the second door, letting it fall open into the store, then knelt down to grab his daily copy of *The Times-Picayune*.

"Morning guys", he said to his two permanent residents as he had each day since he had found them at an estate sale in Shreveport. "You two have a good night? Didn't make too much mischief, I hope." He continued to make one-sided small talk with them as he lugged the two massive, carved granite trolls to their post by the doors. They were a matched set at twenty-four inches high and nearly two hundred fifty pounds apiece. Their knubbly skin was the color of wet cement and tattered, severely faded britches and vests had been painted on to them. Their postures were frozen with their backs slightly hunched, broad shoulders just a bit rounded, massive arms folded, and self-satisfied smirks dominating their long flat faces. Their job-and they did it well-was keeping the doors from swinging shut in the wind or banging against the walls as patrons passed in and out of the shop throughout the day.

He told curious patrons that he had found the pair at the estate sale the week before he opened Blessed Be, but it was more like they found him. Practically buried under a number of tapestries, the little voice in his head told him to dig in and see what lie beneath. He had been excited to find them, falling instantly for their eclectic charm, even though he could think of no real use they could serve. Archer found himself shelling out the asking price to the incredulous executor. He didn't know exactly why they seemed to call to him, but his inner voice had become an increasingly more prominent part of his life, learning long ago to act on those feelings and hunches when they made their presence felt. Not only did he overpay for the pair, but he nearly gave himself a hernia trying to move them until the estate had let him borrow a hand truck and an assistant to get the trolls into the back of his beat up Isuzu Rodeo. He brought them to the shop and had Trick come over to help him unload the behemoth brothers. He named them Trold and Berg, for their Swedish and Danish forebears, and planned to eventually restore them to their full color and glory.

Until then, the twin trolls stood silent vigil and bid every prospective customer a quiet greeting upon entering the shop. When he had no customers in the shop, he would occasionally run suggestions by the taciturn pair about how something should be placed or decorated within the store; after all, they lived there too. Since opening, he had received numerous offers from passersby to sell Trold and Berg, but he knew he could never do that, despite some of the outrageous tenders made.

Archer pulled a feather duster from behind the glass display that also served as his cash register and credit card portal area and gave the assortment of candles, books, and herb jars a quick brush. Every time he did any work upstairs plaster dust, fine as sand and light as ash, managed to coat nearly every square inch of everything in the shop, even when he prepared and laid drop clothes over shelves and displays. He watched the motes of dust swirl away like small galaxies floating through the streaks of sunlight that penetrated the plantation shutters over the display windows.

Recognizing that chasing the powdery silt around the store was an unwinnable war, he quit the battlefield and went outside to his cozy courtyard checking on the small garden he had started. It was here that he hoped to soon have his own patch of protective herbs for personal use or retail sale, depending on his yield and need.

He had squeezed as many together as he thought could thrive in such close quarters. Even though he knew better, he was hoping to see buds of basil, dill, bay, cinquefoil, yarrow, and sage breaking the rich loamy soil before Spring. He had avoided planting rosemary, not knowing if his allergic rash and hives would return just by working with it.

Much of the courtyard's old growth shrubbery and trees had died or were unhealthy when he moved in, so he had invested in some trees and ground cover that would be functional as well as ornamental. Beside the small trickling fountain that flowed into a slow drained cistern, he had planted a pair of willow trees, hoping the copious amount of fresh water would encourage rapid growth. Along with the willow, he planted a slender rowan tree and a silver birch on one side of the courtyard and a healthy oak and ash tree on the other.

On the pathway to the garden from the small refurbished slate patio, he had planted rows of marigolds, lavender, and sunflowers. Along the far wall of the courtyard, he found space to plant a juniper tree, a blackberry and an elderberry bush, and a section for ginseng and mandrake. The wisteria and wild jasmine that were in the courtyard when he bought the property grew ubiquitously up and across the trellises to help keep the courtyard cool and smelling fresh when the days grew hot.

Until spring, he just let his imagination take over and pictured the entire space in full bloom. Under Toinetta's insightful tutelage, he had learned the value of positive thought in mastering skills and subtly shifting the ripples of reality. With fate in his favor, as well as enough wortcunning and herbal knowledge, he felt confident in his solo planting forays. Thinking good thoughts in his garden would have seemed like an exercise in futility to him before his fateful battle with a psychic revenant. In the aftermath, he had learned that absolutely nothing was a waste of time, and as finite beings, not even the smallest of things should ever be taken for granted.

He doted on his planting layout for a few moments and was contemplating a transplant of the elderberry to allow it more space to thrive when he heard the high tinkling note of his customer bell going off. Dipping his hands quickly in the cistern and grabbing a small grimy hand towel he walked back inside, drying his hands along the way. Tossing the towel on the long empty table near his cluttered desk, he stepped through the rag curtain that separated his floor space from his office and private apartment entrance.

Flicking his eyes to the wall clock over the door, a wooden rendering of a gallows with a hanged man swinging as the pendulum, he realized it was still too early for what he used to call 'lookie-loos' when he was a cop, but now simply referred to as foot traffic, or tourists. Hopefully, it was a legitimate paying customer, but he saw no one browsing his book shelves, examining his candles, or even smirking at the more exotic curios that the average shopper would find more amusing than useful. Perplexed, he turned to make his way behind the high glass display case and counter, and bumped squarely into her as she rose from examining his collection of amulets and pendants.

She was absolutely stunning, and something about her fired Archer's senses on a higher level than he had ever felt. She was tall, a touch over six feet, her body lithe and willowy but with a hint of iron in her open easy stance. Her complexion was olive, with raven black hair shot through with highlights the color of burnt almond, and the most stunning limpid blue eyes he had ever seen. Archer had an unexpected overwhelming compulsion to growl from deep in his throat, take her lustily in his arms, devouring her sensuality, tearing off her clothing and…holy shit! He shook his head to clear his mental slate of those carnal images and reassert his self-control.

He had taken her all in at a single glance as he recovered from the physical contact and reached to steady her from their collision, but she stepped away fluidly, a quirky, knowing, yet shy, smile flitted across her rosebud lips as she took a moment to eye Archer from his toes to his suddenly perspiring brow.

"Sorry," Archer said as he moved to put the display case between them. "I'm not usually so clumsy as to stampede my customers, I was just out back in the courtyard checking on some things." He blushed slightly as he realized he was blithering, but the lust, he noticed, had faded some as their proximity decreased.

"So this is Blessed Be? I have walked by here a number of times and have not had the opportunity to come inside." Her voice was full, throaty, and lightly accented in a way that sounded alternately Spanish and Baltic. Archer had never heard anything like it and couldn't even hazard a guess about her origins. He realized she was no longer speaking and was looking at him expectantly.

"This is my day to be sorry, I guess." Archer replied stupidly, trying not to let his voice sound as distracted and off-center than he was. "I have had so much going on recently, a lot of things on my mind and hardly any sleep, I kind of zoned out for a moment. It's nothing personal; believe me. *Yes it is. She's driving me wild!* "Could you repeat what you said after you said you had been by but hadn't had time to stop in?"

She frowned slightly, her delicate slightly upturned nose wrinkled almost imperceptively as she did. Archer thought she seemed disappointed. Here was a man who might be different, but like so many others he was thrown off balance by her looks. Wondering if she might have been hoping for better, he lost his train of thought as she reiterated, "Yes, I was saying it was convenient for this store to be open so near to where I live. I am in constant need of good quality herbs and items, and this location is as convenient to me as an ATM machine situated next to a tavern; perfect placement. Do you own it, or just keep an eye on the place?"

Even her speech was different, accent not withstanding. She seemed to be practicing her informal banter and only succeeding part of the time. Her carriage screamed refinement, maybe privilege, but her attire and attitude tried with little success to make a different statement. For the first time in his life, Archer found himself uncomfortable around a beautiful woman, but if she lived so close and would frequent his store, he had to get over that, and fast.

"My apologies. It seems my manners are as clumsy as my body this morning." He extended his hand over the counter, grateful that he had wiped it dry and clean before coming back to the shop. "My name is Archer Sweet, and I own Blessed Be. Welcome, feel free to browse. I don't have everything I've ordered in stock yet, but most of it is here. Let me know when you are ready and I'll be happy to help in any way I can."

She enveloped his hand in a firm grip but did not shake it. Her long tapered fingers lingered under on his wrist, as if checking his fluttering pulse. She caught his gaze with her own and held it for a moment before releasing both simultaneously. "A pleasure. I will look while you prepare my order if that is acceptable. I need one ounce each of Dragon's Blood, Purple Loosestrife, Frankincense, Blood Root and a three-ounce cutting of Mandrigora. Do you have all of these things?"

"Yep. And if by Mandrigora, you're asking for Mandrake Root, I have that too. If not, I'd have to say no. Did I pass?"

"An easy test, that." she replied, her voice ominous yet mischievous. "I've no doubt there will be others," she added distractedly, appearing completely absorbed by the labels of the pre-made tinctures on the display carousel.

"I do believe I'll be looking forward to it," he responded playfully, then grunted as he reached for the top shelf and the container of Dragon's Blood. "That means you'll be coming by now and then?"

"So long as you have what I need, Shopkeeper. So long as you have what I need. I noticed you did not ask me for my name or about my accent." She turned around and faced the counter, re-evaluating the man as Archer measured out each ingredient individually onto a small apothecary scale. "Most men ask me these things as soon as I open my mouth."

"You didn't ask how much I charge for what you've ordered, which is usually the first thing I hear from anyone in here. Unless you're paying me on credit, I don't need to know your name, but if you're going to be a steady customer, and you decide to tell me, I'd be pleased to know it. As for your background, well, the past is a tricky thing. Sometimes it's private, sometimes it haunts, and sometimes it simply gets in the way. What you choose to tell me is all I will ever know, even though I may be curious."

Archer replaced the Dragon's Blood container on the shelf, wrapped her purchases, and collected cash from his client in silence, all the while stealing surreptitious glances at every part of her, using that time to drink her in slowly. The fiery desire in his belly had cooled more with her attitude. Relieved to begin to feel more normal, or at least slightly less uncomfortable around her, he decided the vague unease she projected now was much more acceptable to his self-control than the radiant heat she exuded when they first touched. Her salmon pink sweater, denim jacket and pocketless, thin leg, blue jeans were stylish and accentuated her every curve, but how she wore her attire was something he could enjoy, not a feeling to dread. As he placed the money in the cash register, made change and handed her the small paper bag with her herbs, he said, "Thanks for giving me the business. I do hope to see you again when you are ready for more."

"I'll be back," she replied crisply as she turned to leave. "When we are both ready." She smiled, then and Archer was struck by her dazzlingly perfect, gleaming pearlies, especially her slightly oversized incisors. "Goodbye, Shopkeeper."

Archer leaned against the counter for a moment, replaying in his mind his encounter with what felt like a force of nature, his senses still tingling with her presence, not just her beauty. He walked over to the front doors. Resting his hands lightly on Trold and Berg, he turned his head in the direction she had walked, and asked the stoic pair what they thought of her, The Nameless One.

He did not see that she had stopped just around the corner from his storefront, leaning against the cool concrete of the building, catching her breath; her pupils dilated with an awkward mélange of lust, joy, and a touch of fear. He couldn't have guessed that no one, man or woman had ever stirred such a profound yearning in the deepest recesses of her solitary existence.

So befuddled was she that she hardly noticed the passenger a taxi cab discharged practically at her feet. An ageless elegant black woman who walked directly past her toward Blessed Be, folded newspaper under her robed arm, necklaces, earrings, and dozens of bangles jingling pleasantly as she moved. The passenger's eyes remained glued to the other's face until she had disappeared from sight. The woman straightened and her nostrils flared wide as she caught the vaguest hint of Archer Sweet lingering about the passenger, reminiscent of a wistfully, distant fond memory of love lost, swirling away on the wind of the new day.

CHAPTER 4

WHO-WEE," SAID Toinetta Carondolet as she fanned the air with her newspaper. "Did your entire stock of love charm break this morning, shugah? There are some serious pheromones up in here."

"Nah, I wish." Archer turned to look at his mentor. "Did you see that goddess in the pink sweater and blue jeans on your way in? I tell you, Toinetta, she put thoughts into my head that I haven't felt for, well, ever. After Liz, I never thought I would have such intense feelings for a woman again, especially for one I don't know. Hell, I don't even know her name. She couldn't be bothered to tell me. How could someone I just met make me feel so helpless? It was, she was, overwhelming. My brain slipped into neutral for a few minutes."

"Ah, don't candy coat it, Archer, how didja really feel" Toinetta asked, a hint of a smile playing across her eyes and lips for just an instant before her jovial demeanor vanished, replaced by worry. "Honestly, shugah, someone with that much energy, that can make you hum like an over wound spring will be back, count on it. I hate using the moth to an open flame analogy, but for the attraction to be that strong in an instant, your auras must have crossed and meshed, if only briefly, and that can be overwhelming."

"Our auras crossed up? Is that like crossing the streams in

Ghostbusters?"

Toinetta looked confused.

"Don't worry, stupid joke. Crossing auras sounds like it could be dangerous if she can feel me on that level, or vice versa. What can I do? I've got to be able to keep her out of my head or I'll never be able to think about anything else. I can't afford that right now."

"Try not to think about it. Until she comes back, there's nothing for it, and worry just wastes time and energy. Meanwhile, have you seen this?" She plopped her copy of *The Times-Picayune* on the glass display counter, turned to an article in the Metro section on page one, beneath the fold.

Tulane Roommates Found Dead.

Two Freshman co-eds, Joella Rodsell and Cynthia Crow, both 19 and natives of Kenner, Louisiana were found dead late yesterday evening in the home of Rodsell's deceased grandmother. David Rodsell, the father of one of the deceased, stated that the two girls had been cleaning out the home of Mr. Rodsell's grandmother and did not return home for dinner. The bodies were discovered in the attic by Rodsell who quickly called 911.

The pair was pronounced dead on the scene by the Parish Medical Examiner, cause of death unknown, pending autopsies. The M.E. refused to speculate on possible causes of death stating only that the nature of the deaths appeared to be "highly unusual…".

Archer stopped reading and gazed up at Toinetta. "So what does this have to do with us? It's a shame, but it doesn't sound too ominous."

"I got sick yesterday afternoon Archer, just overcome suddenly with a violent fit of panic then nausea. What did the word 'unusual' mean when you were a detective and had to release a story to the media?"

Shaking his head, Archer replied, "Usually it meant there was something we knew about the crime, some aspect or clue that we were withholding from the public, to prevent copy cat killings or to use as a fail safe if some loon turned themselves in confessing to the crime. If they didn't know the details we had held back, they got a boot in the butt right out the door. If they had those little nuggets of truth that went unreported, then they got to stick around for a while.

"I thought so."

"Smug is not a good look for you, Toinetta, but you're right. There's something missing there, but it's not our place to follow behind a police investigation every time something like this catches our eye. I'm not a cop anymore, Toinetta. Trick may still be a consultant for the Treasury on cases, but that day-to-day part of my life is over."

"I'm not convinced, Archer. Once a cop, always a cop. It's part of your makeup, who you are. You couldn't keep your nose out of a mystery if your life depended on it."

"Just watch me. I can ignore the nagging voice. I'm still not convinced there's anything otherworldly about the murder of those two girls. There's enough evil in man; let's not go looking for something worse."

Toinetta sighed. "I suppose you have a point. There's a difference between what I know I know and what I think I know. But mark my words, we're going to see a whole lot more of these kind of articles, and soon."

Archer's shrug betrayed his ambivalence. "So noted. Now what's on tap today? If my lesson can wait a little, if you have time, you can talk to me while I finish a little bit of stocking and inventory, and I can show you the courtyard. I think you'll like what I've done. It should be awesome come the spring."

Toinetta had been an invaluable resource since the incident with the psychic revenant. When they first met, she opened her heart to Archer as if he were the prodigal son, sharing her wisdom, experience, and knowledge of the supernatural. She had remained a staunch friend after his wife, Liz died, becoming not only a mentor, but a dear friend. With her help and more mental exercise then he cared to admit he had been able to hone and expand his abilities, primarily strengthening his shielding and cultivating his intuition to the level that he could accurately anticipate the word and actions of others. The fact that he could live in such a psychically active section of an area as old as the French Quarter was testament to the many things that, now, seemed second nature. He let the dead speak when he needed to hear them. His psychic ability had sharpened to the point that not even Toinetta could get into his mind all of the time, and he was even able to move small objects short distances, a limited form of telekinesis.

Privately, Toinetta hoped that skill would never develop; it was a potentially dangerous and powerful weapon. Fortunately, the effort of such small successes taxed him so greatly that he would usually pass out.

During the tour of the garden, she quizzed Archer on his lessons, mixing old work with new queries.

"How do you find spirit companions when you meditate?"

Archer sniffed indignantly. "It depends on your preference and what you're looking for. Personally, I visualize a tall, ancient, tree with wide spreading boughs and branches that disappears into the clouds. The branches are easy to climb and as I ascend, I either concentrate on my questions, or empty my mind completely to make it easier to create a bond with a new entity. Once the top is reached, you wait until an animal finds you, a spirit ally in the guise of the totem that can most help you."

Toinetta reached out with her mind, testing Archer's shielding, trying to penetrate them and throw him off-balance. Archer reached up and pulled a crisp brown leaf from the rowan tree and rolled it through his fingers, appearing intent on the tactile sensation of the leaf disintegrating. He felt his mentor testing him and opened himself to the energy around him, drawing an extra boost for his shielding. Toinetta gasped involuntarily as she thought she sensed a tiny gap, a crack in his mental shield that she could worry like a loose thread until she had unraveled his defense. Then she could lecture him on the importance of practicing and constantly striving to improve.

"Archer, Archer, I found my doorway. I'm coming in, shugah, best prepare for a headache."

Archer didn't reply, letting her widen the hole he had left for her, then he visualized a spider, dropping in behind her, weaving an elaborate web at her back. When Toinetta noticed what had happened, she marshaled herself and pushed forcefully into the hole, widening it slightly. The web held and the trap was sprung as he allowed his mental picture to split, adding another spider directly in front of her, casting its web with manic precision.

Toinetta shook her head and Archer broke the contact. "That's just wrong, shugah. Trapping an old woman like that and using her worst fear to do it!"

"I haven't had a lot of time to work on anything new lately, but I've been practicing what I know. I didn't know about your dislike of spiders until you tried to sneak into the loophole I left for you. It just kind of came to me."

"You've surpassed your teacher yet again, boy. Sensing others' fears and phobias through psychic contact? Whee-oo! I've read of adepts being able to do that after years of study, but you are no adept."

"Was I just complimented or insulted?"

"Shugah, I don't know. I wish we knew who your birth parents were, they've bred someone in you that to my way of thinking is boundless in potential."

"I don't need to know anything about the people who created me, the ones who raised me are just fine," he replied tersely, and walked back inside the shop.

"Archer, c'mon you know what I'm talking about, don't be so pig-headed about it. You can do things without tutelage that I've only read about." The door squeaking closed as Archer walked back inside was his only reply.

The tour obviously concluded, Toinetta followed Archer back into the store and joined him in the cozy little office area where he was warming a pot of fresh brewed dandelion tea on a hot plate. He poured two cups and carried them over to the table where Toinetta was sitting. Toinetta took a grateful sip, then set her cup down and waited until the taste of the bitter brew passed her tongue.

"Archer, shugah, I hope you come around a little quicker to my way of thinking about those two girls. That nice man who tried to rescue Liz, he's still a cop, isn't he? Could you maybe have him look into any murders in the adjoining parishes that could fit the description of 'unusual' and keep you informed? He still has access to the reports with the 'unusual' details and could spot any trends, maybe give us a jumping off point."

Toinetta was referring to Archer's last partner, when he was with the Jefferson Parish Narcotics Task Force, Wendell Pierce. Pierce was present when the a psychic revenant, had attacked Archer; he had helped investigate the disappearance of Archer's wife, and suffered grievous injury from multiple stab wounds when he fought to the death with Liz Sweet's kidnapper. Unfortunately, things didn't go according to his on-the fly rescue plan and Liz was mortally wounded, dying in Pierce's arms as he struggled against his own injuries to bring her to aid.

An Internal Affairs investigation found Detective Wendell Pierce not culpable in the death of Liz Sweet, and the shooting of her kidnapper/killer to be righteous. His personal guilt, not to mention the nine grueling months of skin grafts, cosmetic surgery, and painful rehabilitation, had played havoc on his mental constitution. Pierce began to drink heavily during his convalescence. When he reported for his first day back to work reeking of bottom shelf boilermaker fumes at seven a.m., the department had suspended him indefinitely with pay. He was reinstated after he completed a certified detox program and counseling.

Wendell Pierce attended and finished what he called "clown college" and left the detox and rehab center at Oschner a seemingly better-adjusted if not changed and contented man. He did well hiding his binge drinking from his co-workers, but not from his wife, who took their two children and moved to Baton Rouge, filing for divorce and sole custody. A sober Wendell Pierce would have fought tooth and nail for his children and his marriage. He let both go and chose self-pity.

A sober Wendell Pierce would have prevented these events from happening, but revisionist history was never something Pierce enjoyed contemplating. He was a functional drunk, and so long as his wife didn't let his condition leak to their mutual friends on the force, he decided that he was okay with being left alone at home and pushing papers in the archive rooms at the station where he had little human contact. Archer had attempted several times to reach out to his old friend, and once tried an intervention with him, face to face. The end result was basically the same; emails, phone, and text messages went unanswered, and a right cross in the chops was Archer's reward for not respecting Pierce's private life.

Archer knew that Pierce still felt guilty for Liz's death. Nothing Archer could say or do seemed enough to convince Pierce that he bore no grudge or malice in his heart over his actions or the outcome. Archer had backed off and had given his friend six months and counting before trying to reach out again.

"Maybe doing a personal favor for you is just the thing Mr. Pierce needs to start working off the debt he feels he owes you, Archer."

"I'll give it a shot, you never know. Think I'll visit him though. He's less likely to make a scene if I go see him at the station and he's among colleagues," Archer replied.

"Okay, shugah, you do that and I'll be satisfied. Keep your eyes and ears open, too. A magic shop is the ideal place to hear about anything out of the ordinary in our circle."

"I agree wholeheartedly, but I need to have customers in the store before I can take notice of anyone talking about oddities. My hearing isn't that great."

"Hush now, Archer Sweet. Things are going to pick up for you soon. You've only been open a few weeks; it takes time for word to spread. Trust me, I tell all of my friends that you are head and shoulders above the other shops in town." Toinetta swirled the dregs of her tea and gazed impassively at them for a moment, then set the cup down with a chuckle. "The tea leaves say I'm going to meet a tall dark stranger soon. I always hated dregs for divination, it's too dirty, too nebulous." She looked up at Archer. "Now the last time, we were working on how to better identify your spirit allies and how best to use them once they reveal themselves to you. You said you haven't been doing your homework, but you gave me a good answer when I asked before."

Archer grimaced as he set his cup down and replied, "Between trying to get the store stocked and running, planting my garden, and renovating the upstairs, I haven't had much time for leisure activities, even ones as important as that. I've climbed the tree before and waited, but no animals have come to me."

"Okay, this is Magic 101, Archer. You already possess knowledge of a couple of your spirit allies. Who are they?"

"You mean Liz?"

"She's already proven to be a worthy guardian, a true champion, willing to cross the veil between worlds to help you. She's given you your life back, twice."

Archer smiled warmly, his memories of Liz coming to him as he lay comatose in the hospital, coaxing him out of himself, back into the world of the living, and then appearing to him again in his darkest moment of grief and despair, to tell him he had to move forward on his path.

"Yeah, I suppose if I have one true guardian, it would be my Lizard. Then there's the inner voice that guided my intuitions; I just haven't placed a form to it."

"In time, shugah, you'll come to meet and know them all. Some drift in and out of your life many times. Some are around for the long haul because of some pact you struck with them before you decided to take up this path of the Earth Walk, to mingle with humanity."

"You mean my imaginary friends weren't imaginary?"

"Probably not, at least until someone told you they were."

"Earth Walk, huh? Sounds like something you do for AIDS, or to wipe out hunger. My soul collecting canned goods for the needy, too?"

Toinetta's face tightened and she started ranting, rolling up a section of the newspaper into a wand, bangles clattering together in her fury. "Boy, don't you go sassin' me now; I'll wear you out. I swear, if I didn't know what you could do, I would walk out this door and quit wasting my time with the likes of you."

Archer hooted as he easily ducked the hollow tube of news she swung at his head, but wasn't quick enough to avoid the rap on his knuckles. Nothing hurt but his pride, he supposed.

"You gonna listen to me? You're still not left thinking. The swat to the head was designed to set you up for the hit on the hand." Toinetta dropped her makeshift club, muttering, "Fool boy still one step behind. How can you learn if you don't start using that pretty head for more than a place to store your eyeballs?"

Archer took her adorned and bangled hand in his own, patting it affectionately. "I apologize Toinetta. You know how much I need your guidance; I won't always be one step behind, but you've got to lighten up. I joke to blow off steam sometimes, like now. You've known that since the first day we met. That woman from this morning still has me firing on all cylinders. I can't concentrate anything else."

She took his hand, clasping it between both of her own. "I know, shugah, I know. Sometimes I forget how young you are, how new this still is to you. My guides told me a long time ago that you were coming and I was to help you become a force in this life, not just another lost spirit with nowhere to haunt. That's why I get frustrated."

"We've got time, Toinetta. You may be here to help me grow, but did you ever take time to consider that maybe I'm here for you to help you unclench, just a little? You've been wound tight as a nun at a strip club since the day we met. I can count on one hand, and have a finger or two left over, how often I've seen you relax and just flow. It seems to me your gifts often cloud your joy."

"I've got a finger for you to count, Archer Sweet. Guess which one it is?"

"There you go," he laughed, as she let him go and sat back, a wry smile flickering briefly across her face as she smoothed out her clothing and readjusted her bangles and bracelets. "Do you want another cup of tea?"

"Nah, shugah, I'm going to have to run, and you've got house work and studying to do." She walked around the counter and gave him a ferocious bear hug, rocking him affectionately from side to side. "Besides, your tea tastes like shit." Archer listened to her high-pitched, tinny laugh all the way out to the sidewalk, wondering if he didn't prefer her to be serious after all.

CHAPCER 5

ARCHER WAS ON a step-ladder, grooving to WTNO on his clock radio, plastering some cracks and rough patches on his office wall when his cell phone chirped, literally. He had downloaded a ring tone that sounded like a flock of song birds warbling. It was much less jarring than any of the harsh buzzing, beeping, ringing, or belching the phone did on its own, and he found it soothing. He glanced at his hip to see who was calling, then set down his small bucket of plaster and trowel, and flipped the phone open.

"Hey you Cajun bastard, how they hangin'?"

"Long, low, and complainin' 'bout their lack of use, *mon ami*. Did I hear your message right? You wanna grab th' clubs t'night?"

"You've got no idea, Trick. I've been busting my balls trying to get this place squared away, and Toinetta's been busting my balls trying to get me squared away. I've got to let the animal out of his cage, you know what I'm saying?"

"If tha's a euphemism for some body part you're tryin' ta bust, I don't wanna see it. But if you're wantin' a wingman, I suppose I can clear th' decks for a night."

"Alright, alright," Archer replied, feeling fifty pounds lighter with the proclamation. "Can you swing by here around six? We'll hit a couple of three for one specials at The Cat's Meow or Razzou, then maybe hit Howl at The Moon Café or the House of Blues, see if anyone good is playing."

"I have too many tree fo' one specials, won't be no later for this ol' boy. I jus' can't hang like I used to. I think it's somethin' they put in th' water while you's in college. Once you leave, wham! It's a permanent, irreversible condition to ease ya inta middle age. You're all growed up with no tolerance ta stayin' out late. I'll be there, see you 'bout six."

Archer flipped the phone shut and smiled as he returned his phone and eagerly picked up his implements again, stirring the plaster vigorously so it wouldn't set. There was something to look forward to other than more work.

The electric chime sounded again just as he was preparing to tackle a significant fissure in the wall. Grateful for the diversion, his mind already on the evening's camaraderie, he set aside his tools and stepped onto the sales floor as his mobile phone tweeted again. Archer peered down and saw that Trick was calling back. *Uh-uh buddy, you aren't going to back out on me,* he thought as he ignored the call and went to meet his customer.

The first thing he saw as he entered the sales floor was a bald, disembodied, egg shaped head, slightly flattened in the back, with craggy in features from the side. It seemed to float behind the highest shelving he had in the store. The head was so black it was nearly purple, its skin shining healthily, the eyes white and clear as pristine snowfields, their gaze boring into Archer's without a change in expression as their eyes locked. Archer could see a wide nose, offset slightly sideways on the broad face, as if it had been broken more than once, wide thick lips that when moved, revealed a set of straight white teeth, and a heavy immutable brow that seemed incapable of revealing anything the man behind it was thinking.

Archer moved quickly over behind the sales and display counter waiting for the man to come around the corner. He was impressed by the man's chiseled upper body accented in a black Under Armour compression shirt. Archer guessed he was just over six and a half feet tall and probably pushing three hundred pounds with no space to spare for fat. "Good afternoon, welcome to Blessed Be. How can I help you today?"

"You Archer Sweat?" came a surprisingly high-pitched voice, not unlike that of Aaron Neville.

"Archer Sweet," Archer corrected, "Yeah, I'm he. And you are?"

The giant stuck out a huge hand the size of a pie plate that enveloped Archer's up to the wrist with a gentle but firm grip. "My name's Tellico Trufant. It's my pleasure to meet you, Mr. Sweet."

Archer took back his hand, wiggled his fingers nervously, checking to make sure that they were all still attached and functional.

"What can I do for you today, Mr. Trufant?"

"Oh," he looked down at his size eighteen shoes for a moment before continuing, "I thought you'd be expectin' me. Trick Boulieux sent me here to axe ye for a job. See, I just got outta Angola couple of weeks back, and I've been pitchin' in at The Mission, tryin' to keep my parole officer off my back 'til I could get me a job. Trick took a likin' to me, I guess, an' told me he'd talk to you about maybe lettin' me be your assistant or help you run errands or something."

Archer was tempted to grab his phone and punch the flashing message key to see if Trick was belatedly telling Archer to expect company. Now he knew why Trick had agreed to a night out so easily, he had wanted something. Archer had been to overjoyed to pick up on the ease of which he was able to convince his normally socially-reluctant friend. Instead, he looked up at the man before him and replied, "Mr. Trufant, I haven't heard boo from Trick about you yet, but I'm going to be seeing him. If you'd like, you can drop by tomorrow and we'll talk, but honestly, you caught me off guard today."

Trufant's face remained stoic but his voice reflected disappointment. "Well then, I'll be on mah way. But just so's you know, I'm a good handy man; if it's broke, I can fix it. I know th' entire city like th' back of my hand, and you'd never have to worry 'bout me gettin' jacked up for delivery money. And your store? It'd be as safe as a baby in its momma's arms so long as I'm here. Shit. I know that came out all wrong. All I'm sayin' is I bring a certain, calmin' influence ta folks thinkin' about actin' up."

"I'll bear that all in mind, talk to Trick tonight and let you know. Come on back any time after I open tomorrow, hear?"

"Alright then," Trufant replied softly, turning slowly away, plainly not used to being dismissed. "Thank yah for your time today, Mr. Sweet, I 'ppreciate it."

As soon as the big man was out of sight, Archer ducked back into his office to listen to the message from Trick. It was indeed about Tellico Trufant, and he really was recommending Trufant for a job as a Man Friday of sorts.

"I'd take him on here if I could, but he needs payin' work as condition of his parole, and I don't have a single openin' right now. He's good people. Look who I'm tellin', you prob'bly already have him sweepin' up th' place. See ya tonight."

Frustrated that Trick had put him in such a position, Archer paced in small circles fuming. He was to the point where he realized he needed help, but knew he couldn't actually afford anyone just yet. Trick was right, Archer had sensed a strong aura with dominating colors representing goodness and strength. He also felt a strong and honest spirit in Tellico Trufant, but that spirit had been wounded badly somehow. It was a festering hurt, still raw and ready to bubble over, with only the thinnest veneer of scab protecting him. That emotional gash was what had caused his life to take the wrong turn that had landed him in prison. Could Trufant heal and thrive with a job at Blessed Be? There was an equal chance that Trufant's proximity to Archer, the psychic shit magnet, would be the fuse on the powder keg that set him off again. Sighing, Archer wondered if working at Blessed Be would lead the man to greater paths of self-destruction.

CHAPTER 6

THE SUN HAD set in spectacular hues of red, orange, and magenta before giving way to a soothing indigo dusk. Trick picked his way up the narrow path leading between buildings into the courtyard and the outside door to Archer's home. He had gone around front first but found the doors to Blessed Be closed, a sign indicating he was trying to gain entrance after operating hours. He decided Archer was lucky to have found this location. It was still in the French Quarter, but slightly off the beaten track for the average everyday tourist.

While Archer might make a sale or two each week to some organized religion vacationer, looking to freak out friends or neighbors at home with some knickknack or curio plucked from the murky depths of America's voodoo heartland, his real bread and butter would be bringing in the city's significant Wicca and Neo-Pagan populations. The magic crowd didn't necessarily have the money the average tourist had, but they were loyal and bought in bulk. Archer was still on the fence when it came to stepping into the twenty-first century and creating a web site, but Trick had been nagging him enough that he felt Archer might be wearing down and becoming more receptive to the idea. It could only help.

It would be good to see Archer prosper where others had stumbled.

Mystic Curio had closed its doors, and Esoterica and Mojo Rising were hanging on by a thin string. It was only a matter of time until Blessed Be would be the largest or last legitimate mystical supply shop remaining in the French Quarter. Marie Laveau's and Reverend Zombie's were touristy places, fine for retailers dealing more in souvenirs and voodoo than spell craft; no competition to Blessed Be.

Archer had fallen in love with the slightly run-down property directly across the street from The French Quarter Bistro and Fahy's Irish Pub. Seeking advice and opinions from his friends as to whether or not the other sites he had found were better for the store's location, he had agonized over the condition of the building in comparison with the others. Ultimately he made the decision with his gut and heart and seemed to be right on the money so far.

"His gut is so damn good, it should be consulted on issues of national defense," Trick muttered to himself with a smile as he leaned on the buzzer and heard Archer yell down for him to come up. He turned the battered brass knob, noting the amount of play in it before it gave way and opened. He slipped inside, then pushed the faded mauve-colored door tight closed behind him.

The old wooden stairs creaked and squawked as Trick ascended quickly, pausing at the top of the landing to stomp his feet free of the plaster and saw dust before opening the door that led into a brief foyer and short hallway. There were two rooms on each side of the hallway, and two doors at the end of the hall. One led to a bathroom, where he could hear water running in the shower, the other opened out into a large master room This room had once been a bawdy house's parlor, the office of a tax attorney, the home of a shopkeeper, a bar owner, and most recently a squatter's paradise. Small singe marks from hobo fires dotted the resilient cypress floorboards in a haphazard way accenting the room's faded yellow-brown interior. The curtains that had been up when Archer had discovered the property were probably a century old, heavy, rotted, red velvet dating back to the days of the bordello. They looked and smelled as if they had actively participated in the day-to-day adventures of the place instead of hanging around observing.

Until he could afford something better, Archer had gone to the Army and Navy surplus store and purchased nylon pancho liners, which he had attached to the rusted curtain rods by their tie strings. It was a serviceable temporary solution, and they cleaned up with just a shake or two. Patterned in jungle camouflage, they were good enough until Archer had the entire home fixed the way he wanted.

The rest of the place was still rough, but slowly taking shape. Archer had managed to patch and smooth nearly all of the cracks and fissures in the plaster walls and ceiling of the great room. The crisp white of the new plaster contrasting the dingy yellow of the wall like fresh bandages on a badly wounded soldier.

Archer had been saving this room for the last of the indoor work, which, in Trick's mind, meant that he had finished most of the heavy-duty repairs on the rest of the interior space. There was still a lot to be done, the floors needed to be sanded and sealed, and the outside façade to refurbished, but he could begin to see Archer's vision of the place.

The master bedroom and bathroom had been simultaneous projects for Archer, and when the job proved beyond him, a plumber and electrician were summoned to make sure that a leak or a fire didn't undo all of his hard work. Trick had joked with Archer that if he had a fire and plumbing mishap occur simultaneously the two would probably end up canceling each other out.

The Viex Carre Commission, the venerable, oft hated, group that had brought The French Quarter back from the literal edge of demolition during the administration of Franklin Delano Roosevelt would be his final judge. The commission enforced and maintained the historic integrity for the famous section of New Orleans in a state of perpetual external permanence. All renovations required approval; outdoor building facades were mandated to remain exactly the same color and surface it had been when the Commission was incepted. This included every detail of the structure, including siding, shutters, and windows. Archer had a slate tile roof which, fortunately for him, remained mostly intact. The few cracked tiles had been removed and replaced by a local artisan who recycled them as unique canvases for his paintings of the Saint Louis Cathedral and other French Quarter cityscapes.

The door to the bathroom opened; steam billowed and rolled outward, as if the door were a portal that held the advance of Hell's Fury, not Archer Sweet. Tall, ropy, slightly pale, but well muscled, in his late twenties, he emerged from the wall of creeping, vaporous tendrils with an oversized, white cotton towel spooled around his narrow waist, long black hair dangling or sticking limply to the middle of his back. A second smaller towel draped across his broad shoulders was being used for blotting, trying to work the excess water from his hair before setting it into his customary ponytail.

"Th' place is startin' ta take some shape, Archer, no lie; lookin' less and less like a bombed out Storyville brothel ev'ry time I see it. The camouflage is a nice touch, too. Kinda like bein' in a duck blind for tourists. You bag your limit yet?"

"Fuck you very much, Trick," replied Archer as he moved out of sight for a moment into his bedroom, emerging moments later in a pressed pair of khakis and a soft heather grey cotton T-shirt that proclaimed, "My imaginary friends think you're stupid." Archer flipped his hair into one hand, twisting tightly to wring it out, then grabbed his shoulder towel and ruffled his hair with it for a minute or two before combing it straight and running Frizz-ease with a generous dollop of holding gel through it. "Give me three minutes, I'm good for the door," he said as he drew his hair straight back into a ponytail securing it expertly with a thick thong of leather.

Trick walked deeper into the living room, shaking his head, calling over his shoulder, "Please tell me that's some of Liz's ol' stylin' accoutrements. Please tell me that th' Stud of th' Spirit World is not flouffin' his hair like some sissy metrosexual."

"It's all mine, *mon ami*. It keeps my hair from curling or taking too long to dry. You don't like it, wait out in the courtyard and don't watch, or stick around and pick up some pointers on being sharp, instead of your same old shabby self."

"This ain't no date. We jus' goin' to Th' Meow or Razzou for happies. Ain' nothin' says I gotta look good for your sorry ass or vice versa."

Archer swept into the living room, grabbed his wallet and keys from the table by the edge of the door.

"Alright Trick, time to shear some of the wool that's been gathering in our brains."

"It's on bruttah. Let's go kill us some brain cells."

The pair walked down the stairs out into the courtyard and Archer took a moment to double check the locks on his doors before setting out. "Strangest thing," he muttered peering briefly through the murkiness to his store's front doors.

"What, someone sacked out by your door or somethin'" asked Trick, pressing his nose against the cool glass, leaving a face print that he knew would piss his buddy off when he cleaned the next day.

"I'm probably just really kicked. Yet more evidence that I need this night out. It's just. . .those door stops? My trolls? They're not in the same place I left them. Did you . . .?"

"Whatever the question is, th' answer's no. I ain't been in your shop without you," Trick guffawed. "Maybe you should give 'em a good talkin' to tomorrow, tell 'em they break up your store, it's comin' out of their paychecks."

Archer shook his head. He hated leaving when there seemed to be something wrong in the shop, but the real mystery was how he had worked so hard for so long without his imagination playing tricks on him.

The pair walked across St. Phillip to pick up Bourbon and traversed their way up to some of the more entertaining watering holes for big beer and little cost.

"Speaking of paychecks, thanks for letting me know you were sending someone by today. The dude about scared me shitless when he came sauntering in. He's got no neck, Trick."

"I know, ain't it weird? Sorry I didn't get ya word quicker, I didn't think he was gonna roll right to your place from Th' Mission today. He's desperate to work. I know you're gonna need some help, so I figured he'd be a good fit for ya'. The man's got some issues twistin' his soul, and a felony conviction for dealin', but he did his time and his head's on right. I wouldn't palm a nut job off on ya, Archer. He's good people. Just needs of a fresh start's all."

"I don't doubt it for a minute, Trick. You read people better than most I've known, so he's in, as long as he doesn't try to bone the proprietor when I'm bending over for something.

"Your ass ain't half as nice as what he coulda got when he was in th' joint. 'Sides, that's where some of his problems come from, an abusive upbringing. Ya ain't gotta worry about him playin' a game of Where's Waldo? when your back is turned. Hell, you treat him good and I wouldn't worry 'bout anythin' goin' down while he's got your back."

"Okay, he's supposed to come back to the store tomorrow. I'll take him on for a trial basis. If he's got his shit together, and I can afford to keep him on, he can stay."

"Excellent," Trick enthused. "I always like seein' guys matriculate from Th' Mission and integrate back into th' real world. Hey, Arch, gotta ask ya before I pollute my blood stream and forget."

"Yeah, What's that?"

"You hear about somethin' weird goin' on lately in town? There's been some strange stories comin' in to Th' Mission last couple of days. People are gettin' attacked, some gettin' killed, some just knocked around a little and let go, but every one of them sad sack survivors say the same thing. They hear a voice in their head, talkin' 'bout bein' tainted, or that one looks just right. The ones that look jus' right seem to up an' disappear, or wind up in the cooler trays at the morgue."

"Toinetta showed me a *Times-Picayune* article about two girls found dead under 'highly unusual circumstances'. She put you up to this?"

"Hain't seen Toinetta for a couple of weeks, bro. Two totally different reports, there."

"Alright. Well, as I told Toinetta, I'm not a cop anymore. This isn't any of my concern, so I say let it slide, keep our eyes and ears open, and if something else happens, we try and get Wendell involved."

They stopped outside of The Cat's Meow, a karaoke bar offering three long necks for the price of one. Walking inside the dark and roomy main bar, they pulled up seats by one of the tables near the rear service area. Karaoke was the true heartbeat of The Cat's Meow's beer sales, and it was a briefly entertaining, novel show, never the same two nights in a row. Archer and Trick drank cheap Bud Lights in companionable silence as a steady stream of marginal to awful talent got up and gave their shower stall renditions of songs Archer found himself never wanting to hear again, ever. Everyone in the audience was polite, which is the trademark of the bar, giving encouragement to the shrill off-key warbling, applauding politely when the singers finished.

Archer couldn't decide if they were acknowledging the courage it took to step up to the microphone, or if it was an outpouring of relief that one particular version of torture was behind them. In actuality, Archer thought, encouraging sloppy drunks to warble show tunes then making them believe they didn't sound like a trapped cockatiel in a hot waffle iron was just plain mean to everyone involved. That is, unless you enjoyed having your ears pinned back on a regular basis by a two hundred-fifty hundred pound beauty queen belting out *I Will Survive* in three disparate octaves.

After two rounds, Archer needed to pay the rent on his beer, so he wandered back through the courtyard, used as a second open air bottle and shooter bar, to the bathroom. When he returned, a fresh round in his hands, Trick was nowhere to be seen. Archer scanned the growing crowds, and looked at the bar on the far end of the room for his friend. He set the bottles down on the table and was digging for his cell phone to call Trick when the first jazzy notes of Cab Calloway's famous version of *Minnie the Moocher* erupted from the stage. Archer was surprised to hear a legitimate classic and with the first notes of the vocals, pleased to hear a skilled, smoky, soulful voice lending life to the song's inherent playfulness. Looking forward to the stage, cell phone still in hand, he nearly dropped the device, staring stupidly for a moment as he realized he had found Trick.

Standing loose and easy at the microphone, paying no attention to the television screen with the words he seemed to know by heart, Trick stared out to the back of the bar near the DJ stand and belted out the difficult song with effortless style. He seemed frozen to the center of the stage except for a brief pull at his bottle of beer during an interlude, in complete opposition to most other frenetic performers who danced and cavorted wildly about the stage, trying to make the most of their moment in the limelight. For just a moment Trick seemed to be a throw back to the time when nearly every bar or club in New Orleans had marquee acts, small combos, or spasm bands. The vocalists were often the feature draw of the group. Those talents didn't feel the need to further entertain than with their singing voices. The crowd had grown silent too, listening intently, deciding quickly that they were in for a treat and clapping their hands or participating in the brief scat runs that marked the belly of the tune. The host, usually paid to comically caper about the stage as a distraction from the low quality of the talent stood stock still by one of the giant speakers, his head bobbing along to the rhythm of the song.

The song ended and for about three seconds, Trick just stood there, silence buffeting him so completely that Archer could hear the clink of bottles bumping together as the waitress across the room stacked empties on her serving tray. Then, suddenly the spell was broken and the emcee was standing beside Trick, hand up for a high five as the crowd went absolutely berserk. The emcee threw his arm around Trick and screamed into the mic, "Well shit-fire and call me a hemorrhoid! We've got ourselves an honest to goodness performer in the house tonight. Let's hear it one more time for Loo-siana home grown talent, Trick Boulieux!"

Throughout the song, people had been streaming in from Bourbon Street drawn by the performance and the unabashed fun the crowd was having. Trick made his way through the throng of new arrivals, sudden admirers, and well wishers back to Archer and the table. He shook his head, slowly, a sheepish grin playing slowly across his broad, slightly flushed face as he leaned heavily on the table.

"Man, I didn't know you had pipes like that! You were fuckin' awesome Trick, the next American Idol, dude. C'mon, you've got to do another one before we go."

"Nah, ain't nothin' special 'bout it. My Momma always used to have me singing every place she could. Didn't matter to her, contests, auditions, whatever was there; she signed me up and expected me to be her songbird. She forced me in to chorus and jazz-fusion in high school. Guy up on stage's a cat I knew in school from th' fusion group. He spotted me an' dragged me up there, soon as you went to hit th' can. Speakin' of which, where is it? I never liked singin' in front of big groups, and th' beer I drank's buggin' me for a one way ticket on th' porcelain bus."

Archer clapped Trick on the back, pointed him in the right direction, watching as he set sail through a tide of folks who hadn't congratulated him yet. Archer finished his beer quickly, figuring that Trick wouldn't want to stay after this, no matter that he had been the best of what they'd heard all night and would probably remain so. As long as he had known Trick, he had always been an intensely private man. Archer felt he had seen a whole new facet of his friend, unfortunately it was not something Trick would want to discuss later.

Trick returned and took a couple of deep quaffs from his bottle, set it down, belched loudly, then said, "Let's you 'n' me blow this popsicle stand an' go find us a quiet spot to relax a bit. This place is getting' crazy, and I'm primed from th' speed boozin' we been doin' here."

"No problem. Where do you want to go?"

"I don't care man. You want music, we can go to Howl at th' Moon. Atmosphere, there's th' Absinthe House; or just dark and quiet, we can go to LaFitte's Blacksmith Shop."

"Well if we want music, we can always stay here and you can sing some more." Archer smiled, but when Trick glowered, he quit poking fun and said, "Enough noise for the night, let's hit LaFitte's. The only excitement there is usually the tour groups coming in for their half time drinks"

"Let's roll," slurred Trick, already moving, weaving slightly, toward the door, eyes downcast to avoid being corralled again by his high school friend.

The two walked down Bourbon Street in amiable silence, watching the tourists who had left their inhibitions in their hotel room as they celebrated the nightly bacchanal that was the French Quarter. Archer kept glancing sidelong at Trick, curious about why singing was such a sore subject. Trick remained closed, his posture so defensive that Archer decided to leave things alone until they had downed a couple more drinks and let the experience fade slightly from his memory.

John LaFitte's Blacksmith shop stood near the end of Bourbon Street, intersecting St. Phillip Street. A ramshackle two-story building with warped and fading storm shutters, its foundations seemed to sag literally under the weight of its age and historical significance. Lafitte and his brother had opened the shop as a front for their slave trade and piracy, granting them some small amount of legitimacy. No one at the time really cared, since most enjoyed living vicariously through their exploits. It had been preserved and after numerous incarnations, became one of the few nearly guaranteed profitable ventures in New Orleans, a watering hole with bygone-days kiche.

Trick looked blurrily at Archer. "Am I really that bad off already, or is th' bar leanin' seriously ta th' left?"

"No you're correct, the building is definitely off cant. You're still a drunk motherfucker, though."

"Issit safe, ya reckon? Looks like it might fall around our ears if someone farts in there."

"If the bartender runs off, I'll get worried. Until then I think it's alright," Archer replied, sounding much more sober than he felt.

They found two seats at the end of the bar and ordered a pitcher of Abita Amber, toasting each other silently as they watched a few tourists filter in and out. Trick seemed to relax somewhat and Archer decided to try again, "Come on, Trick, give over. How is it I have known and worked with you for two years and this is the first I knew you could sing. Hell, I never heard you so much as hum in all of the time we've spent together."

"Jus' leave it Archer, okay? Jus' let it be."

He was silent for so long that Archer was ready to change the subject.

Abruptly, Trick shook his head, took a long pull from his beer then set it on the bar, focusing intently on the sweat rolling off the glass, soaking inexorably into the cardboard coaster. He said quietly, "This is all you're ever gonna hear 'bout this subject from me so listen up. My Momma loved to hear me sing 'cause she was just awful at it. Soon as she found out I could carry a tune in a bucket, she started gettin' me lessons and havin' me perform at public functions like school chorus or family picnics. She was pleased as she could be, but I hated doin' it in front of folks. Tell ya' we used to fight bitterly 'bout it constantly. She was the only witch I knew that loved hymns, religious junk. She was forever trying to teach me new ones."

"So what happened Trick, did you quit because you didn't like singing those songs, or didn't like singing, even for yourself?"

"Nah, deep down, when I thought 'bout it later, I really think I enjoyed singing, but I didn't like th' attention everyone heaped on me. Th' pressure on me to perform, to always be good, really weighed on me sometimes. Th' day my Momma died, we had a big fight about me singin' a stylized version of *Th' Ol' Rugged Cross* at th' old amateur show durin' Jazz Fest. I was at that age when I thought my friends would poke fun, and pleasin' her was no longer high on my list a' priorities when it came to her versus my social life. She left me alone, grounded me to my room 'til I'd reconsidered, then she went off to gather some herbs on th' bayou."

Archer felt his throat constrict as Trick shifted his gaze from his beer to lock liquid eyes with his friend. "My last words to her were hateful; jus' a kid being plain mean, and I never got to apologize for what I said or any of th' other hurts I put on her. That loss stemmed from my singin', so I figured it best if I just quit doin' it. I don't know what possessed me tonight. That's why I don't ever sing or cotton much to organized religion. Did you know my Momma had a Jesus Christ statue on her shrine as part of her Parthenon of deities? I always secretly thought she dug him 'cause he kinda looked like a hippie."

Archer was quiet a moment, unsure how to act in the face of his friend's discomfort and pain, then said, "I won't tell anyone, Trick, my word on it. Since I know you don't want to talk about it, I'll just ask you one question and you can ponder it or ignore it. Would your mother want you to hide your talent, something you and she worked on together, as the legacy to all of her effort and love, or would you honor her and let her know she's in your thoughts by letting a note or two go now and then?"

Trick didn't reply, except to signal the bartender for another pitcher, as a tall burly man with a deep olive complexion, a shock of thick, black hair, and a well groomed, but still bushy beard sat down on the other side of Archer. Trick looked at the man once, then stole a second glance, noting his black slacks and shirt, sheltered by a summer weight, black, waist-length jacket. With the new arrival, the conversation quite obviously was over.

Archer knew his friend well enough that despite his taciturn response and the disruption of talk, he would take the time to turn things over in his mind and come to his own conclusions, in his own way and time. Archer would just be whistling in the wind if he tried to broach the subject again. Instead, he said, "So what's the story with the guy you sent over to me today. You say he's okay, but what's his deal?"

"To say he's th' quiet type doesn't seem to do him justice. Th' man's a mystery. All I know's what I saw of him and got from his parole officer, and I didn't get much from him. Tellico Trufant's got a knack for engenderin' respect and loyalty from people he meets, even on a passin' basis. All of th' people at Th' Mission like him, myself included. His P.O. would only say he got caught up in a drug sweep year before last, and th' prosecutor had tried to make an example of him 'cause he was usin' as well as hustlin'. Made a point of tellin' me that Trufant's been a parole officer's dream since he got out, and has been clean and sober since the day he was arrested."

"Well, I said I'd give him a chance and I will. Good to hear he's comes with a warranty."

Trick laughed and set his glass down on the scarred, ebony colored bar, "I doubt you'll get money back if not delighted." In the gloom across the bar, he could see two women, sipping martinis and watching them with casual interest.

"Nah, guess not, but I feel better knowing he's not just another ex-con that I'd have to keep an eye on."

"Trust me Archer," said Trick, as he slid off the seat and began to sidle off in the ladies' direction. "You tell him what'cha want him to do, what you expect, and let him git to it, no extra care or feedin' required." He nodded in the direction of the women, who were still shooting curious glances at them. "I'm off to see about baggin' a bird. Want one?"

Archer shook his head, gave him a mock salute and watched as Trick walked across the bar planting his slightly weaving frame directly between the two giggly blondes, giving them a beer-Adonis smile. *Ah, to feel bulletproof,* Archer thought, watching the scene unfold, unable to tear his eyes from the upcoming shoot down. Trick had picked his favorite and was laying on his Cajun charm. He didn't notice either woman's growing disinterest, or that the one he had cut out of his patter was leaning over the bar into the garnish tray for a fat stuffed olive. Trick never saw it coming.

Raising the olive to her glossy lips, the girl drew a deep breath and exhaled, her cheeks puffed, face reddening with the effort. There was an audible 'shwoik' as the pimento exploded out of the olive, a little red projectile that struck Trick on the chin and disintegrated all over him. The women dissolved into gales of raucous laughter as Trick's blush quickly matched the color of the goo dripping from his face. He took up the girl's napkin and swabbed himself clean, then walked away without a word.

Archer had stifled his own smile by the time Trick came back to his seat. He paused to look at the bearded man before settling back in his seat, sighing.

"Some days are better than others, man," Archer said as he finished his beer. "Just be happy those things were already pitted, or you'd have a cleft in that chin."

Trick ignored him, refilling their glasses and setting down the empty pitcher. He leaned forward and murmured to Archer, "Does that guy look familiar to you? He was in Th' Cat's Meow before we left, I remember that faggy lookin' jacket."

Archer was about to reply that the man seemed to be just another tourist, and didn't seem at all familiar, when Trick frowned, extended his arms to his chest height, then lifted his two index fingers together for a moment and slowly drew them apart, keeping Archer framed in the middle as the fingers separated. His expression opened slightly and he dropped his fingers, looking at the top of Archer's head.

"Wha' th' hell, man? Your aura is really fucked up, fractured, splittin' in two diff'rent directions." Trick slurred slightly but Archer knew his eyes weren't deceiving him, Trick had been reading auras since he was old enough to know his colors.

"Something happened today, a woman came in the store and she's been in my head all day. It's not a big deal; she's hot enough to cook on, but she thinks I'm a waste of space."

"Might be more to her than you know, *mon ami*, she left a bit 'a herself in your slipstream. She'll be back, whether she knows it yet or not."

"Yeah? Well I'm not going to worry about it until I see her again," Archer replied glibly as he took a long pull from his fresh glass. "It is what it is; I'm not going anywhere. She wants to see me again, she knows where I am."

"Speakin' of disappearin'; have you noticed the amount of folk been comin' up missin' in the last week? I've heard all kind of numbers from ten to dozens"

"This shit again? C'mon, man, give it a rest. Toinetta came in all hyped about a couple of college girls *The Picayune* reported dead and says more will come. I promised her I'd talk to Wendell Pierce tomorrow and ask him to see if he can link anything, but I haven't heard any stories or felt anything psychically unusual. Let's just drop it okay? I'm more relaxed than I've been in months, and you look like you're feeling no pain; let's not spoil that."

When Trick didn't reply, Archer glanced over at his friend, then at the big man sitting beside him at the bar who was seemingly just staring off into space before turning to Archer and nodding to him. Archer nodded and smiled back at the man drunkenly as he realized that Trick had become a little too relaxed and fallen asleep upright on his bar stool, the long hours and long necks finally catching up to him. Archer sighed, paid the tab and called a cab to take Trick home.

Archer was close to home and clear-headed enough that after Trick was safely on his way, he decided to walk back. He found himself wandering slightly, meandering through the more residential area of the French Quarter, enjoying the silence and serenity that these streets offered. He had hoped it would give him some time to think about the things that had happened today most notably, Mystery Girl as he was forced to call her until she gave him a name, any name. The more he thought of her, the more confused and befuddled he became. He soon found himself sitting on the banquette in front of his store pondering nothing but the slight breeze pushing its way through lethargic tree branches. By the time he dragged himself up and slumped into his bed, still in his clothes minus his shoes, he couldn't tell if it was the alcohol, the late hour, or the damned woman that had exhausted him the most.

He reached out, extinguishing the small, thick, white column candle he had burning on his makeshift altar before letting his eyes close, and with them, the book on the events of the day. There was always tomorrow to figure out what the hell was going on, and he had to be up early to make sure Tellico Trufant got his paperwork started.

CHAPTER 7

DIFFUSE SUNLIGHT STREAMED through his thin poncho-liner curtains as his alarm—set for maximum volume so he'd be sure to drag out of bed— welcomed his day with the eclectic sounds of the college station, WTNO. Some college student was hemming and hawing his way awkwardly through a public service announcement about the importance of getting yourself and your partner tested for HIV because, as the announcer said, "Knowing is, like an, um aphrodisiac and that's kinda cool, you know?"

Archer peeled himself out of his clothes thinking darkly as he ran the water for his shower that the HIV test was only cool or sexy if the results came back negative. He tried to remember any lucid dreams. Most likely the alcohol dulled that part of him, and he was okay with that on occasion, but a sick feeling deep in his gut that was far worse than any hang over raged inside him. Archer wound his ponytail into a shower cap adorned with little laughing skulls and grabbed the bottle of aspirin from his medicine shelf. Shaking out a pair of tablets and stepping into the shower with its spiky needles of pressurized water, he kicked them back with the bracing frosty water that washed down his throat.

Sputtering, and now shivering, he went about his morning hygiene as quickly as possible, vowing to break down and get the water heater repaired so he could have two hot showers in a twenty-four hour span before the weather got any worse. He shut the water off, grabbed a thin, nearly threadbare towel signaling the need to hit the laundromat and soon. After combing his hair out and pulling it back into his customary pony tail, Archer shaved, brushed his teeth, then grabbed fresh jeans and a T-shirt from his dresser. The jeans were faded and tattered and the shirt held the question: "WWJB? Who Would Jesus Bomb?"

He heard his phone beep, indicating a message that must have come in while he was freezing his bits and parts. Looking at the screen, he saw two messages and went right to voicemail. The first was a woman placing an order for an afternoon delivery and Archer jotted the list down on a piece of scrap paper as he listened. The last was from Trick. The man did not sound like he was ready to be up and at 'em just yet, but if nothing else, Trick was a trooper.

"I'm jus' checkin' to make sure you got home safe las' night. I feel like somebody whomped me upside the head wit' a two by four, but I don't think that Abita Brewery is in th' lumber business. No doubt, I got Bourbon faced on Shit Street. Anyway, call me when you get 'round to it. I know you gave me somethin' to think about las' night, but I'll be dipped in shit and rolled in cookie crumbs if I remember exactly what it was. Maybe you can explain the bits of pimento I found in my hair, too. I'm off to throw up now. Call me."

Archer chuckled as he pocketed the phone and trundled down the stairs to open his shop for the day. He walked around to the front of the store glanced up and down the empty, sleepy streets, then fit the key into the lock to open the first French door. As he stepped inside, he felt a stir of air behind him. Whirling around, he found himself standing face to chest with Tellico Trufant. "Whoa, you startled me Mr. Trufant. I didn't see you on the street, where'd you come from?"

Trufant shrugged and Archer realized the man didn't feel it to be an important question; therefore Archer had received his answer.

"Well, I did some checking around and got nothing but good things about you, Mr. Trufant. You appear to be just the man for this job. It's yours if you want it."

"Thank you, Mr. Sweet," Trufant squeaked, "You won't be sorry."

"First thing first, call me Archer, I'm not a mister, never was."

"Okay then, call me Tell or Tellico, as you like," Tell responded as he reached into his pocket for his work papers. He presented them to Archer impassively, waiting for what came next.

"C'mon in. I'll call your P.O. and let him know you're working here. I'll say this once, I don't care about your past history. As far as I'm concerned, so long as you didn't kill or rape anyone, your slate is clean. Anything you choose to tell me about yourself is up to you. Even though I do care and I'm available to listen, I'll never ask for your life story. Just work your hours, be good to the customers when you have to interact, and most of all enjoy yourself. This is probably different than anything you've done before."

Archer paused to wait for Tell's response. After a nod and a flicker of a smile, Archer continued, "I can only pay you minimum wage for now. As the store takes off, job one is to give you a raise. There is also some extra work coming in the future, doing repairs to the outside of the building and some cosmetic work upstairs if you're interested. You can let me know later. Your first official task, while I call your P.O. is to finish opening the doors and brace them open with the statues. I'll be back."

Tell gave him an odd look, then nodded and turned to unlatch the second door as Archer went to his work desk to call the parole officer listed on Tell's papers.

Following instruction, he signed off on the work affidavit and faxed it to the number the parole officer gave him. He was told the convict, Tellico Trufant, had a bi-weekly check-in that was to occur on Wednesdays at ten-thirty. If he failed to make the appearance, a bench warrant would be issued for his arrest and he would return to Angola to serve out the rest of his term on the work farm, not in general population. Archer told the dispassionate voice on the other end that he had been a cop and knew the procedure, he'd make sure Trufant had that time off to meet his commitment. The voice seemed unimpressed that an ex-cop was hiring an ex-con, though he admitted it was a rarity. He asked Archer if he had any questions. When Archer said no, the man thanked him for calling in and rang off.

Archer came back into the store and was surprised to see Tell carefully dusting the candle section, the feather duster looking like a sparrow in the man's massive paws. Archer was struck by the delicacy of his movements and the precise, nimble dexterity he displayed as he shifted slightly now and then to avoid bumping into racks or shelves as he worked. The doors were locked in place, but Archer had never thought to turn the trolls so they faced slightly different directions, one looking out to either end of the street. "I like the trolls that way, Tell. Good idea."

"I had nothing to do with it. They're arguing, and don't want to look at each other."

"O-kay," Archer replied dubiously. "Well you're doing fine. I'm going to be at my desk checking invoices. When you're finished dusting, I'll show you the cash register and we can run through an order I have to fill. Part of your job is to make deliveries in The Quarter. Any tips are yours."

"Got it," Tell grunted as he turned back to his dusting.

Archer shook his head as he went back into the office and sat down. *The trolls were fighting? What was that about?* He hoped fervently, as he picked up the stack of invoices and began doing his line comparisons, that he hadn't hired a nut job.

Soon, a shadow appeared across his desk and he looked up to see Tell standing expectantly by the door. Happy to set down the paperwork, Archer beckoned Tell to follow him behind the glass counter, where he withdrew the apothecary scale, scoop, glassine envelopes, and a paper bag. Archer filled the first half of the order, demonstrating how to weigh the ingredients correctly and to wipe the scoop clean after each item, explaining that a remnant of an item accidentally mixed with another could be catastrophic, or at least make a customer's spell craft fail. He wiped the scoop down and said, "You fill the rest of the order and I'll watch. It's really pretty simple, and I know you can handle it, so I'm not going to do anything slow, with anything here. Just ask if you have a question."

Tell nodded and quickly got the hang of the filing system for the herb jars, adroitly filling the rest of the order in short time. As he set the cleaned scale and scoop back under the counter, Tell asked, "Why don't you have any rosemary stocked? It's a good, simple, protective herb, cheap, too, so the mark up would be better."

Archer was impressed. "You're a man of hidden talents, Tell. You're going to like it here, and I think we can learn from each other. The reason I don't stock rosemary is I'm allergic to it. I can't even touch it without breaking out in hives that would make bees proud."

"Oh. Okay. What's the address this stuff is supposed to go to?"

"Uh, hold on," replied Archer, reaching across the counter to pick up the order slip, momentarily taken aback by the shift in conversation. "Here it is, just a couple of blocks over on Governor Nicholls. I'll see you when you get back."

Tell took the bag and the order form and was out the door quickly, returning fifteen minutes later with the money for the order. Archer was pleased to see him return so fast and was more pleased that he had been able to sell two charms while Tell was gone; sales he would have missed if he had closed the store to make the delivery. It also gave him the chance to show Tellico how to ring up sales, pretty much completing the rudiments of his training.

Archer checked his watch, picked up his car keys and said, "Tell, I have to run an errand over in Jefferson, should take about an hour. Keep an eye on the place, and don't let the trolls fight, okay?"

Tell nodded and moved to stand behind the register as Archer went around back, climbed into his beat up Rodeo and pointed it in the direction of Jefferson Parish Police headquarters. *I think Trick was right,* Archer thought as he merged with the light traffic out of the city, *Tell is good people. I hope he sticks around.*

CHAPTER 8

ARCHER PULLED INTO the visitor parking at the Jefferson Parish precinct building and killed the engine. He had been running every scenario and outcome he could imagine for when he stood face to face before his old partner. He hoped Pierce was in a good mood.

He walked into the station and signed in. The bustle of activity transported him momentarily back to his own time in this building and all of the memories, good and bad, that he had accumulated in his brief tenure. Contrary to what he told Trick and Toinetta, he missed being a cop sometimes. He had been good at undercover work, but after Liz's death, he simply felt that his time in law enforcement had run its course. It had been time to seek out a new destiny for himself.

Archer was buzzed through the waiting area and as he walked through the bullpen, he saw some familiar old faces and plenty of new ones. He didn't remember turnover on the force being so high when he had been there, but then again, if he could walk away from it, he supposed anyone else could, too. Reaching the end of the pen, Archer exchanged greetings, handshakes, and claps on the back, and was introduced to some of the new troop by his veteran friends. Archer gamely met each one, knowing that they already knew his story; every cop here knew the details by heart. It was the kind of tale that would be told and re-told long after everyone who had been in the department when it had happened was gone. It was also a big reason why Wendell Pierce had not been shown the door. Every cop in Jeff Parish knew that while it was unlikely they would go through what Archer Sweet had endured, there was every chance that they could end up like Wendell. He was their living proof, their cautionary tale and example, the focus of every cop's worst nightmare.

Archer made his way to the hallway of offices and stopped at the first one, rapping his knuckles on the frosted glass, with gold lettering, opening the door when a gruff, "Enter" was called. Slipping through, he closed the door behind him and looked at the seated form of his former boss Chief of Detectives, Mark Rosenthal.

"Archer Sweet," boomed the large ruddy man, as he stood up to shake hands. "What brings you by? Nostalgia? No wait, you were never big on that. What's shaking?" Rosenthal sat down again, motioning Archer to one of the folding chairs in front of the desk.

"It's good to see you Mark, you're looking well."

"If you call gaining twenty-five pounds and working on ulcer number two good, then yeah, I'm peachy, the picture of health. How about you?"

Archer replied and they made small talk for a few minutes, catching each other up on the little things. Finally, Archer was able to steer the conversation in the direction he wanted.

"How's Wendell doing, Mark? I hear some things second hand, and I tried to visit him once at home, but it didn't go well."

"He's maintaining, for whatever good that does. At least he's switched to gin; he doesn't reek nearly as bad when he comes in. That why you're here? To ask after Pierce?"

"In a manner of speaking. I was hoping to talk to him and figured he was less likely to blow me off or get violent in the station house. I love that man like he was my brother, Mark, and he's so convinced he let me down that he can't countenance talking to me."

Rosenthal absently twirled a pencil in his beefy hands. "He's not the same man you knew, Archer. He's twisted so tight inside, I don't know if anyone or anything can reach him again. At least until he's ready to give up some of the self-loathing he thinks he owns the market on."

"I need to try to talk to him. Just once more. Tell him again that I miss him and never blamed him for anything."

"I think in his gut he knows you don't blame him, Archer, and if our positions were reversed, I don't know that I would be so forgiving. He can't exonerate himself for what happened. Department shrink says he's got to come to the realization that the only person disappointed in Wendell Pierce is Wendell Pierce. He needs to come to that on his own time and in his own way. Until then, he's going to continue punishing himself and those he cares for, by poisoning himself daily."

"Thanks Mark, I'll keep that in mind. I always focus on trying to convince him that it was okay, that I was okay. I'll do all I can this time to let him know that he needs to be okay." Archer stood up, shook his old boss's proffered hand and turned to leave.

"Last door on your left, end of the hall. He should be back from lunch."

Archer nodded and closed the door behind him. Striding down the short hallway, he stopped when he reached the door marked Records and Archives. Taking a deep breath, he knocked twice on the glass, opened the door, sliding inside before receiving permission, and quickly closing it behind himself. Turning to face the file room, Archer found a disheveled Wendell Pierce in a rumpled, wrinkled, food stained uniform, that carried a strong enough odor to make Archer start breathing through his mouth.

"Well lookee here, if it ain't my old partner, coming to check up on his alchy buddy. You slumming, or what?"

"It's good to see you, Wendell. I'm not going to ask you how you're doing. You look alright. The beard is growing in a little nappy through."

"You're not going to ask how I am? That because you're afraid I'll tell you? Well here it is: My wife and children are gone, my career is in the shitter, I'm on the sauce, and oh, yeah, your wife is still dead, all because my head is planted so deep up my worthless black ass I'm using my fucking navel as a peep hole. How the hell are you?"

"I'm getting by Wendell, but I miss seeing you, hanging out and bull shitting like we used to. Truth be told, I'm here because I need some help and you've always been there for me when it counted. Can I sit down?"

Pierce had plopped back into his seat and rocked it back and forth, the hinges and springs protesting with every movement. Finally, he made the briefest of motions and Archer took it for an invitation, seating himself quickly across from his old partner. Pierce stared over the top of Archer's head for over a minute, then barked, "Well? I haven't got all day. Case you haven't noticed, I'm not high on the list of promotable officers anymore. I can't waste my time jacking my jaw when I should be working."

"There's something going on in New Orleans. It might be nothing or it could be a serial killer with a serious timetable. Now that you're the Records man, I was hoping you could check some things out for me."

"I'm listening, you've got thirty seconds."

"I need you to look at the homicide reports for Jefferson, St. Charles, Livingston, St. Tammany, St. John, and Orleans Parishes in the last two weeks. Key on Orleans and Jeff, but see if there is a common thread that the papers have been leaving out. *The Picayune* calls it 'highly unusual circumstances' and we both know what that means. The police are holding something back."

"What's it got to do with you? Why should you care if we're holding back a detail or two? You know the drill."

"Yeah, I do Wen, that's why I need you. I can't crack the blue line as a civilian. If there's a common thread, you can find it and let me know. That way I can put some minds at ease if you come up empty, or have a clue about what's happening if you find something."

Pierce pointed to his metal wire In Box that was overflowing and in danger of tipping over. "I've got a lot to do and I don't get overtime anymore. If I get a chance in the next couple of weeks, I might be able to look into it. Don't hold your breath though. Now get the fuck out and let me get back to work."

Archer stood up and opened the door. "It was good seeing you again Wendell. Thanks for talking to me. Take care of yourself now, that's what you do best, right?"

Archer was two steps down the hall before he heard what sounded like a chair slamming into a wall, but he didn't look back. He hoped Wendell would stew for a little then with any luck, he might look up the information tonight or tomorrow instead of looking up from the bottom of a new bottle.

CHAPTER 9

WHEN ARCHER WALKED through the office door and onto the store's sales floor after his drive back, he was stunned to see Tellico standing across the counter, talking with Her. Their tone was quiet, almost intimate, like two old friends. She smiled and rested a hand gently on his massive forearm. There were two other customers browsing unhurriedly at his books on display. Archer turned when he heard a squeaky, staccato choking sound emanating from Tell. It took a moment to register that he was laughing, or else he was really enjoying Archer's distress.

Needing to do something, Archer walked over and greeted the browsing customers, solicitously inquiring if they sought anything specific.

"Well," came the reply from the middle-aged woman with poorly colored rust tinted hair, "it would be nice to be able to shop for five minutes without being hassled by everyone who works here. Now please, shoo. If we have a question we'll ask." She turned back to her husband who had continued to read the various titles Archer carried, muttering something about pushy salesmen, and was soon engrossed in her own search.

Chastised, Archer walked over to stand by Tell and Her. She was as stunning today in faded jeans, mismatched Chuck Taylor's, a tattered Tulane sweatshirt, matching the battered green and white back pack that she had the previous day. "Sorry, boss, I was going to tell you I had already offered my help, but you went over before I could get your attention."

"Don't apologize, Tell. You did exactly what I hired you to do. It's my fault for not remembering how thorough you are. Besides, you looked busy with this customer, so I wanted to be sure . . ."

Tell snorted, "Customer? Her? Nah, she's here to rob the place, you should call the cops while she's detained."

She swatted good-naturedly, but sharply at Tell's arm and said, "Archer knows I wouldn't do anything like that. Why I was here just yesterday and hardly stole a thing."

Archer smiled, playing along, feeling her restrained energy just below the level of consciousness. "We might have to call the cops anyway, Tell. She was here, it's true, but maybe it was to case the place, find out where the best stuff is so she wouldn't get nailed for trinkets." The woman's mouth opened in indignation and was ready to say something less than flattering when Archer continued, "Hell, she wouldn't even tell me her name. How paranoid is that? The least she could have done was drop a fake one. She must be up to no good."

Tell seized her arm teasingly, earning him another, more strident smack from Her. "You goon! You know good and well what my name is." She replied, wrested herself free of Tell's grasp, pausing to flip him the bird discreetly. "We'll talk later, Tell. See you soon, Shopkeeper." Turning, she glided out of the store, pausing to pat one of the trolls, on the head as she departed.

"What the hell was that all about Tell? Who is she? Why is she giving me such a hard time about everything?" Archer shook his had, clearing the mental Etch-a-Sketch® "Let's start simple: What's her name?"

"Daniella."

"And...?"

"And what, boss?"

"Oh, you're a fountain of knowledge, you know that? What the hell is her last name?"

"You didn't hire me to chat."

"Then what was that with Daniella?"

"Good point, boss."

"For the love of Hecate, don't call me 'boss'. I've seen you work, and you're good, but I feel like you don't care about this place or me when you call me 'boss'. Now c'mon, tell me a story."

"Her name's Daniella Andrej. I've known her for a couple of years. She lived here when I was coming up, then she left. Obviously she's back. Why's she breaking your rocks? I don't know, but she got jumpier than a frog on a hot plate when you came in. Maybe she likes you."

"Daniella Andrej, huh? Pretty name. Where's she from? I still can't place her accent. The surname name sounds Slavic."

"You'd have to ask her, and good luck. You now know as much as about her as I do, except she loves red wine and chocolate."

"How do you know that?"

"The bottle of Merlot and the Hershey bar she stuffed into her backpack when she recognized me, before she hugged me."

"Alright. Well, I'm going back to my office to finish those lousy invoices. Give a shout if you have a question about anything."

"Will do, Bo...uh, Archer."

Archer had no more than leaned back in his chair, pen in hand checking off his orders and sales for the week when his mobile phone burst into song. Gazing down, he noted it was Trick and debated whether or not to answer. The nice thing about the bird chirping ring tone was it didn't annoy him to the point that he flipped the phone open just to make the noise stop. Sighing, he cracked the phone open. "Hi Trick, how's the melon?"

"Killin' me, but any day above ground is a good one. Speakin' of which, you need to meet me at Armstrong Park ASAP."

"I'm trying to run a business, Trick. I can't up and leave it whenever I want. It's Tell's first day, and I want to see him through it."

"He doin' alright? You trust him yet?"

"He's doing fine, but how do I trust him after one day?"

"It's your call Archer, you're Mr. Intuition; but you remember th' guy I thought was followin' us last night? Well, he was jus' found floatin' in th' pond at Armstrong."

"Just now? How did no one find him earlier? Someone just toss him?"

"Nah, don't look that way. His body's all folded up. It's ugly, Archer. Kinda looks like he got stuffed into a drain pipe along with about a dozen others an' he got pushed loose by th' water pressure and the lack of space. There's more bodies floatin' up behind him. Something is major-league fucked."

"Are you there now?"

"I ain't pullin' these details out of mid-air, buddy. There's more, but I'll wait until ya get here. I'm out."

Archer didn't get to reply; the connection was already severed. Sighing, he dropped the paperwork back on the desk. "Hey Tell? I hate to do this again on your first day, but are you okay to mind the store for a bit longer?"

"No problem, already did it once, wasn't too bad. I think I've got the hang of it."

"It really won't be like this everyday, I promise. There's just some really weird stuff happening today."

Tell nodded and Archer left for Armstrong Park. It was only a short distance over to Rampart Street and easy to find, considering the volume of the First Precinct patrol cars, motorcycles, and bicycles parked haphazardly wherever there was space. Archer entered through the foot gate at what was once Congo Square, close to the St. Louis I cemetery. The Morris Jeff Municipal Auditorium and the Mahalia Jackson Theatre of the Performing Arts loomed in the distance as he traversed the wide cobbled expanse of the clearing.

He passed the massive, majestic oak tree that dominated the center of Congo Square and had been a resident of Louisiana long before any French settlement. Thick and lush, even in the last full bloom of Autumn the ground cover of ferns, monkey grass, and other indigenous flora around the tree served as a natural barrier to all but the most determined of vandals or tree huggers, helping to preserve its health and longevity.

Archer continued up the footpath of gray granite paving stones until he emerged from the tree lined lane at the edge of Louis Armstrong Park. Ducking under the yellow crime scene tape that had been strung across the entrance he made it as close as the large bronze statue of Satchmo before a uniformed officer stopped him. As the young cop began to herd Archer back beyond the tape perimeter, Archer heard Trick call his name. Archer dug in his heels and stopped the officer's prodding until Trick emerged from a larger throng of crime scene specialists, pathologists, detectives, and assorted medical examiner's office staff. Jogging to where Archer stood, Trick lifted the flap of his neck hanger to display his Department of Treasury identification. "Thank you, officer. This man's with me."

The patrolman turned and walked away without a word, resuming his patrol. Archer and Trick walked over a large wooden bridge that spanned the small pond in the park's center, stopping as they reached the center of the viaduct. From their vantage point, they could see the coroner's assistant zipping closed two black body bags then reaching into the equipment truck and pulling out more. Archer realized he recognized their silent bar mate from the night before. He looked much different today. His skin was almost translucent in death, his clothing and hair bedraggled from his time in the water.

"Any idea who he was?" Archer asked, nodding toward the man's body.

"According to his passport, his name was Giacomo Francione, an Italian national. Arrived here day before yesterday. Th' more interesting thing is this." Trick held up two evidence bags with sodden papers inside.

Lifting his left hand slightly, he said, "According to this document here, our boy was a priest. A Dominican, dispatched here by his order in Vatican City. Th' other paper is th' address and a crude map to where he was stayin'. Th' address is right up th' way at Our Lady of Guadalupe Church over on Basin Street. I was thinkin' maybe we could take a walk over there."

"Won't N.O.P.D. do that? I mean this isn't exactly a case for a part-time Fed, Trick."

"Oh, I'm sure they're already there talkin' to whoever they need to, but I don't think they're gonna axe th' right questions."

"Yeah? How'd you figure that?"

"Two things. First, it's personal for me. Th' other body bags down there have two Moonlight Mission folk in 'em. One was a volunteer, th' other a guy who has been clean for three months now jus' startin' to turn his life around." He paused, looking at Archer, trying to decide how best to broach the second of his reasons. "I overheard th' medical examiner talking to one of th' detectives after she pegged th' liver of th' first floater with th' meat thermometer. She said, there was no lividity or pooling on the corpse. Not a drop of blood in th' wound she caused with th' thermometer when she spiked th' liver. There are strange ligature marks on th' neck, consistent with strangulation, and twin puncture marks on th' back of th' shoulder near th' subclavian vein."

"I'm sorry for your people Trick, I am, but they were murdered. I'm not a cop anymore and you have no jurisdiction to run an investigation. Let the police do their job, alright?"

"You ain't been listening to me, Archer, you're missin' th' point here."

"What point? That someone grabbed these people by their throat, turned them around, and stabbed them so they'd bleed out? Sounds messy, maybe ritualistic. It seems to me that we have a sociopath running wild, killing in a pattern."

"Therein lies th' rub, Archer. Th' killings aren't messy a'tall, an' no one's been stabbed or choked ta death. Th' punctures are all shallow, and there's not much blood left in th' bodies of any of them. Those're bite marks, Archer, and my gut tells me that Francione th' priest was some kind of a vampire hunter."

Archer burst out laughing, sobering quickly when he saw the black look on Trick's face. "You're serious, aren't you? You're actually fucking serious. Vampires? Oh man, Toinetta's going to love this one. What do you want to do?"

"I think I want to talk to someone at th' church 'bout their vampire hunter. You wanna come along?"

"Not especially, but like I said, Toinetta's going to love this. Lead the way."

CHAPTER 10

ARCHER AND TRICK walked in silence the short distance to Our Lady of Guadalupe Church and the Shrine of Saint Jude where the famous limestone cavern Lourdes Grotto sat between the church and the rectory. Trick took the lead, insisting they enter the rectory first because that was where the priests resided. Archer, who had grown up thoroughly agnostic, admitted he didn't know his rectory from his apse. Archer silently followed Trick into a cozy, simple, little reception area with egg shell white plaster walls and wheat colored industrial berber carpeting. Items from the Saint Jude gift shop attached to the rectory decorated the walls and receptionist's desk.

An elderly black woman, somewhere between eighty and old enough to have known Jesus personally, sat behind the desk, all blue tinted hair, mismatched polyester, and lipstick stained false teeth. Trick approached the desk and leaning in, said, "Good afternoon, I was hoping to see th' Vicar. Is he here?"

The woman squinted up at him and replied, "I'm sorry Brother, but there's no liquor here. I can give you a voucher to The Moonlight Mission down the street. They can give you a hot meal and maybe a place to sleep." Opening a desk drawer she rummaged through a thin sheaf of files, pulling out a church referral form that Trick's predecessor, Baird Mooney had created when he first opened the Mission.

"No ma'am, you misunderstood me," Trick replied as she thrust the paper toward him. "I need th' Vicar, Father Lucian. Is he here today?"

"Oh, my, bless me, I'm so sorry," replied the old woman, adjusting her hearing aid. "Father Lucian is over in the church hearing confession until three thirty. Do y'all have an appointment to see Father today?"

"No, but it's very important that we speak to him. We'll just go to th' church and wait for him to finish."

"It would be better if you waited here, honey. We can't have folk going in and out of the church disrupting our parishioners and visitors."

Trick looked at his watch. "It's only thirty minutes until he finishes, we'll go and pay our respects to Saint Jude. Thank you ma'am."

She waved her gnarled, arthritic, hand at them but they were already heading back into the bright afternoon sun. They walked through Lourdes Grotto, a first for Archer. He was struck by all of the small wood and bronze plaques, and nameplates affixed at random all over the walls and ceiling of the small limestone cave. A separate niche held devotional racks and an honor box, where votive candles of various sizes could be purchased and burned. The ceiling and wall behind it was blackened with years of carbon build up.

Emerging from the other side, they passed what looked like a restaurant size coffee urn with an ornate cross deeply etched into its side, a small spigot protruding from the front. A woman with a nametag identifying her as a gift shop worker was drawing water from it into tiny vials labeled with the church's name, identifying it as Holy Water, A gift from the Shrine of Saint Jude. Trick was past her and opening a heavy wooden door, waiting for Archer to enter the church.

Inside was cool after the bright sun, the inky dark was broken only by candles and the diffuse sunlight creeping in through the multitude of stained glass. Their eyes adjusted quickly as they stood looking around. The first thing Archer noticed was the exquisite gray and brown marble altar bracketed by twin images of angelic beauty and splendor, wings high and straight behind them, seemingly ready to launch into the heavens with any and every prayer offered by the faithful. To their right was another niche with row after row of votive holders at the feet of statue of Saint Peter and Saint

Theresa. Trick nudged Archer and murmured, pointing to the statues, "You know who those two are?"

"Not a clue. I'm guessing you're going to tell me," Archer replied.

"They're Saint Florian and Saint Dymphna. They stand watch directly over them," Trick inclined his head to the opposite wall. The votives and candles burned brightly enough that Archer could see the plaques listing the names of policemen and firemen who had given their lives protecting the city and her citizens. The list was far too long, Archer thought somberly.

By his side, Trick elaborated, "Archer this church was once a lowly little chapel. When th' epidemics hit th' city in th' nineteenth century, all th' victims of Yellow Fever or Yellow Jack, as it was called then, were brought here for rapid last rites before being carted across the street for interment in Saint Louis I Cemetery. This part of th' church was re-dedicated in 1971 to Saint Jude, to honor th' men and women who had made the ultimate sacrifice in the line of duty, be it military, police, or fire fighters."

"Sweet Jesus, Trick," Archer blurted then blushed as a parishioner glared daggers at him.

Motioning for Archer to follow, Trick led them down the side of the church's near wall, away from the altar, and the rows of simple wooden pews interspersed with parishioners and guests kneeling in prayer. Stopping in the back of the church where the holy water fonts stood before the main doors Archer couldn't wait anymore. In a quieter tone, he asked, "Did you just channel a tour guide or something? I thought you weren't religious. How do you know about this stuff?"

The umber colored marble gleamed in the afternoon sun and Archer followed Trick's gaze to two confessionals on the opposite wall, one with a small red light glowing over the top, indicating it was in use. Trick smirked and said, "I got th' tour from th' Padre. You'll see, he likes to talk."

Within moments, a stooped elderly white man pushed the door open and made his way slowly to the front of the church with the assistance of a gnarled wooden cane. He sank at a snail's pace to his knees and Archer hoped someone would be close by to help the infirmed man to his feet when he had made his penance. Trick touched Archer's arm pointing to his watch. It was three thirty on the dot and Archer noticed that the red light, which had turned green when the old man had departed the confessional, was now dark.

A door on the far side of the confessional opened and a middle-aged man in ceremonial raiment stepped out and turned to close the door quietly. Trick walked over to the man and Archer heard a murmur of surprise as the priest held out a hand and Trick took it warmly in his own. They spoke for a moment, then Trick motioned toward Archer with his head. The priest looked across the room at him, then nodded. Trick and the priest made their way over to Archer and Trick introduced Father Lucian Finnernan.

The priest had a receding hairline of once brilliant copper locks that had faded with age to that of a rotten carrot. His sharp nose showed the broken capillary roadmap of a man who enjoyed more than a casual relationship with the bottle, and the knowing eyes of a man who had witnessed all things good and evil in the world, yet still believed in the inherent decency of the human species. His handshake was firm, dry, and friendly as he greeted Archer then motioned the two men to follow him out the front door, where they were again blinded by the change in lighting.

Father Finnernan led them back to the rectory, waving cordially as they passed the old receptionist, and into another room that turned out to be a cozy sitting area. A younger, less care-worn looking priest entered from the far end of the room and offered to bring tea, and biscuits for Father and his guests. With a nod of assent the priest was gone and Finnernan shifted in his seat until he could see both Trick and Archer.

Gazing sharply at them for a moment, he finally broke the silence with the faintest trace of an Irish brogue. "Well Patrick, what can I do for you today?" He looked at Archer and said, "Patrick is one of the finest folks I've had the fortune of meeting in my time here, even if he isn't Catholic." The three men chuckled convivially and Trick squirmed slightly in his posh high backed chair, uncomfortable with the attention. Brushing away the compliment Trick directed the conversation back to their business.

"Lucian, I'm not here in an entirely social capacity, though I always enjoy seeing you."

"Would this be about poor Father Francione, then?" Finnernan crossed himself. "God bless him. The police were here earlier inquiring about him. Terrible thing to happen. Terrible."

"We were hoping you could tell us why a Vatican City Dominican was stayin' here. Was he on sabbatical, or maybe researchin' somethin' at th' Archdiocese archives?"

"I believe he spent some time at the archive, yes, but I'm not sure how comfortable I am telling you any more than that. I confess, I don't know much about him or his reasons for being here. He had just recently arrived, we didn't have the time to sit and talk at length."

"It's th' rest of what you do know that we're lookin' for, Lucian."

"Are you here as a federal agent or a nosy neighbor, Patrick?"

"A bit of both, but more of th' latter. You see, Father Francione was found with two of my people from th' Mission, and I'm trying to put a couple of odd pieces together."

"Ah, I was afraid of that Patrick. I can't disclose church business to a layman, not if I ever wish to advance myself. I hope to make Archbishop before I'm through."

"I guess I never saw priests as particularly ambitious, Lucian. C'mon. We're really in a bind here. You know you can help, why won't you?"

"Ambition is part of the human equation, Patrick and perfectly acceptable so long as aspiration doesn't become covetous. That's where the church draws its distinction." Lucian Finnernan tried, but failed to look apologetic. "I am sorry, Patrick but I don't know what else to say. I've spoken to the police and The Archdiocese before them. I have my directives on the matter."

Archer noticed a buzzing in his head, almost as if a horsefly had become trapped nearby starting just as a second priest returned with a tray of refreshments. He set it on the coffee table that served as the center for all three chairs. Father Finnernan poured tea for them all, and passed around the sugar bowl and creamer. The second priest excused himself and the buzzing seemed to subside as Archer reached for his cup.

Trick stirred sugar into his cup absently, then looked at Finnernan. "These murders weren't your run of th' mill, Lucian. I don't know how much th' police told you, but they were all killed th' same way and stuffed into a drain pipe down in Armstrong Park. Francione's body dislodged somehow and set over a dozen other corpses free to float in that pond. If you could help stop anyone else from dyin', then what's the harm?"

Looking distressed, Finnernan replied, "I truly wish I could help, but I have been instructed by the Archdiocese to direct all inquiries regarding Father Francione to them. That is what I told the police, also."

Trick set his tea down on the table, his exasperation at the reticence of his friend growing by the moment. Archer asked, "Excuse me Father, but it sounds like you're keepin' something from everyone who is asking. Could you at least tell us what a Dominican priest, fresh from The Vatican was doing here? Was he to be a new rector or vicar?"

"I'll answer this last question then I must bid you good day. Historically, at least since World War I, the Oblates of Mary Immaculate have served predominantly as rectors of Saint Anthony's then Our Lady of Guadalupe, but it is not at all uncommon for a Dominican Father to serve here in any capacity. As for Father Francione's business here, I'm sorry I can't be more forthcoming, truly I am. I simply can't help you." Father Finnernan stood, offered his hand to Trick and Archer and said, "Feel free to finish your tea. I have other matters that I am late attending. Patrick, may God bless you and permit you to keep up the wonderful work you are doing at The Moonlight Mission. Mr. Sweet, it was my pleasure to meet you. The Lord bless and keep you. I hope we meet again."

When he had gone, Archer and Trick stood up and walked out of the rectory without a word. Walking away from the church Trick grumbled, "Well he was just a baptismal font of information wasn't he?"

Archer nodded and said, "What did you expect Trick? It's not as if he can lay out church business for you because you ask nice. He's an ambitious man given an agenda by his superiors. He may be shaken up about the murder of a fellow priest, but he's not inclined to talk about it, at least not with us."

"Yeah, well it seems to me he'd be more interested in helpin' bring th' killer to justice than protectin' th' sanctity of a dead man's privacy."

"To me, it's another sign that we are not supposed to poke our head in this one Trick, maybe move forward with our lives. Let's go back to doing what we do, not what we did."

"Maybe," Trick conceded. "Hey Archer, it's time to be gettin' the Mission fed and buttoned down for th' night, and I'm down two sets of hands. Can you help me out for an hour or so?"

Archer looked at his watch and sighed, "Yeah, sure. I can help. Just let me call Tell and ask him to latch the front doors when he leaves. I'll lock up proper when I get back."

CHAPTER 11

IT WAS MODERATE bedlam for the next two hours before the doors closed for the night. Archer took up an apron and helped to serve the last trickle of the indigent and down-on-their-luck who came for a hot meal and a warm bed. After that he helped dole out the individual plastic bags of toiletry items for the men and women before helping Trick set up and place the last of the cots in the main hall. It was a strenuous business running a shelter. Everyone had to be in bed by nine o'clock and turned out by five the following morning.

Trick motioned Archer to follow him down the hallway toward the business wing of the building. Unlocking his office door, Trick switched on the lights, and dialed down the controls on the window-box air conditioner to knock the mustiness from the air before plopping heavily into the big padded swivel chair behind his scarred pine desk. Archer sat across from him and let the cool stale air wash across him for a moment.

"You know we gotta call Toinetta an' tell her about this."

"Yeah," Archer replied tiredly. "She's going to crow for a month that she was right, but we need her."

Trick hit the button for the speakerphone on his desk and dialed Toinetta, who answered on the eighth ring.

"Yeah, hello?"

"Hi Toinetta." Archer and Trick replied in unison.

"Hmph. 'Bout time you called me. I heard they found some more bodies today. Archer, did you talk to your friend?"

"Yes ma'am, and he said he might work on it, but we came across something a little more intriguing."

"Oh? Well out with it. I'm an old woman. Shouldn't keep the elderly waiting, it frightens us."

"We think we have a vampire problem, Toinetta. You know anything about them? What's real? What's Hollywood fantasy?"

"Lawdy. I didn't think it was going to be something like this. I really don't know much, I'll have to do some research—"

Toinetta was interrupted by Archer's cell phone chirping. Looking at the caller ID he saw it was Wendell, so he stepped back away from the conversation and activated the receiver.

"Wendell buddy, it's good of you to call. I appreciate you helping me like this; I didn't know where else to turn."

"Yeah, whatever Archer. Just shut up and listen okay? I found fifteen other deaths like the Tulane girls. They're the only two that made the paper. The police are keeping a lid on this situation, man, I mean there are no leaks in this boat. With few exceptions there doesn't seem to be a pattern to the times or killings except most happen sometime after—"

"Sundown."

"Give the man a cigar. They all have the same characteristic of attack, listen to this."

"Wild guess, ligature marks on the throat and puncture wounds on the back?"

"So why the fuck did I go wasting my precious time if you already know all this shit? Goddamn you Archer, you were just trying to make me feel, what? Useful? Like I was helping my old buddy, like old times? Well fuck you very much for wasting my time pal."

"Wendell hold on. Everything you found was dead on right, exactly what I was looking for. It's just that N.O.P.D. tumbled to a mass dumping ground of corpses today. All of the bodies match the attack signatures and I happened to be close enough to see one of the bodies. Believe me, I needed to hear this for my own sanity. You did great. Thank you."

"Well, okay. I'll buy that, I guess. What are you guys dealing with so I can tip the right set of eyes if there are any more deaths like this."

"Are you sure you want to know Wendell? It's way the hell out there."

"Fuck." Pierce paused briefly, "What? You think getting mauled by a psychic revenant was normal? Go on, hit me with it. I haven't had a drink yet tonight; I could use the excuse."

"Vampires," Archer replied softly, "We're dealing with vampires."

"Vamp-? Why do I get the feeling you're not talking about that cult of whack jobs down in The Quarter? Oh, I can't wait to drop this on the homicide guys tomorrow. 'Guess what? You're not after human killers, you're chasing Anne fucking Rice's Noble Dead!' Just perfect." Archer heard Wendell sigh across the phone line. "Do you need me for anything else Archer? I've got to bail."

"No. Thanks for getting back to me so fast. I appreciate it. We might need your brains when we start tracking these suckers down. Count you in?"

"Suckers? Man that's bad, even for you Archer. Yeah, call in the cavalry if you need me. I'm not a total wet brain yet. I'll try to be sober enough to make a difference."

Archer hung up and returned back to the speakerphone where Toinetta and Trick were arguing over whether any movie or book from pop culture seemed to have an underlying theme for destroying vampires.

"Sunlight, fire, a stake through th' heart, and decapitation are th' only ones I can remember. What about you Archer?"

Archer was about to reply when they were interrupted by a manic pounding outside on the closed garage door down the hall. It seemed to make the entire building shake in an unending staccato of metallic noise.

"What is that?" Archer heard Toinetta ask. Archer looked over to see his friend freeing a sawed off pump-action twelve gauge shotgun from under the scarred wooden desk.

"Sorry Toinetta, gon' hafta to give you a call back," said Trick as he disconnected the call, opened his desk drawer and pulled out his service weapon, a nine-millimeter Beretta, semi-automatic. He tossed the pistol to Archer and said, "Clips full and th' pipe is hot, you know th' drill."

Archer had never known Trick kept a shotgun hidden so deviously, but had little time to ask as he found himself trailing behind Trick down the short hallway back into the main room. Every man and woman was awake, some hiding their heads beneath their pillow, screaming into them, trying to drown out the din around them. Some were sitting on the side of their cots feet dangling or touching the floor, blankets huddled around their shoulders; others were shuffling aimlessly around the common room as if in a daze, their hands on their ears.

Stopping abruptly, Archer felt a buzzing in his head, and a metallic taste in his mouth as the adrenaline hit his stomach like a sucker punch. Something magical was afoot, the air seemed to prickle with energy, and he was doubtful they had the proper weapons to handle the situation.

Trick ran past the main entrance, a garage door, to the man-door; a single entrance for simple access without raising the garage door. Next to the smaller portal he had installed a simple black and white monitor that was connected to a static camera and one-way intercom system. Flipping it on, he saw five people. Three of them were dressed like they could have been Mission regulars. The other two, a well-dressed man and beautiful blonde woman showing more skin than clothing, were most likely Bourbon Street revelers who had staggered a few blocks too far. All of them were pounding on the corrugated steel garage door, frantically looking over their shoulders, their faces aglow with the common heat of naked terror. Trick lowered the shotgun to depress the talk button. "Y'all gon' hafta move on. Doors are closed for th' night, no exceptions."

The reaction on the screen was immediate and heart rending. The couple slumped as if defeated and reconciled to facing whatever had frightened them so. The three street denizens began to scream louder in addition to the pounding, tearing the skin on their knuckles and palms, leaving bloody smears on the door as it clattered like a hail storm on a tin roof under the beating. One of the men stopped pounding, craned his head back as if he had just heard something, then turned and ran for the man-door just out of range of the camera. Trick watched the doorknob turn and rattle, the shotgun still resting under his arm.

Archer caught up to Trick. "We've got to get them inside. There's something out there, possibly the vampires. I can feel something—"

The rattling on the doorknob stopped and Trick caught a quick glimpse of the man as he was suddenly hauled back into the camera frame, just behind the other four people. The body was suspended at least two feet from the ground. Archer was shocked to see the man's leg's flailing uselessly, like watching a lobster as it gets dropped into a boiler pot.

Falling silent, the others turned to watch in rapt horror the macabre spectacle, mesmerized by what they were seeing. The victim's agony rose to a crescendo then the energy seemed to sap from the man as he ceased struggling altogether. Within seconds, the limp pliant body was flung aside, out of the camera's range. The horrifying spell broken, the screams of the survivors swelled and grew quickly to a fevered pitch, audible through the thick door.

Trick released the intercom and stepped back, helping Archer as he flipped the dead bolt open, unlatched the chain and slid the bottom bolt. Turning, Trick pushed back the frightened tenants who had been watching the drama unfold and now pressed forward to see the tiny screen, using his shotgun at port arms, roaring for them to move and stand away from the door. He racked the pump action on the shotgun and looked at Archer. "What's th' plan, big man?"

"On three, I'm going outside to bring them in. You stand against the door frame and cover. Be ready to pull it closed with or without me on the inside. Once I'm out, I'll lay down some pistol fire and with any luck wound or at least frighten the vampires enough to buy the time we need to get everyone back here." Archer checked the pistol's safety and Trick motioned with the shotgun. "When I get out there, you see something that isn't me or those people, start blasting. Got it?"

"You're outta your mind, but I got your back. We go on your count buddy," replied Trick.

"Alright, let's go. Now!" Archer tumbled out the door in a low roll, coming up in a combat crouch, tracking for targets. "Everybody, come to me, we have the door covered. Hurry!" The roar of Trick's shotgun, the pellet spray close enough to make Archer flinch, obscured his last command.

The scene outside was utter chaos. Archer saw the first victim crumpled in a heap against the far wall, the two remaining homeless men seemed rooted in fear at the garage door, but the couple saw their freedom and sprinted for the open door. The man pushed his lady friend in front of him and she rocketed past Archer, through the doorway to safety. The man drew even with Archer his eyes bulging in his panic, but still managing to give Archer a grateful look as he reached for the door. Suddenly, he screamed high and loud as he was raised off the ground. Archer drew a bead above the thrashing man's right shoulder and feathered the trigger once, twice, a third time as the man began to quiver uncontrollably, his screams dying to a weak mewling. Archer fired again, and Trick, taking Archer's lead, let loose with another blast from the shotgun. They were rewarded with an inarticulate roar of pain as the man was suddenly free of the grip that held him.

Archer felt a prickling sensation and the hair on his neck raise as he sensed something totally new, nearby, more malignant than anything he had ever encountered. He motioned and yelled to the homeless men again and they ran for him, the gunfire having snapped them out of their galvanized state. Trick fired over their heads as they gained the doorway, then swiveled back to cover Archer as he went to collect the fallen man who was moaning in a heap on the cracked sidewalk.

"C'mon Archer, gotta move, gotta move! I can't see a goddamn thing out there, you're vulnerable. Grab him and haul ass."

"Vulnerable. How perfectly articulated. Their fear is intoxicating is it not, brother?" The voice had come from directly in front of Archer and he was hit by a wave of psychic paralysis so intense, his mind seemed frozen, like a fly in a drop of amber. His weapon came up instinctively, searching for a target, his sense of self-preservation still functioning.

"Come brother. Drink of the one who has stung you. It will restore your constitution." This voice came from directly behind Archer as he felt a vice like grip clamp on his throat, cutting off circulation to his brain and lifting him, his feet flailing like a marionette on a drunken puppeteer's string. He couldn't scream. Couldn't draw the breath to do so. Black spots began to flit in Archer's vision and he knew he was seconds from blacking out. Raising the pistol Archer pointed it over his shoulder at the same time he thought he heard Trick yell his name and the roar of another shotgun blast. Archer thought it was the roaring of his blood through his ears, but a brief stinging pain on his face, hand, and shoulder told him otherwise.

With the last of his strength, he squeezed the trigger of his own weapon spastically thinking as his consciousness detached that he would have to talk to Trick about not peppering him with the shotgun in the future. He heard one more faint blast and everything faded to black as he slumped in his attacker's grasp, his pistol clattering useless, to the sidewalk.

CHAPTER 12

Archer came to his senses slowly, pain leading his way back to consciousness. His eyes flew open and he jerked upward as his last memory surged back into his head, pictures of the final moments before darkness took him. Strong arms held him down and a familiar voice was saying over and over, "Its okay Archer, you're safe, relax."

Archer slumped back onto the cot closing his eyes in relief, but not before noticing the circle of concerned faces behind Trick. He felt sore from head to toe, and his face, neck, and shoulder blazed with a stinging sensation. "Did everyone get in safely?"

"You're here, ain't ya? Th' guy you brought in is on his way to th' hospital, but the medics aren't holding out much hope for him. They thought he had pretty much bled out."

"What happened? It just let me go?" He reached around and felt the sore spots on this face and neck, his fingers coming away bloody. "Aw, shit, it bit me? What does that mean? Am I going to become one of them now?"

Trick chuckled nervously. "Take it easy. When you hear what happened, you'll be too relieved to be pissed. First things first; ya didn't get bit, that's where I grazed you with th' shotgun blast. Don't worry though, I only load rock salt into that thing, so th' bumps and stinging will go away as th' crystals absorb or push their way out."

"Rock salt? You know, you could have told me that was all you had before I went out there thinking you had my back. Jesus on a jet ski, dude!"

"Chill, alright? If it wasn't rock salt, you might be dead right now, and I doubt that buck or bird shot would have done any damn good against the vampires anyway. I heard one of them say it had been stung, so I am guessin' it was my salt, not your lead."

"Did anyone see anything? Even when those fucking things were right in front and behind me, I could hear them but not see them. What's up with that? How do we fight something invisible?"

"Some folks could see them. Th' homeless guys we snagged saw them and th' lady that was with th' guy said she could see something, but not as well as th' guys from th' street."

"What'd they see?"

"I'll tell ya later, when the cops leave, but they're waitin' to talk to you."

"What do I say when they ask me how I got away?"

"Tell 'em the truth, you blacked out and woke up here, that's also a story for later, got it?"

"Yeah, but why do I think I'm going to hate this even more when you tell me?

"Probably because you will. Don't sweat it for now. You ready to talk to th' blue boys?"

"Yeah, bring em' on."

Archer sat up flinching as he felt the salt shift in his wounds. He knew he had more than a few hours of discomfort and some interesting stippled scars when the wounds healed. Just more to add to the collection. Sighing, he imagined finding a nice blind woman who could read his body in Braille. With luck, she wouldn't be shocked by the scars accumulated in less than thirty years courtesy of the military, the police force, a psychic revenant, and now a run-in with invisible vampires. *Better make that a blind girl fresh out of an asylum, then I might have a shot.* He swung his feet off the cot and stood shakily, the room spinning for a moment, before the floor steadied beneath him.

He pushed past the circle of well wishers and blue uniforms taking statements from those willing to talk. Following Trick down the hall to his office where two detectives sat, he found one reclining in Trick's chair, his feet up on the desk, the other stood behind him, shifting from foot to foot. They gazed at Archer with inscrutable countenances.

"Archer Sweet. We meet again," said the man sitting behind the desk.

"Defective Corgan, what the hell are you doing here? This isn't your jurisdiction."

The other officer answered as Corgan flushed crimson. "*Detective* Corgan is here as part of a city-wide task force formed to solve the spree killings in the city. Now please, have a seat and tell us what happened."

Corgan snorted, "This oughtta be a pip."

"Well in a gesture of good will toward you, Corgan," said Trick blandly, a glint of malevolence in his eye, "I'll ask you once nicely to get'cha dirty feet off my desk and your fat doughnut lookin' ass out of my chair."

Corgan went from crimson to vermilion stumbling to get his feet off the desk and make a lunge for Trick as the other cop put his hand on the outraged Corgan's shoulder.

"Remember, Detective, you are here in the spirit of cooperation with the other districts. You're off your turf. I don't care one gnat's nut what personal issues you have with Mr. Sweet or Mr. Boulieux. Now play nice."

Trick slithered around and took his seat as Corgan moved to stand and fume against the wall near the office door. Archer took the guest chair and a bottle of water that Trick retrieved for him from the mini-fridge by his desk.

Archer ran through the story, leaving out no detail up until he lost consciousness. "What else can I say, everything went black."

The two detectives exchanged glances and the first one, a First District gold shield named Al Willig, closed his notebook and tucked it into his blazer pocket. He withdrew a business card from a slim gold case and set it on the desk. "If you two remember anything else, give me a call please." He smiled as Corgan walked out of the office without a word. "Unless you'd prefer to talk to him," he said as motioned toward Corgan's back. "Take care now."

Willig left and Archer took a long drink from the water bottle, then passed it over to Trick, who finished it tossing the empty in the recycling bin. "So what'cha think Archer?"

"That Corgan's still an ass munch."

"That's old news. They have a task force convened. They know something is real fucked up in th' Crescent. You think they believed us?"

"Probably not, but we were the only sober or straight people that had front row seats. Besides, Wendell told me there is a total press black out on this right now. Tourism would take a big one in the ass if folks knew they weren't safe and couldn't be protected."

"Wow. You should hear the description th' girl gave of what was after 'em, the other survivors, too. Least they were consistent 'bout what they think they saw. If it's true, then we've got problems sho'nuff."

"Well? I was kind of out. Want to fill me in?"

"Oh, right. My bad. How does seven foot tall walkin' slabs o' muscle with yella colored skin stretched so tight over a triangular skull that th' face looks almost Chinese? Huge catcher's mitt hands with wicked claws that seemed to be able to retract. Oh, yeah, nearly forgot, a big honkin' mouth, that can stretch completely across th' top of a grown man's back when it's opened alla th' way? Th' jaws seem able to unhinge when th' mouth opens. Believe it or not, th' teeth ain't that big, which I guess explains th' lack of depth in th' puncture wounds."

"Sounds like the way the jaw comes unhinged they can bleed a body dry pretty quick, kind of like a suction pump, especially if the teeth are hollow."

"Like snake fangs, except instead of injectin venom' they're drawin' blood?"

"That would be my guess. And trust me, I believe the part about them being tall and muscular. The damn thing picked me up like a paper doll, and was pinching my neck with what felt like one hand."

"Tha's somethin' at least; you lose consciousness before they put th' bite on you. Kinda humane, in a sick way."

"Nothing humane about it, Trick. It helps them get to the blood faster."

"How's that?"

"Your brain demands a constant flow of oxygenated blood or it ceases functioning. The pathways to the brain come up from the shoulders into the neck. What happens when you kink a garden hose when the water is still running?"

"Th' pressure builds..."

"Yep, the heart keeps beating and pushing against the clamped veins and arteries, so when they bite into the shoulder, on the subclavian vein, there's an immediate gush and tension release. They don't have to work as hard or as long. I'm guessing the vampires toss their victims like we do toothpaste tubes. There is still a little left, but it's too easy to just open a new one."

Trick shook his head, trying to absorb Archer's hypothesis. He said nothing for a few moments, then shrugged. "You're prob'ly right on th' mark, I sho'nuff can't think of anything else that makes more sense. I also think I'm swearing off squeeze ketchup for a while."

"Trick? How did I get away? Why was I spared? We both heard the same thing, and I don't think the rock salt would be enough to kick me loose and make them run off. Why go through the process of dimming my lights and not taking their meal? Kind of like going to a drive-thru and forgetting to pick up your food at the window?"

"It's just a guess mind ya, but I'm thinkin' th' wolf had a little somethin' to do with it."

"Wolf?"

"Mm-hmm. At least, it looked like a wolf. Came outta nowhere, snarlin' and snappin'. I'd just fired my last shell and was trying to reload when this thing came barrellin' out of th' dark right from th' alley on th' far side of th' Mission. Big ol' thing, black pelt, maybe six or seven feet tall on its hind legs. Graceful brute; it leapt like it could see what it was aimin' for, and thud. That thing made some serious contact with th' vampire, 'cause your whole body shook like a cotton shirt on a clothesline during a hurricane wind. Then you were kissin' concrete. Th' wolf landed light as you please and kept circlin' itself between you and where I guess th' vampires were. It kinda yelped out once and flinched, looked like maybe one of th' vampires took a swipe at it with them claws. Anyway, th' cops started comin', and th' wolf waited another minute or so before it turned tail and ran off. I went outside and brought you in."

"You said vampires? Plural? As in we're dealing with more than one?"

"Witnesses said they saw two. I know my English ain't so hot, but my math is better. Two is plural and more than one."

"Son of a bitch, I was hoping it was talking to itself. I heard two voices but books and movies usually make vampires out to be solitary hunter types."

"Guess continuin' to use pop culture books as valuable reference guides are out of th' question."

"Oh, you're a wit tonight, Trick."

"And you're about as fun as a barrel of sea sick monkeys, Archer."

"You're not the one who got attacked by a vampire and have a melon full of rock salt melting into your body."

"I already said I'm sorry 'bout that. Ain't gonna say it again. Nobody asked you to go running out there like you did."

"Someone had to and I didn't see volunteers lining up."

Oh, so now I'm a coward because I don't have a death wish? That's rich Archer, that's jus' rich."

Archer stopped short, the bitterness of his retort nearly choking him. Was Trick right? He had quit being a cop and went into safer environments, but did he still harbor a latent desire to join his wife on the other side?

"Did I thank you for saving my stupid ass?"

Trick was looking off at something Archer couldn't see and replied quietly, "Nah you didn't, but don't sweat it." He turned to look at his friend. "Listen, I got no call to be judgmental. You did a damn brave thing, goin' out there like that. I hope if the situation were reversed, I'd have the nerve to do what you did."

"There may be something to what you said before. I haven't given it much thought, but maybe you're right. I don't recall being that brave when I was cop. Reckless, yeah, but brave?"

Trick laughed, hearing the playful self-deprecation creep into his friend's voice, "I'm gonna go set you up for th' night. Nobody's leaving here 'til th' dawn, sho'nuff. Vampires may not care about big groups or massive exposure like they had with th' cops here before, but I'm not takin' any chances. You can go home when th' sun is up."

"No one's arguing with you partner. I'm fried, not to mention salted. I try to walk home, some drunken revelers are bound to hallucinate I'm a walking bag of pork rinds."

Archer heard Trick's laughter as he left the office to go set up an extra cot. "What is it with me and freakin' wolves?" he mused aloud as he pilfered another bottled water from Trick's fridge.

CHAPTER 13

ARCHER WOKE UP on the floor, stiff and sore with a splitting headache, the result of falling out off the narrow cot and face planting on the cement. He sat up, disoriented, bloody, and frightened by his pain until he realized he had spent the night at the Mission, not in his cozy twin bed at home.

Memories of the previous night flooded back when he went to stretch and rub his face. Walking over to the small shaving mirror hanging on the wall, he gazed at his face, neck, arm, and shoulder where the rock salt had peppered him the night before. Had he not known better, he could have convinced himself that he had suffered an outbreak of acne on one side of his body. Silver lining: thanks to the salt the wounds would not get infected, and while the open skin still felt raw, the salt no longer burned. He washed the blood from his split lip and gingerly dabbed it dry.

Dressing quickly, he left the small room and entered the main room where the bustle of the morning meal was at its height. Most people brushed past him without a second look, their thoughts already on their day. Some looked at Archer with a mixture of awe and fear. Trick came out from behind the counter at the far end of the service line, shucked his plastic serving gloves and clutched Archer's elbow.

"G'mornin' there he-ro. Glad you're finally up. Th' people you saved last night wanted to thank you before they left. I figured it might be a good idea for us to hear their version of what happened up to th' time we stepped in. Th' regulars we can catch anytime, but th' woman doesn't belong here and she might be harder to track down later." He lowered his voice and leaned in closer to Archer. "Her boyfriend didn't make it. Cops were here earlier to give her th' news."

Archer was upset the man was dead. He knew that rehashing what could not be changed would only make him crazy. "Shit, that's too bad. Hey, before I do this, can I get a cup of coffee? I don't have too much time; I have to get to Blessed Be. I didn't even get to lock the place up last night."

Trick nodded, signaling for a mug of coffee to be brought over as he led Archer over to a table where he was greeted by pale haunted faces.

The blonde was disheveled, rocking herself gently in the chair, her smeared make-up the only color her face could generate. Looking up she smiled at him gratefully, tears brimming down her cheeks, runnels of mascara caked on her chin and jaw. She stood and flung her arms about his neck in a ferocious bear hug that made his head spin and shoulder scream as she sobbed her gratitude messily into his ear. He patted her reassuringly, uncomfortable with the familiarity of the embrace. Pulling away, looking embarrassed by her outburst and the mess of make-up and mucus she left on Archer's shoulder, she found her seat and stared miserably into her coffee mug. Mumbling shyly by way of introduction that her name was Theda Hyde from Lewisberg, Pennsylvania.

Archer took the coffee mug brought to him and sat down amidst the group of survivors, completing the set. He looked at them all and sighed. "So can anyone tell me what the hell happened last night?"

"Hell," mumbled the filthy white man at the end of the table. "When the man's right he's right."

"And you are..." Archer asked when the man fell silent, his gaze fixed on his coffee mug.

"Bobby Betcholly," replied the sullen man. "At least I used to be."

Archer's gaze hardened as he tried to match this mess of a man to the boy he knew in high school, a star point guard who had earned a scholarship to Mississippi State. "Bitch hole? That you?"

The tousled, unkempt man cringed at the nickname but nodded hazily, refusing to look Archer in the eye through the mess of lanky, stringy, baby-shit brown hair.

"He don't like that name so much, no more. Don't mean what it used to," said the black man sitting across from Archer.

"And who are you?" Archer asked as he shifted his gaze away from the strung out shell that had once been a finely tuned athlete.

"Name's Cracker. Didn't get a chance to thank you for savin' my ass last night. You'll be understandin' if I don't hug you like Ms. Thang did."

"Cracker, eh? Kind of an ironic moniker, isn't it," Archer asked with a wry smirk, trying to lighten the mood.

"Oh, it's not like *cracker*, like he'd call you or me." Betcholly said, glaring at the dark face. "He used to pimp out his own sisters and their friends, got 'em all addicted to Mr. Brownstone. Every single one of 'em, including Cracker, ended up with HIV, from sharing needles. If any of his stable of whores got out of line or sassed him, he'd crack 'er across the face with a leather sap he keeps in his pocket. Depending on his mood he'd cut her, rape her, or shoot her so full of horse she'd O.D. Keeping his pimp hand strong."

"You gonna be gettin' a taste of my hand yourself, you don't shut your mouth about my bidness. 'Sides, you're one to talk, went to school on a full ride to dribble and shoot the fuckin' lights out. All you hadda do was keep it together and shove that orange rock down other team's bitch hole to shut 'em down, but ya couldn't even manage that. Now look at you, a fuckin' washed out, strung out loser. You more like Cornhole now, doin' whatever or whoever it takes for your next fix."

The two stood up and glared at each other, ready to square off when Archer slammed his hand down on the table to get their attention.

"Excuse me kids, but I really don't give two shits about your personal issues. You do whatever you want when you leave. But you know the 'You fight, you're banned' policy here. All I care to hear from you guys is what you saw last night. If you have nothing to tell me, then get to walking."

"We saw the same shit you saw, man. Why'd we be any different," said Cracker, his breathing still hard and ragged as he sat back down and reached for his coffee.

Archer looked at the gathering of pathetic faces before him and saw they were in accord. "Well I didn't see anything, neither did Trick. We were kind of winging it."

Theda, put her hand to her eyes and said, "You're the lucky one then,

Mr. Sweet. Every time I close my eyes, it seems like they're waiting for me. Those eyes, that mouth, biting and squeezing Todd like he was a drink box or something."

Cracker and Betcholly nodded mutely as if there was nothing more to add and sat staring into their nearly empty coffee mugs.

Trick wandered over and set his hands on the two transients. "All right men, y'all need to pull up roots and blow. Neither of ya are clean, so until you are or ya need help gettin' that way, y'all can't stay."

Cracker started grumbling as he stood to leave and Trick looked at him sternly. "Ya care to repeat that, Cracker?"

"Yeah. The fuck man? You think I'm scared of your, scrawny ass or your power trip here? Hell, I've run up in tighter pussies than you just gettin' my dick wet."

Trick was a blur of movement as he rammed his body into Cracker's torso, forcing the bigger man into the nearest wall, spinning the surprised man in one motion until Cracker's face met the white-washed wall. Trick's forearm thrust into the nape of Cracker's neck, pinioning him, the pressure splitting his lip against the concrete block.

"Some folks don't count their blessin's," Trick snarled into Cracker's ear. "In case you forgot, we saved your ass last night. I let your strung out ass stay under my roof against house rules, fed your pathetic, grubby, pan-handling ass and," he lowered his voice to save some of Cracker's dignity, "gave you fresh pants 'cause you fudged what ya came in here with last night. Any time you want to party with me, we'll boogie down bro', but right now, you're leavin'. You feel me?"

Cracker relaxed, more out of necessity to breathe than abated anger, but he knew what had just happened saved face for both parties and was content to let things slide-for the time being.

"Yeah, I'm cool, jus' let me go, I'm bleeding."

Trick released his grip and took a guarded step backward. "C'mon back when you're clean and sober Bobby B. You, too, Cracker It ain't never too late. When you're ready, we'll be around, hear?"

Betcholly stood without a word, thanked Archer and Trick and started to shuffle his way toward the door. He stopped and looked sideways through his hair at Archer. "I still don't understand how you couldn't see those things, especially when they had hold of you." Turning, he pulled a battered Dallas

Mavericks hat from a cargo pocket, and fitted it to his greasy head as the door closed behind him.

Theda looked at Archer again as if just realizing. "You really couldn't see those goddamn things? How do you miss something that's like, seven feet tall, no hair, ears like a Vulcan, and teeth like a Klingon?"

Archer looked questioningly at her and she shrugged. "Sorry. Todd loved Star Trek and it kind of rubbed off on me. Can I go back to the hotel now?"

"Sure, sure. Whatever you want, we can call a cab for you. One last question, though," Archer asked as he saw Trick open his cell phone to summon a Yellow. "Where were you last night when those things attacked you?"

"Todd and I were walking Bourbon Street just to see how long it ran. After we passed Marie Laveau's it started getting kind of quiet, you know, sort of residential. We ran into that white guy who just left and he tried to bum a smoke and a couple of dollars from Todd. About half a block later as we were ready to turn back to the party, we ran into the black guy who sold us a couple of joints. I figured we're in New Orleans, party time right? I fired up my jay and smoked it while we were walking back toward the bars. Todd wanted to save his for later, to get mellow." She stopped to take a long drink of her now stone cold coffee, "Next thing we know, the white guy is zipping past us, screaming. I look up and see these two freak show-looking things bearing down on us. I may be from the country, but I'm not country, so I took off with Todd right beside me. We met up with that Cracker dude and the other guy who got eaten as we were running by. The white guy ran to your door and started pounding. You know the rest."

Trick wandered over to the table. "Ms. Hyde? Your taxi is here. Do you have enough money to get you where you need to go?"

She glanced down at the purse that hung drunkenly from one unbroken strap and saw it was still closed. "Yeah, I'm good. I think I'll be checking out when I get back and flying home today. This kind of vacation, I don't need." She looked at them both and did her best to smile. "Thank you again for my life and for trying to save Todd. If it wasn't for you guys..."

"Happy we were there," replied Trick. "Now get yourself back to where you feel safe."

"Safe? No. Somehow, I think I'm fresh out of yippee right now. I don't know if I'll ever feel safe again." She shivered and ducked her head into the cold morning air. "Goodbye."

When she had gone, Archer walked over to the receiving counter and handed in his empty mug. "Hey Trick? What about the last guy, the first one the vampires grabbed?"

"Raoul Fuentes. He was a chef in town and lost his job when th' restaurant closed. He didn't have any family 'round and lost his apartment. He was livin' here to have a stable address for his job applications. Last I had heard, he had an interview yesterday. Not quite sure why he was late for curfew, but it don't matter now, does it?"

Archer shook his head. "So, we've got a partied-out stoner co-ed and her musician boyfriend, a clean blue-collar type down on his luck, a bottom feeding rock smoker, and a spike riding pimp. I leave anyone out?"

"Nope. What do they have in common, other than wrong place wrong time?"

"Damned if I know, but I've got to beat feet and get the store open. I'll think about it today, and you can call Toinetta. We'll all put our heads together later, figure it all out."

"You want a ride? I mean you should be safe with it bein' sunlight and all, but they're prob'ly a little pissed with us."

Archer headed for the open garage door and turned. "You're forgetting we don't know when some of the murders occurred. Some of them could have happened in the daytime, so sunlight isn't necessarily a factor for them. Could be they prefer the dark for hunting and work on their tan by day."

"Fuck a duck," Trick murmured. "Are we gonna catch a break with these things or are we just snacks on the hoof for 'em, anytime, anywhere?"

"Just hope Toinetta has some useful things to tell us about them," Archer replied and he was gone.

CHAPTER 14

THE AIR WAS so crisp, Archer felt he could reach out and snap it in two like a slice of ripe apple. Looking down at his watch he quickened his pace. He had to hurry or poor Tell would be left standing around since he didn't have keys to the store yet. Rounding the corner on Burgundy he was surprised to see Daniella step out of a building across the street, closing the door behind her with a hollow thud. Calling to her she looked up startled, then waited for him to approach her.

Archer took in her beauty, enjoying the corona of sunlight behind her, making her hair look brilliant and angelic. He stopped short when he saw the black eye and livid scratches across her cheek. "By the Goddess, Daniella, what happened to you?"

She didn't respond, but turned and began to walk up the street, dragging her right leg slightly as if her ankle were sprained. Archer hurried after her and set his hand on her shoulder, hoping to stop her and make her look at him. As soon as he made contact with her, he was struck with a light-headedness and weakness. His hand slipped off her and he stood there, stunned, his body swaying like a willow in a windstorm.

She walked away from him and turned. "Never touch me Archer, unless I allow it. It can be bad for your concentration, and mine. Well come along, Shopkeeper, I was heading to your store anyway. You may as well walk with me."

Archer shook his head and the mental cloud quickly lifted as she waited for him to catch up. "You're not going to tell me what happened to you Daniella? I know I said I would never ask, but I'm concerned. There are some really bad things happening around here lately."

"I read the papers, and I heard the sirens last night," she replied coolly.

"Well then, what? Did you lose a best-two-out-of-three falls in the Jello wrestling finals last night and are embarrassed to tell me? Let me help you."

"Oh," she laughed humorlessly, "you're one to talk. How'd you get the road rash on your face and neck since yesterday? Get dragged down the block by a disgruntled customer?"

"Something like that."

"Something like that?"

"Yeah, I had something he wanted and didn't want to give it up."

"Ah. Won't stay open long that way."

"It was after hours. I didn't want to be opened."

"Well be careful. That face is too handsome to wreck," she replied, causing both of them to blush.

They walked in awkward silence until they reached Blessed Be. Tell was sitting on the banquette, his tree trunk-like legs sprawled out into the gutter. He flowed to his feet in a single movement as Archer fit the key into the locks.

"Wow, y'all look like you was deep into some extra-curricular activity last night. Archer, you've only known me a day so I can't blame you for excluding me, but Daniella, I am sorely disappointed. Unless you two were on a date, then I don't even want to know."

Daniella glared hard enough for both of them as Archer pushed the first door open and unlatched the second. He reached for Trold and Berg, the troll statue, and recoiled.

"Tell? Did something happen while I was gone yesterday afternoon?"

"Nothing unusual, Archer. Customers came in and out, some people bought, some didn't. I emptied the register and put it in your bank bag. Something wrong?"

"I honestly don't know. Why is Berg snarling and Trold sticking his tongue out? How do statues make faces?"

Tell walked past Archer and easily picked them both up, looking at their faces before placing them in their customary positions guarding the door. He gave both rock hard heads a playful swat before walking back to Archer. "Either they're angrier than they were yesterday or they've made up and are entertaining each other. They'll get over it."

"You didn't answer the question Tellico. How do statues make faces? I mean, they're called statues because they are immobile, you know, unmoving. Am I right?"

"Archer, so far as I know, statues are just that. What you have here are trolls."

"Bad day to pull my leg, Tellico. I got these statues in Shreveport and they've been statues ever since. I'm not buying trolls."

"Hey man, you asked, but I think what you have here are two immature rock trolls. I don't know why they went dormant but they seem to be wakin' now. It's nothing to worry about, they look healthy."

"Nothing to worry about? Throw in a cheesy animal facts and you sound like that damned Jeff Corwin on Animal Planet. How do you know so much about them? I didn't even know they existed!"

"You think ya have to be an expert on all things mystic, just because you own a magic store? I've been around some in my day. Kind of surprised these little fellas were all the way up in Shreveport. They usually stick to the Bayous, unless they got trapped down here, went dormant and made their way there asleep."

"Ow, my brain hurts! If I walk back out and come back in again, can I start my day over again? How do I know they aren't going to trash the shop or hurt you or my customers or come for me in the dead of the night?"

"They're a fey creature, Archer. They might play a trick or two now and then, but they're harmless, and very loyal if you treat them right. It's probably all of the magical energy in this place that's rousing them. Trust me, they're very shy, so customers won't ever see them do anything. If they do, so what? They'll think they're imagining things like you were."

Daniella had been listening to this exchange and seemed nonplussed by the topic. "What happens if those little guys wake up completely and decide they don't want to be here?"

"Good question," Archer murmured, noting with some irritation the tone of humor in her voice.

"They're bound here, actually. And believe me, you'll never have a need for a security system with them here."

"They're bound here? How can that be?"

"You purchased them from whoever captured them. A lot of the time, when a troll, gargoyle, or other fey creatures in the servant class are captured or taken from their home, they go dormant like this so they can't be of any use to whoever caught them. Since you bought them, and they are choosing to wake, chances are they're yours to command. I don't know for sure if they'll listen, but the fact that they are waking up is a good sign that they like where they are."

"Jesus. You make me sound like I purchased a pair of slaves, Tell."

"Well, you did. You just didn't know it. Now you have a choice."

"Keep them in servitude or set them free, is that it?"

"Yessah massah Archer sah," jabbed Daniella wryly.

"Well of course, I'll set them free. It would be wickedly wrong to hold them, not to mention the bad karma."

"When they're fully awake, you can give them the news, but don't be surprised if they stick around."

"Man, oh man," Archer chuckled darkly. "I think I have a more normal life in my dreams than I do waking. Trolls, witchcraft, and mass murderers. Who would have guessed my life would spiral into such a scary little freak show? What next? Maybe ghosts or goblins? Hell, the opportunities seem boundless today."

Tellico stiffened, his demeanor suddenly icy. Daniella looked at him, like someone caught in the middle of a crowd when an ethnic slur is uttered. "If you'll excuse me, I'll be cleaning up," he said and walked away.

"What was all that? He's acting like I asked him to bend down so I could fart in his face."

"You don't know, so I won't hold your ignorance against you, and chances are neither will he. I've known Tellico Trufant for years, and I've never been able to get the whole story, but he either is, or believes he is, one half Great Smoky Mountain Troll."

"Smoky Moun...what?"

"Evidently there are a lot of types and tribes of many different fey creatures. For whatever reason, real or imagined, he thinks he's fey."

"So I insulted him when I said my life was turning into a freak show?"

"I knew you couldn't be as dumb as you looked," Daniella said, punching him lightly on the arm.

"Nah, that's not possible," he replied. "Shit. How do I apologize without letting him know that you set me straight?"

"Just give him some space and later on ask him some more about those two little guys at the doors. You can probably ease into things from there."

"Sounds good to me. Thank you. Now, what did you come in here for this morning? I know it can't be because you just had to see me."

"Not entirely," she demurred coyly, "but come on. I need some things to help heal my bruises, as well as my everyday list of stuff."

"You've treated me like a leper every other time you've been here. What's different about today?"

"I was trying to decide whether or not I liked you."

"So I'm people now? You like me?"

"I didn't say that," she replied with a shrug of her shoulders. "Try not to get ahead of yourself."

Archer's smile was thin as a pencil as he began reaching for her regular items. With his back turned, he missed the laughter in Daniella's eyes and the color that rose in her cheeks.

CHAPTER 15

THE REST OF the day was busy, surprisingly so, until Archer realized that the news must be out about the vampires in the Quarter. A lot of tourist types buying up his stock of garlic and crosses. The crosses he had in an abundance of styles and sizes, but the garlic was in short supply. Archer was amazed at the variety of things that the more serious practitioners were asking for, recognizing many of the ingredients sold as partial or entire lists for protection charms and spells. Based on the variety of what was purchased, there seemed to be no consensus on what might work best to repel a vampire.

Tell proved to be a valuable commodity for Archer. He was not the lumbering simplistic field hand that he appeared to be; Archer simply hadn't had that much of an opportunity to see him interact with customers the previous day. Tell was an adroitly able salesman who managed to disarm people's apprehension about his appearance with a quick wit and a ready smile.

About an hour before closing, Toinetta glided into the shop past the trolls, carrying a burlap shopping bag stuffed to overflowing with books. She looked curiously at the statues, but made no comment as she walked through the store and, plopping the bag down heavily on the display case, picked up Archer's phone and called for take away from Fahy's Irish Pub across the street. Then she called Trick and told him to pick it up before he came over.

Tell was trying hard not to appear interested in what Toinetta had in the bag,

"C'mon over here, shugah," Toinetta beckoned to Tell. "You're among family here and that gives you every right to know what's going on."

Archer looked uncomfortable for a moment as he caught Toinetta's eye. Her eyes were naked in their message; he's one of us, accept that. Tell shuffled over and stood uncomfortably by Toinetta until Archer scooped up Toinetta's bag with a sigh and led them into the back room where he sat down at the long table, gesturing for the others to sit. Trick joined them a few minutes later with a couple of large take out bags from across the street. Everyone started rifling through them, spreading out the assortment of food. The last customers took the hint, brought their purchases up to the counter, paid, and left. Tell closed the doors and locked up.

The food was sorted out and eaten in relative silence as if no one wanted to broach the subject of why they were assembled. Finally, after Trick launched a trumpeting belch and Toinetta shot him a laser glare of reproach, Archer decided the ice, at least, was broken.

"Alright, we all have full bellies and feel a little more relaxed. I suppose it's time we get down to business."

"Yep," replied Trick, stifling a second outburst with his fist. "Wha'cha got Toinetta?"

Wordlessly, she reached for her bag and upended it, spilling books of all sizes and thickness across the table top. "Take one and start reading the passages and sections I've marked." Toinetta said blandly. "A lot of it is historical and just gives names and countries. For example," she grabbed a book she had marked and opened it up to the right page, "the very first vampires in recorded history were purported to be in ancient Sumeria and Iraq. Iraq also has ghouls, living creatures who feast on human flesh. According to *Vampires: The Occult Truth* by Konstantinos, there are a lot of ethnic vampires; the Bulgarian version is the *ubour*, for the Hindus, it is the *langsuir*, Malaysians, the *penangglan*. In India, they are *raksashas*, *vrykolakas* in Greece, *nachtzehrer* for Germany, *strigoi* in Romania, *upior* and *upyr* in Poland and Russia. The biggie to note here is the Polish and Russian versions only hunt during the day. Mexico has a vampire called a," she held out the book for everyone to see the word, *tlahwelpuchi*.

"A what? How in the world do you pronounce that?" joked Archer. "By the time you scream for help, you're a dry husk."

"Suffice it to say," said Toinetta with a humorless smile, "I found references in nearly every country and culture throughout history, except oddly enough, Native Americans. Other than the ethnic names, there is not an awful lot of information available that isn't contradicted elsewhere."

The hours fell away, the remnants of their meal long gone, the only sounds heard beyond the waking noise of the nightlife in the Quarter was that of pages turning. Occasionally a chair creaking as someone shifted, sometimes uncomfortably as something they read made them squirm, sighs of frustration, and occasional soft muttering were the only sounds anyone made. Finally, Archer closed his book and said, "So gang, what do we know?"

"I know we're in trouble," replied Trick as he shut his book with a snap.

"Heard that," Tellico concurred. "Not a whole lot in mine."

"Well," Archer said slowly, drawing the word out, "we already know from personal experience these particular vampires don't seem to be harmed by sunlight. Based on sheer volume of victims, they're not necessarily nocturnal, and salt seems to do little more than irritate them. My book said that garlic, moving water, a stake through the heart, and beheading was effective. Also, burning the head and corpse separately."

Tell shook his head. "Mine said garlic was worthless, sunlight was good, holy water, staking, beheading, and burning worked."

"According to mine," Trick said, "holy water and garlic are less than crap, but silver, holy or blessed relics, and weapons might work. It says here that th' stake is more to keep the creature pinned down whilst you separate th' head from th' body, which makes sense. Burnin' th' head and body separately is the only way to guarantee a second, final death."

"So, our commonalities are staking—though the reason varies—decapitation, and burning. I think we have some things to work with," Toinetta said with a sigh. "However, it would seem that the biggest problem lies in finding them."

"Yeah, I wonder why it is that none of these references or any pop culture stuff I've ever read says these damned things are invisible," Trick said disgustedly.

"Y'all are forgetting something here," Trick chimed in quietly. "They're not completely invisible. Th' cops do have some eyewitness accounts."

"He's right," Archer said. Some of the people who were attacked outside the Mission gave a pretty consistent, not to mention, graphic description of something that we couldn't see."

"Th' cops will dismiss th' eyewitness accounts, Archer. All of 'em are junkies or live in th' bottle," Trick replied drumming his fingers angrily on the table top.

"Well, don't you think that in itself is a good starting point? These people's brains are polluted with their favorite poison; maybe being jacked up lets them see these things."

"Keep talking, Tell, I think you're onto something," said Toinetta excitedly.

"Well, it seems like the victims, including Archer, couldn't or didn't see what hit them. People with polluted blood—HIV, drugs, booze, whatever—get to see these things, but they get to walk."

"So what, we got to get stoned or doped up to see these things in order to fight them? I can see a high rate of success there," Trick snorted.

Archer shook his head, his frustration rising. "There has to be another way. I mean, what was that priest they found dead in Armstrong Park planning to do? Somehow I doubt his big plan was to find them and become a Happy Meal. I can only sense them when they are real close, but then they were too close to escape or mount a defense. No way could I attack."

"Just spitballin' here," said Trick into the silence, "but that dog or wolf that jumped in when you went down...maybe animals are the way to go; track 'em like game."

"Somehow I don't think it'd go over to well, us roaming town with a bunch of coonhounds much less werewolves," Toinetta replied, chuckling. "Even if the local lycanthropes were willing to lend a paw."

"Trolls can sense them, even see them if their powers are strong enough," Tell added quietly.

"Are Trold and Berg close enough to being fully awake? Do you think they could help us?" Toinetta asked, suddenly animated.

"Nah. Besides, they're immature, not into their real powers yet. Me, on the other hand, I think I could probably be able to find them. The point is moot, anyway. What'd I fight them with? And who would have my back? I'm pretty sure I could take on one, but two or more would get pretty ugly for me."

"I say we go back to th' church tomorrow and ask Father Finnernan some more questions. We may also want to visit th' antique weapons shop on Chartres to see if we can find some good blades."

"Good thinking, Trick. As conspicuous as we'd look carrying broadswords, I think chainsaws would draw more attention," replied Archer.

"Well," Toinetta said briskly, collecting her tomes, placing each carefully back in her bag so they all fit, "it looks like we have a starting point. I'll delve a little deeper to see if there are any mind altering herbs that might fit the bill without leaving you incapacitated. You boys talk to that preacher and see if he's willing to help you any further. I need to get home and get to work. Patrick? Would you be so kind as to drive me home? I really don't want to be alone outside until this is over. I just hope vampires can't enter a home without being invited. I didn't see that in any of the books."

Trick took the bag from her. "Archer, I'll give ya a shout tomorrow and we'll go see Lucian together." He waved goodnight to everyone and led Toinetta out the door.

Tell was marking out the till totals and logging the totals for the deposit slip when Archer joined him.

"You stick around here long enough, you're going to see some weird stuff. I tend to be a supernatural shit magnet," Archer said, trying to get his new employee's attention. "Look, there's something else that happens a lot around here. If you have trouble seeing me walking around with my foot in my mouth, it's probably for the best that you find someplace else to be. I say a lot of things I have no right to say, mostly out of ignorance. If I said anything today that rubbed you the wrong way, I want you to know I didn't mean anything by it." Tell looked at him, his hard eyes, smoldering but thoughtful, boring into Archer's. "I want us to be friends, Tell, and I'd like you to stay here for as long as you want. If that's going to happen, we need to be upfront with each other about things. I know you have your life outside this place, but I expect when you are here that you give me your opinion about things. You can be sure I'll let you know if there's something going on I don't care for."

Tellico regarded Archer for another long moment, then nodded his head slowly. "Alright Archer, from now on if you piss me off, I'll let you know."

"So we're solid?"

"Like a rock, Archer."

"Alright then. As soon as you finish the till you can call it a day."

Archer was to the entrance of his back office when he heard Tell say, "Thanks for including me tonight."

"I'll remind you that you said that when the shit splats through the blades, my friend."

CHAPTER 16

Archer TOSSED and turned all night, dozing fitfully until some small noises broke into his dreams. He listened for a few moments, wondering if he had squirrels on his roof again, then realized the sounds were coming from down in the store area. He took his Glock from the nightstand drawer, slunk down the stairs quietly and nudged the apartment door enough to slip through. Padding barefoot silently across the courtyard, he stopped short of entering the shop itself. Peering through the rag curtains he saw two small figures pursuing each other slowly around the shelves and cabinets. At first he thought children had found a way inside and were chasing one another around the store, but then a cloud that had been obscuring the moonlight skirted away just enough to allow him to see the faces of the two capering figures. Their faces were contorted in what seemed like unbridled joy as Trold and Berg chased each other around the store.

As Archer watched, he noticed they began to move faster and faster as their long period of slumber fell away. One of them, Berg he thought, noticed him in the window and gave a quick wave, then ducked as Trold swatted a hand playfully toward Berg's troll's head.

Shaking his head, Archer made his way back across the courtyard and trekked back to bed. The noises faded as sleep came, but with slumber came vivid dreams: heat and sand, bloody death, the glitter and flash of steel, the clash of bodies against wooden shields and spears, and the desperate cries of the wounded and dying. He awoke as dawn was breaking, diffuse light poring through his make shift curtain. With a groan, he got up and staggered across the room and took a shower. He had to get the store open, then meet Trick to go see a priest about some dead people.

CHAPTER 17

ARCHER AND TRICK journeyed easily in the gentle morning sun to Our Lady Of Guadalupe Church, kicking their strategies back and forth about approaching Father Finnernan, creating the best chance at getting the answers they needed. They stopped a half a block short as they saw the church surrounded by squad cars and EMS, the flashing blue lights pinwheeling off the white exterior. The whole place was bustling with men and women clad in blue jackets, the yellow lettering on their backs identifying them as members of New Orleans' Crime Scene Investigation Unit. Parishioners and the morbidly curious stood huddled in small knots up and down the sidewalk. Trick found a familiar face in one of the larger clots of onlookers and bumped his way into the buzzing cluster pulling his acquaintance aside. They spoke for just a moment, then Trick came back to Archer, shaking his head.

"So what's the story?"

"We can scratch th' theory that vampires need invitations to get in some place. Old Lucian lost a coupla pounds last night, and not in a healthy way."

"Great. We've lost our link to them in exchange for debunking another myth. Now what?"

"I think we need to find th' priest that served us refreshments th' day we spoke to Lucian. He may have been a personal assistant or whatever Catholics priests have."

"He didn't seem too involved. He didn't even stick around to listen. You think he knows anything?"

"C'mon, you walk into a room and people are havin' a serious discussion about dead priets? Tell me you wouldn't hover just a little bit unless you already knew what time it was? That's a tough sell to me."

"Okay, say he knew what we were talking about and wasn't minding his own business. How do we find him, especially in this mess?"

"We're going to have to hang back a bit 'til CSI and th' Task Force clear out. I think if Detective Willig saw us again so soon at a crime scene, he just might start listening to that paranoid pile of walkin' dog shit, Corgan and put us under th' microscope.

"Hell, we've got nothing to hide, Trick. All we're doing is running a parallel investigation."

"True, but when you were a cop, did you want civilians mucking around in your active investigation?"

"Yeah, you're right, but . . .Hey! Isn't that the guy?" Archer pointed as he noticed a familiar figure emerge from Lourdes Grotto and cross into the church.

"Sho'nuff looks like him. Let's take us a gander inside."

Walking past the still-milling crowd they ducked in to the cool darkness of the apse, letting their eyes adjust. They walked up the aisle and went to the left of the altar where a small door led them into a spartan narthex with an office chair, small desk, folding chairs, and a closet-sized washroom, the only amenities. The priest seated in the faded green padded office chair, his back to the door, feet up on the small, scarred, wooden desk, was speaking in Italian over a small satellite phone. Archer cleared his throat and the priest jumped in his seat. Turning to face the intruders he ended his conversation in a hushed tone before making the phone disappear.

"I'm sorry gentlemen," the priest said in lightly accented English, "but the Church has suffered a great tragedy today. Perhaps if you could return in a day or two?"

"I'm sorry, Padre, but we haven't got th' time to come back. Fact of th' matter is, we're here to talk to you," said Trick, closing the door behind him.

He seemed surprised. "Indeed? Have we met?"

"We were in the rectory with Father Lucian and you served us refreshment," replied Archer.

"Ah, yes, the men who were inquiring about poor Padre Giacomo. Yes, Father Lucian mentioned you were interested in his death."

Archer grimaced. "Not interested, exactly. We were investigating the manner of his death."

"I see, then you are policemen? I have already told them all I can about poor Father Lucian. If I discover anything that can help, I will call the investigator who gave me his card. Now if you will excuse me?" The priest gestured toward the door, indicating that he wished them to leave.

"Hold on jus' a minute, partner. We still have some questions for you," Trick started, stepping toward the priest.

Archer put his hand on Trick's shoulder and said, "We're not police Padre, but I know you're leaving something out." Archer's senses suddenly throbbed in his head, almost but not quite like what he felt before he was attacked outside the Mission. Something was definitely not right. "Why don't we start with your name?"

"My name? That is of no concern." He drew Detective Willig's card from his pocket and produced his phone again. "I believe I shall call the police and have you removed from here at once."

Trick took a quick step forward and in one fluid movement, swept the card from the man's left hand and knocked the phone from his right with a backhand motion. The priest flinched as his phone clattered against the plaster wall then shattered on the marble floor.

"Wouldn't do you much good, Padre. By th' time they got th' call from dispatch and got over here, we'd be a distant, bad memory. We just have a few questions, and for th' life of me, I can't understand why you have a problem with that."

He sat back down, his eyes locked on Trick, as if gauging the gravity of the events unfolding.

"Let's start with your name," said Archer, the thrumming in his ears becoming strong enough for him to swipe at it like an itch. He didn't notice the amusement that danced in the priest's eyes as he rubbed irritably at his lobes.

"My name is Alberto Luca Scalese. Father Luca will suffice."

"Did you come here with the priest who got himself ghosted in the park?"

"Padre Giacomo? No, I have been at the Archdiocese here for the past few months, if that matters, attending to affairs on behalf of our new Pope."

The buzz subsided in his head as the priest spoke, but resumed as Trick asked the next question. "Luca, you're telling me that a priest who serves as an envoy to th' Pope was servin' tea to a parish priest? That there's no protocol or hierarchy? That dog just won't hunt."

"I am not sure what a hunting dog has to do with anything, but it was a courtesy to Father Lucian since he was allowing me to reside at his rectory without any extra duties. Now please, will you go?"

The buzz in Archer's head had ceased once again as the priest spoke and, in a moment of clarity, the puzzle fell into place. Luca moved to stand when Archer suddenly lunged forward and pushed him roughly back into the padded office chair. The chair rocked dangerously, threatening to overturn and spill the surprised priest to the floor.

"Hey Archer! What th' fuck?" was all Trick could say before Archer was on the priest, picking him up by the collar and jerking him to his feet.

"You want to play? C'mon with it! Now that I know what you're doing, let's see your best shot!"

Luca looked desperately at Trick, beseeching him with his eyes, but Archer shook him hard enough to make his teeth rattle.

"Don't look at him, look at me. What's the matter, can't do it when your victim can defend himself?"

"Archer! What are you doin'? He may be a liar, but I don't cotton to th' notion of beatin' up a priest. What th' hell?" Trick was stunned at Archer's sudden violent behavior.

Archer threw the priest back into the chair, grabbed a folding chair from against the near wall and swiveled himself down so his body weight opened the chair, the legs hitting the floor with a muffled thud. Archer's eyes bored into Father Luca's so intently that he no longer even noticed Trick. Pulling up another folding chair, Trick perched himself by the wall, content to watch, ready to intervene, curious to see what Archer had unearthed.

Padre Luca seemed more surprised than scared as Archer's eyes tore into him. Archer squinted as Luca narrowed his eyes, returning Archer's gaze evenly, cocking his head slightly to the right, a look of defiance on the priest's face. The tension between them was electric, literally. Trick noticed every hair on his arms and neck were on end and he would swear that he smelled ozone. Seconds became minutes and Trick watched as sweat erupted from Padre Luca's forehead followed more gradually by a trickle from Archer's brow.

The strain proved to be too much for Padre Luca as he finally moaned, looking away from Archer, his shoulders slumping in defeat. Archer let out a long shuddering breath as his opponent began to shake and sob uncontrollably. Standing, Archer walked unevenly over toward Trick, stopping when his back was resting against the wall. Archer was breathing hard and heavy, as if he had just finished a dozen wind sprints.

"Mind lettin' me in on jus' what the holy hell that was all about," Trick asked quietly.

"Oh, I'm fine. Thanks for asking buddy. Nothing an Advil the size of a volleyball won't cure."

"Did your Vulcan mind meld make you deaf? What the fuck jus' happened?"

"Holy hell, that was a good one, Trick. Hey Father! Quit your sniveling and answer the man's questions." Archer turned toward Trick. "You baptized Catholic?"

"Nah. C'mon you've heard 'bout my momma. Think she woulda taken me ta church?"

"Okay, then it's safe to leave you alone with him for a minute or two. I'm going to go splash some cool water on my face while he starts explaining. I'll be right inside, listening in case he starts lying. Start by asking him why you're safe and what happened to Lucian."

Archer walked into the small wash room and Trick turned to the drained and drawn priest sagging into the thick padding of his chair. "Sounds like I'm in for a right fine yarn. So tell me, Padre, what gives?"

Father Luca glared through the open door, the squeak of the faucet and tapping of pipes could be heard as Archer began rejuvenating himself. "You're not Catholic, so I can gain nothing by your presence. Only those who bear the mark of Holy Roman Catholic baptism are susceptible to my needs. As a heathen, you are spared."

"Hmm. Chalk one up for my momma. Guess once you go Vatican, you never go back again, izzat it," asked Trick, bewildered, as he glanced over at the wash room, hoping Archer would be out soon to help him decipher what seemed for the moment to be completely beyond his comprehension. "Why don't you start with what happened to Lucian and we can go from there?"

"Lucian was a fool, a brave one, but a fool nonetheless. He thought he could reach out to them and they would be grateful for his guidance. Father Giacomo and I both advised against it, but after Giacomo died at their hands, Lucian felt time was of the essence."

"You know about the vampires? When did you find out? How did Lucian plan to contact them and keep his skin intact? I thought the Catholic Church had a standing war with all things supernatural and evil." Trick was astounded, momentarily overwhelmed by the cascade of questions that all wanted to tumble out at the same time

"The Vatican sent Father Giacomo here to assist me. The Holy Father felt their presence the moment they stepped through the rift from their world into ours." He shook his head forlornly. "But it has been so long, and The Holy Father is so new, he was not sure of what exactly had occurred until he spoke with the New Orleans Archdiocese."

"Whoa! Time out! Jus' back th' truck up. You're tellin' me that th' Pope knew about these blood suckin' sons a bitches and can sense them?"

"It's the truth, Trick," said Archer, emerging from the other room dabbing at his face with brown paper towels then tossing them into the trash can against the wall. "The Catholic Church even has a pet name for them. It seems they don't like the term *vampire*; it's too stigmatizing."

"Believe me, they are no one's pets. A name for beings as perfect as these does not exist in a language that can be uttered with a human mouth. We call them *Invictus Morte*. Invincible Death. Lucian sought the glory of being the first to make contact with them. Instead, I believe, he was a sore disappointment to them. Their displeasure cost Lucian dearly."

"Contact? What th'...? He was gonna do, what? Serve 'em tea!" came Trick's incredulous reply.

"Luca, before you piss Trick off enough to throw you a physical beating to go along with the psychic ass-whupping I gave you, why don't you tell us why you need to make contact?"

"In the past," Luca began quietly, his head resting in the cradle of his fingers, elbows on his knees, "we would regularly summon a small contingent of the *Invictus Morte* from whence they came, a parallel dimension, or a bridge to some other world, we do not know. You see, we are permitted to reproduce, but not in the way you think. A Genesis male, called an Incubus by the less informed, may breed with a human woman. If the child is male, the boy is guided by us through the church and other ways until he hears 'The Calling'."

"Many are called but few are chosen, eh? Is that it Luca? What about the women?" Archer inquired scathingly.

"No. Only the male children are called. The sister orders are there for intermediate assistance tending the flock and on occasion, amusement. Brides of Christ?" Luca's voice turned scornful. "Bah! He had one of his own in his time."

"Perhaps the women who make their vows truly believe in The Holy Trinity," said Archer, as he quietly folded into his chair, "or perhaps they need the rush, too. Look at Mother Theresa. She had lots of opportunity to leave the squalor and suffering she dealt with every day, but still she stayed. Was that saintly goodness in humanity or one never ending orgiastic glut, a feeding frenzy?"

"No, no. She was not one of us, just a fine example of what is decent and right about you humans. She unwittingly supplied some excellent repasts for my people, but she was no vampire."

"Hey!" Trick said, holding his hands up in a time out motion. "Can we focus here? I feel like Jeff Gordon, down a few laps to the lead car. Can I get up to speed here? Priests are vampires but nuns ain't?"

"Our males are sorted through by the process of serving Mass, the urging of families to utilize our educational system, and working within a strict, rigid environment. We observe which among them truly have the gift. The ones who are not strictly brethren, but feel some heed to our call are gently discouraged. Before we take our final vows, truly becoming one with the collective, there is a twelve week reflection period where any of us may be as wild and free as we desire or remain pure through study and meditation. When that time is up, we are ordained."

"'Ordained'?" Sarcasm oozed off the word as it left Archer's mouth, "By God? They're just forgiven their trespasses and become one of you?"

"No, you miss the point. Their time away is useful to all parties. The candidates are encouraged to seek out and impregnate as many Catholic women as they can in this period of time. A small barb in the penis helps to plant their seed deeper and remain near the womb longer. Most methods of birth control created by man will prevent this, hence the Church's stance on birth control. We do not wish to ever have a woman of breeding age using a drug or device capable of reducing our flock or stopping our procreators.

Those who indulge too much in their dark side and taste of human blood become lost to us and must be destroyed by vampire hunters such as myself. The women who bear the children nourish them constantly with their emotions: happiness, worry, anxiety, and the joy of birth or the bitterness of abandonment by the child's sire; food is of secondary importance. In exchange for bearing our offspring, the mothers enjoy an unintentional benefit of living longer and experiencing a more serene outlook on things for the remainder of their lives. Plus any mother of one of our children may produce normal progeny by a human father or fathers."

"So th' orphanages your churches run are repositories for your own bastard demon spawn. If the mother gives up th' child you raise 'em and shape 'em an' th' momma has a chance at a different life then as a single mother? Ain't y'all jus' th' sweetest of folk?"

"Catholic dogma states that killing a child in the womb is a mortal sin, so what are the poor breeders supposed to do? We don't come right out and offer to take them and raise them, but we guide and, when necessary, pressure them through their faith and guilt. We propose an alternate way out of their situation so they enjoy a more productive and Godly life afterward."

"So what about th' mothers who decide to keep the baby regardless of th' pressure? What's th' master plan then?"

"The Church watches over them covertly as they grow and mature. We guide them back to the fold if they should stray."

"Catholic charity! Gotta hand it to y'all, you got th' system down pat. You have a feeder system, a weeding out process, and fresh batches of new suckers being born. Why have th' number of priests been droppin' so steadily over th' years?"

"The only way to keep the line pure and guarantee its continuance is to have our progenitors, the *Invictus Morte* replenish us periodically. In the early days of the Second World War, when Italy was ravaged, the parchment with the only remaining incantation to summon my people's Genesis vanished. The secret remained hidden until later in the war, when Mussolini, *Il Duce,* bragged to Adolph Hitler of the secret behind the Church's success. Hitler arranged to have the parchment seized and a large number of our forebears were summoned and pressed into service with the promise of all the fresh blood they could ever want.

"Working with the Underground movement, the Church reclaimed the stolen prize from the Nazis and spirited the parchment from their long reaching fingers by way of an elderly French couple who were preparing to immigrate to America. Record keeping was not good then and the couple was lost in the melting pot of refugees, dissidents, and deserters who flooded your country, unaware of what they carried. It was not until The Holy Father felt the stirring caused by the incantation being uttered that we knew it still existed and hope for our line returned."

"Some hope," Trick snorted, "They've drunk two of ya dry so far. Kudos on a well-handled situation."

"The *Invictus Morte* have no way of entering this dimension on their own; they must be brought forth. It was part of the pact made with early Christians who drove our blood-drinking brethren to the brink of extinction. Had we known beforehand that they were being summoned, we could have been there to formally greet them in the traditional way and keep them safe until they materialized as humanoid."

"Like Trick said, they've chowed down on two of you so they obviously don't discriminate, or see much of themselves in your watered down version of their people. Any tangible plan on stopping them, or are you just going to start eating rich food so your blood tastes better when they come for you," asked Archer, his patience shortening as his headache gained strength.

"They will still materialize and adapt as humanoid, but they are of little use to the Church now; the attack on Father Finnernan is proof of that. If there is no reshaping their attitude, such blood lust and wanton feeding is most surely irreversible. We may have no other alternative. Perhaps they have to be destroyed." replied Luca with a sad shake of his head.

"Perhaps? There's no *perhaps* here. Those things are responsible for at least three dozen deaths," said Archer with a shake of his head. "I won't call it murder since you're suggesting they're feral; hunting is what they do. But dangerous animals need to be brought down as quickly as possible, no hesitation."

"Dangerous animals can also be caged, and trained. Look at any zoo or circus," replied Luca beseechingly. "Let me at least try to bring them in when they are ready."

"I'd say they're overdue Padre. If Finnernan couldn't tame 'em, what makes ya so all fired sure you can pull it off after they've had even more time, more taste for th' kill, and freedom to do it," asked Trick sharply.

"I must be allowed to try, please. These are the first progenitors of their kind in nearly three quarters of a century; my race's first opportunity to refresh our thinning blood line…"

"They die. No more chances to bring them in alive," was Trick's firm reply.

"I'm inclined to agree with Trick, Luca. Not because they almost killed me, but because there have been so many people killed. No more. If as you say, you have the summoning scroll back in Rome, it shouldn't be too long before you have the new blood and generations you need. Now will you help us or get in the way?"

Luca looked miserable. "I'll help. If they must die, then their burden is mine. I will help you find them, but to slay our own kind, especially one of the *Invictus Morte*…" he shook his head vehemently. "Thou shalt not kill."

CHAPTER 18

"ARCHER, MAYBE WE should adjourn somewhere further away from th' active police investigation and pryin' eyes. We'll take Father Luca with us."

Archer was feeling woozy, but Trick made sense. "Yeah, we shouldn't be found anywhere with the priest so soon. I doubt Willig and Corgan would be pleased."

"What makes you think I would go anywhere with you two lunatics?" Luca demanded incredulously.

"What makes you think you've got a say in th' matter," Trick asked derisively.

"I do this under duress," replied Luca through clenched teeth. "The police should be finished at the rectory by now. We can go there."

"Sounds good to me," replied Archer, rubbing his temple where a headache was building.

Nearly two hours had passed since Trick and Archer had found Luca, and the crime scene was pretty much clear as Luca led them back to the rectory. Archer called Tell and asked him to close the shop and join them, then rang Toinetta, asking her to meet them at Our Lady of Guadalupe Church. Ensconcing themselves temporarily in a small reception room, they could continue their discussion in comfort while they waited for Tell and Toinetta. Trick was nervous about the arrangement. "Kinda like divin' inta a swamp full'a gators wearin' a red meat Speedo, ya ask me."

"Look, it's all good," replied Archer, weariness still a whisper in his voice and manner. "He just got his psychic ass kicked and it's going to be a while before he's ready to try and feed again. I hurt him a little more than I should have, but I wanted an example, so we can have relatively free commerce with his people. The stroll I took through his mind leads me to believe his kind is mostly benign, seeking to coexist symbiotically with us, but desperate to keep their secrets. I have to say though, pumping his flock full of The Holy Spirit is hollow compared to what they get in return. In exchange for a life of guilt, spiritual head games, shame, psychic raping before dying, they find that the afterlife was waiting for them all along. Humans get a brief sense of well being that they're 'saved' and a sense of community."

"Compared to an endless supply of food, wealth, and power that th' priests enjoy from their people, I'd say we mortals are getting' offered th' lollipop that got dropped in the dung heap," Trick spat.

"We are not immortal," Luca interrupted quietly as he paused to let a rectory volunteer pass through the room on her home for the day. "We have significantly longer life spans than humans and physically, we age more slowly. We can appear older if we put a glamour on ourselves. A minor but effective ruse we must sometimes use. It is the reason why we are transferred from parish to parish so frequently, so it is less likely anyone will notice our relative good health and longevity." There was a short, insistent knock, and Luca rose, pulled the side door open and ushered Toinetta and Tell inside. With the arrival of everyone, Luca led them to a quiet room on the second floor where they sat in tense silence. Luca phoned downstairs and requested coffee be brought for his guests. When it arrived, there were a few moments of everyone fixing themselves a cup. Introductions were terse, the tension palpable as they all got comfortable in their proffered seats.

Toinetta had received a brief overview on the phone, but Tell was still puzzled as to why he was asked to come. His skin crawled with curiosity, but he still wasn't sure of his position in the group dynamic. Sitting still and paying attention during the conversation, he decided, was the best way to learn while keeping his place at the table.

They all sat expectantly, quietly, while Archer and Trick fidgeted in heavy silence, waiting for someone to take up the unbelievable conversation. Trick spooned heap after heap of sugar into his cup as Archer stared thoughtfully into his mug, as if the darkness of the drink would help him divine and separate the shadow from the soul of the priest.

Inhaling the aroma of the brew deeply before sipping daintily, Father Luca finally set his cup down. "I have always loved the smell of coffee, but it is so much better in my country." He sighed wistfully and continued. "So. It seems we have a common problem gentlemen, and lady, but one in which I hold a distinct advantage." He picked up his cup again, but did not drink.

"Care to elaborate on that," asked Trick darkly, his mood fouler than Archer had ever seen it.

"You know my secret, the Church's secret, but no one, save a few adepts such as Mr. Sweet, will ever believe you if you go public."

"I could live with that," Trick growled, "so long as I can piss in th' well and make your kind suffer after we take care of th' problem at hand."

"Trick," Archer sighed heavily, "hostility isn't constructive. We need to look at the here and now. There will come a time and a place, but until then I think it's in our best interest to learn everything we can from Luca. It's not like we have a lot of extra sources we can tap."

"Ah, your head is finally clearing, Mr. Sweet. That is good," replied Father Luca, adding grudgingly, "Our battle was extremely taxing for me as well. I have absolutely no desire to fight again. After this, I will require some healing to close my aura again. You are leaking energy too, I see. They are minor wounds compared to what you did to me, still I would be cautious until you can heal yourself. Until then, perhaps some history, hmm?"

Smiling warmly, Archer reported, "We're in this world together, Padre. Until it's safe again, I see us as allies. And you're right, no one would ever believe us if we said priests are vampires. The story is just too fantastic. Two thousand years of dogma is a lot to overcome based on the unsubstantiated word of a few people. It is two thousand or so years, isn't it?"

"Our race is much older than all recorded histories, but it was not until after the ascension to the head of The Jerusalem Church by James, the brother of Jesus Christ, shortly after the farce of the crucifixion that my race—"

"Whaddya mean, 'farce?'" bellowed Tell, forgetting himself and bolting from his chair, his hot coffee spilling heedlessly across his arm and chest as he rose. "You're shovelin' shinola to confuse us, sittin' there telling me that Jesus Christ, my Lord and Savior, didn't die for my sins? You'd better get right preacher. I may not be Catholic, but I was raised in a religious house. You're walking on dangerous ground."

Archer was quickly by Tell's side using his linen napkin to blot his arm dry, and if necessary, be close enough to try to restrain the big man. "Tell, I get the feeling we're in for a lot of surprises, rough ones at that. If we want the unvarnished truth, to really know and understand things as they are now with the vampires, we need to hear him out. Just sit back, try to relax, and we'll all suspend our disbelief until he's finished. Alright?"

Tell nodded, plopping heavily back into his chair. His face set in a deep scowl, he crossed firmly over his chest, eyes boring holes in Luca as Archer said, "Please, continue."

"Mr. Trufant, Jesus was a great man, a wise man, but he was only a man. He had a twin brother named James, and a younger sister. He had children of his own by Mary, The Magdalene, and was a great rabbi to his people. Unfortunately, James was the more politically astute of the two and Jesus, or Joshua as he was truly named, came out on the short end when it came to influencing The Jerusalem Church. In the end, despite his charisma, he agreed to endure a false martyrdom so there would be no further dissention and he could take his family and continue to do God's work in another place."

"Jesus had a twin brother and his own family?" Tell barked incredulously, then burst into a fit of sarcastic laughter. "Archer are we really going to sit here and listen to this load of guano?"

"Yes, we are, Tellico," replied Archer heatedly. "But one more outburst and you're leaving, got it? I've read about the probability that Jesus was married. The feast of Cana was most likely his own wedding feast. According to the Gospel of John, his mother, Mary was present at what scholars interpret as a small village wedding. Jesus had not even begun his ministry so there was no need or pressure to garner notice when Mary called upon him to produce wine for the guests. It wasn't his responsibility unless it was his marriage feast."

"You are correct," said Luca, a hint of excitement in his voice for the first time. "John 2:3-4 says, 'And when they wanted wine, the mother of Jesus saith unto him, They have no wine. Jesus saith unto her, Woman what have I to do with thee, mine hour has not yet come. In verse 5 of the same chapter, her reply was, His mother saith unto the servants whatsoever he saith unto you, do it.' The family throwing the feast would have been the ones responsible for replenishing the wine.

"Lastly, in John 2:9-10, after the wine was brought out, the Governor of the Feast, a master of ceremonies of the era, if you will, 'tasted it and called the bridegroom, and saith unto him, Everyman at the beginning doth set forth good wine, and when men have well drunk, then that which is worse; but thou hast kept the good wine until now.' If the Gospel is to be believed, and the Governor of the Feast called the bridegroom, and it was Jesus who had provided the wine, then one can easily draw the conclusion it was his marriage feast."

"Excuse me, Father," said Toinetta quietly. "This is all well and good, but what does it have to do with how vampires are connected to Catholicism?"

"Ah, I do tend to digress at times. Perhaps I was trying to goad Mr. Trufant, but he is immutable when he decides to be. Back to the tale. James took over the Jerusalem Church and proceeded to bend the apostles of his brother to his own will. Peter was not 'the rock upon which the church was founded'. He was a willing conspirator as was Saint Paul, known as Paul The Liar. Between the two of them, they muddied up the political water so badly that one sect of the church did not know what the others were doing. It was James' ultimate will that a Spartan, somewhat secretive, faction holding to the true beliefs of Judaic law should break away from what was becoming the more popular stance held by his brother. That view was God was not a vengeful, spiteful deity, but a loving and benevolent God who would look past our transgressions and not condemn us to Hell for our sins. Since it was a belief espoused by Jesus Christ, the new sect was named Christianity. James used his brother as part of a longer line of religious dogma regarding virgin birth, death, and resurrection. The cult of Mithra was a Roman fable that the Christ myth seems to mimic most."

"Mithra," Toinetta murmured almost to herself, "I've heard of that legend. He was a sun god. Roman soldiers and sailors prayed to him for life after death. His resurrection was said to be celebrated around the Easter/ Passover season and his birth was December 25th, maybe about 600 BC?"

"Yes! But the story is not only found in that fable. There is Guatama Buddha born to Maya the virgin in 600 BC. Dionysus, who was credited with turning water into wine; Indra of Tibet; Krishna, the Hindu deity; Adonis; the Babylonian god; and Zoroaster, somewhere between 1500 and 1200 BC. The closest in chronological order to Christ is the story of Attis of Phyrgia, born of the virgin, Nama around 200 BC. The seeds for the allegory were already well established before James put his own spin to it."

"All well and good for debate later. How do vampires tie in," asked Archer, shifting uncomfortably in his chair, growing irritated and impatient with the religious dissertation.

"Ah," Luca sighed, "very well. You Americans have no love for a good tale, one that builds slowly. It must be instant gratification or you grow bored."

Scowling, Trick said, "That's why opera sucks; all bluster and noise, a waste of time. Just like you."

Clearing his throat with a hoarse cough, Luca reached for his mug, sipping with a deliberate fastidiousness, his eyes fixed merrily on Trick, savoring his impatience. "Ah, now where was I? For centuries before and up until the time of James, my blood-thirsty ancestors raided, plundered, and destroyed villages, attacked pilgrims and caravans to feast on the crimson soul essence of the living. We were weaker in the day time, indistinguishable from man and usually benignly indifferent to the thirst. When night fell, my people's power, and our great undeniable hunger returned.

"When James ascended to his seat as head of the Church of Jerusalem, he put forth a call to leaders of the different clans of vampires, suggesting a way to end the centuries, maybe millennia of bloodshed and death. Never once in all that time had humans asked for formal parlay. The curiosity of my progenitors was piqued, so they agreed to meet with James in secret. His idea was so revolutionary, so radically beneficial to my people that he had no trouble swaying them. James would take his true Essean followers and depart from mainstream life, living in seclusion, adhering to the strictest interpretations of the ancient Judaic laws. Upon his death, in sixty-two A.D., he had arranged for his son, Jesus' cousin Symeon, to assume the throne of the Jerusalem Church in a titular sense, and my people to rule in blood, sanctified.

"It didn't take long for my people, behind Symeon's banner to begin to move. The Church revolted against Rome from 66 to around 73 A.D. forcing new Christians and Jewish converts to flee. Jerusalem was destroyed in their rampage and the Temple razed. When the dust had settled, they were sated and satisfied, but now they needed someone to write the history of that time with a different slant, one with an eye toward the future. It had to suppress or discredit any who tried to write of what we were, but leave the brutality of the time intact. Between 66 and 95 A.D the gospels of Mark, Matthew, Luke, Acts, and John were created. With the second Jewish revolt, Hadrian, the Roman version of what was to become the Pope, fought our people to a standstill and we left the city under the auspices of being beaten.

"The fighting continued for the next century and a half until May of 325 A.D., when the Roman factions and my people met in Turkey for Vatican I, or the Council of Nicaea. Roman leaders were fewer in number, and when they emerged from that meeting, knowing who and what we were, they quietly melted into varying levels of obscurity or collaboration. Also, that year, the First Church of the Holy Sepulchre was built in Jerusalem." Luca picked up his coffee and sipped, wetting his throat after the long narrative. "Any questions so far?"

Trick was silent, contemplative while Tell squeezed the arms of his chair barely able to contain the rage he felt building. It was Toinetta's reassuring presence and occasional pats on his hand that kept him from leaping across the table and throttling Luca. How could a priest blaspheme so utterly, so naked and vile? *No court on Earth or in Heaven would convict me for killing him,* Tell thought. The logical part of him refused to be overcome by his desire to silence the priest and he found himself wondering if his anger stemmed from his lifelong beliefs being assailed, or that he'd found himself believing the tale?

It was Archer who was intrigued enough to ask, "If your antecedents were blood-thirsty vampires who killed wantonly, then how did they manage to keep their secret so well and for so long?"

"Ah, an excellent question with a simple answer. We have always written the histories of the time as victors are wont to do. We were the bastions of knowledge and keepers of tomes. Do you really think that Viking and Pictish hordes took our wealth and knowledge from our monasteries and priories? We permitted it, knowing it would return to us, in time. Then there were the Crusades to take back and defend The Holy Land from the Moors; long and exceptionally bloody affairs that kept the majority of my forebears sated. The wealthy who did not find the Church life to their liking were protected by it and from it. It was the aristocracy and royalty who sponsored monsignors, bishops, and cardinals to keep their secrets, and helped us to cut a bloody swath across history.

"Quite frankly, the Eucharist for us was much more, 'the blood of Christ' than the wine. The communion wafer was usually used to cleanse the palate after draining some wretched serf gleaned for such an occasion. After the last of the Crusades, we turned to Inquisition and it spread like wild fire through all of the Christian lands. No one desired to be put to the question, and few who entered the inquisitors' tender care ever emerged.

"Oddly enough, it was during the Inquisition that we made the discovery that would revolutionize our existence and consolidate our power into permanence with few ever being the wiser. Our Holy Father was visiting a church near one of the sites of inquisition; histories are unclear exactly where. All accounts say that he was a harsh ruler who put his best face forward only for the masses. During this visit, however, the pontiff was inexplicably giddy and gave no rebuke to even the most deserving of the order. After he had gone, the Holy Father remained pleasant and sated for nearly a day before returning to his curmudgeonly ways and foul humor. A cardinal suggested in jest that perhaps just knowing there was such misery so close by gave His Holiness a great bout of joy. The Holy Father, no fool he, realized that there might be something to that so he returned a few more times, each time clearing his mind and concentrating on the pain and torment that abounded. With each passing attempt he was more and more able to sate his desires for longer periods of time. He said Mass and allowed himself to feed off the feeling of guilt, pleasure and suffering he felt radiating from his flock. It was a boon from the gods themselves."

"So that's when you stopped usin' folk for food and began siphoning off their spirit, that right Padre?" asked Trick swirling his cold coffee around and around in the cup, his gaze not meeting Luca's.

"A papal bull was issued within months decreeing that all of our race were to convert to this new method of feeding. Those who could not or would not adapt were deemed to be considered enemies of the Church and hunted down as Hell's spawn. It gave the masses something to fear and yet another reason to run to the Church for protection. There is still a sect of rogue vampire hunters, but obviously you know that. It was good public relations for the church, taking the battle to the evil in the world, while discontinuing the terror of the inquisitions. It was a master stroke."

"What about all of the off-shoots of religion?" Tell asked, his breathing heavy. "What about the Protestants, Lutherans, Methodists, Baptists and the rest? Are they run by monsters like you?"

"Not all of them. Henry VIII had deeper motives to break with the Church than mere divorce. Throughout time, there have been some who have seen us for what we are or simply grew tired of the heavy hand of the Church. They splintered off to form new sects to conform with how they interpret the Bible. The only down side for us is they are beyond our reach for feeding. The rest of it is quite comical, really. Every Christian religion on earth has the same Holy Trinity of Father, Son, and Holy Ghost, but none of them has it all right. There is a piece of truth to each, but the puzzle will never be complete because of the base human fundamental need to disparage anyone who has a different thought that they accept as truth. Politics, athletics, literature, religion, the list goes on. Mr. Trufant is a perfect example. No offense meant, sir, but you were and still seem ready to rip off my head for telling you the truth about how one religion in this world organized. You don't even seem placated to know that whichever denomination you subscribe to is not affected by me or my kind."

"You mentioned an incantation that brings these sucker heads into our dimension," Trick said, still not in any better mood than when Father Luca had begun his tale. "Where is it now? I want it."

"Why would you possibly want that? It can serve you no purpose."

"Yes it can," he replied quietly, his stare finally coming off the cup to spear the priest with cruel intent. "If your people have it, you can perpetuate this cycle on humanity from now until Judgement Day, or is that another Catholic myth? I can't countenance that notion. I destroy it, and eventually, religion comes full circle and goes back to the people and their interpretation of what God is to them."

"I am sorry to disappoint you, but the summoning scroll was recovered the day the police found those two silly, unfortunate, college girls who began this whole debacle. It was on its way back to Rome with the Papal Nuncio that same night. It is now safely back in our archive vault. There will be a resurgence in the Catholic Church shortly, Trick, and we shall continue to be who and what we are."

Archer stood up and gave Father Luca a hard look. "Like I said before, we're in this together until those rogue vampires are dead. Don't betray us to them and don't taunt anyone here about what the future holds for your kind. It won't matter for you what your people do, because you'll be stuffed in a crypt and sealed inside. I'll call you here tomorrow after we've had time to digest all this and flesh out some plans for how to deal with something we can't see or touch. Kind of like faith, I guess. Be here for my call, or we'll think you're not playing nice. Understand, Padre?"

"No need to threaten me. I have said that I haven't the belly to face you again and I meant that. I have also promised to help you destroy the *Invictus Morte*," he sighed. "And I meant that, too." He walked to the door and held it for them as they filed out. "You can show yourselves out, I'm sure. Good day."

CHAPTER 19

"WELL, IS ANYBODY else's head spinning on their shoulders," Trick asked as he pushed the door to Blessed Be open and ambled through the showroom to Archer's desk, plopping heavily on one of the mismatched high-backed chairs Archer had accumulated. Toinetta joined him, silently seating herself and clutching her beaded handbag, staring intently at it. Tell was a blur of nervous energy as he grabbed a chair flipped it backward and straddled the seat, his head resting on the high seat back, fingers drumming a mindless beat. His gaze flitted around the room; looking at everything, seeing nothing.

"Um, Tell?" Archer said quietly as he rested his hand on the man's shoulder, feeling the tension in the man's muscles, like a python bulling its way through the densest wetland.

"Yeah?"

"You alright?"

"I'll be fine; just a lot to wrap my mind around."

"Glad to hear it. Now, can you tell me why I didn't have to unlock my shop for us to get in here?"

Tell winced and looked sheepishly at Archer. "Daniella said she'd mind the store 'til we got back. I figured you could stay open that way, you know, maybe make a few sales while we were gone. I didn't give it a second thought. I trust her." He looked around then bolted out of his seat. "I didn't see her when we came in. Daniella? Daniella!"

Archer had walked back in to the showroom and looked immediately to his stock of prime revenue, the herbs and spell ingredients he sold, thinking he might have been cleaned out. He found Daniella behind the counter, hastily trying to fold a tourist's map of New Orleans, then just stuffing it in a wad into her pocket, while trying to fit a large amber necklace back onto its rack. "Whatcha doin'" his tone incongruent with the casual phrase.

"N-nothing. It was nothing. Some tourist left this map here and I was going to throw it out."

"And the necklace? Yellow isn't your color. Maybe something in emerald or jade?"

"You startled me. I was looking at your necklaces when you came in. You have some nicely cut crystals. I only wanted a closer look."

Archer brushed past her and opened his till. "Any sales?"

She watched him, her eyes narrowing as he sorted through the bills, "A couple of small things and your last white-handled boline. You'll need to order another. Before you frisk me, no I didn't pocket any of it. And you're welcome for watching the store for you." She turned and stormed out from behind the counter heading for the door.

"Daniella, wait. I'm an asshole." She stopped but didn't turn around. "Thank you for minding the shop, you did a nice thing, an important thing for me today. I won't forget that." She turned to look at him, expecting more. "The truth of the matter is Tell didn't let me know what he had done, and despite my best attempts to change things, you're still virtually a stranger. You come in almost every day; we banter, we smile, and everytime I open my mouth, I am scared to death that I'll start babbling, like I am now." He smiled pausing a moment to allow his self-control to return. "Daniella, I want to trust you, and I hope one day to be included in your life in whatever capacity you'll allow, but we have to be straight with each other."

Daniella stepped forward and melted into his arms like a hot, solid dream he hadn't realized he had been having. Her hair smelled of lemongrass and wild lavender. She looked up at him and said, "I've been feeling the same things. At first I thought being coy and distant would keep you away, but the truth is, I have piles of unused herbs I have bought since the day I first saw you. No one could use as much as I buy, but I do it to have a reason to come and see you. It's just that keeping men at arm's distance has always been a good idea for me. I tend to run, and bad things tend to follow me."

Archer heard Trick clear his throat from the other room and ask if everything was alright. "Look, things are super weird right now and I have to try to work some things out with the people in there. Can I take you to dinner, say Olivia's around eight?"

"You've got yourself a date, Shopkeeper. I'll meet you there."

"Excellent. I'll see you then." He gave her an extra squeeze and peck on the cheek then turned and disappeared back into his office.

Daniella smiled and walked over to the rack of pendants, this time drawing an amethyst quartz and pocketing it with the map. She mentally kicked herself for getting caught practically red-handed. It had been a golden opportunity to be alone in the store but the steady flow of customers and tourists kept her too busy to accomplish anything. She had what she needed most, the amethyst quartz was by leaps and bounds stronger than a worthless scrap of amber, and she now had dinner plans. All in all, her day was looking up.

"She lied to me. I think she was trying to scry for something on a city map when I found her. She might have covered it okay except for the part when she said she was throwing the map away as she stuffed it in her pocket. She's a liar. She's a liar and a scryer, and now I have to have dinner with her. Look at me, I'm going totally mental! How does she manage this effect on me?"

"You done, Archer or would you like to run your gums some more," Toinetta asked mildly, a hint of her usually jovial tone in the barb.

"What is it with her? I didn't feel anything like that with Liz and she was the only woman I've ever loved. I don't get it."

"For starters," Tell interrupted, "you ever hear of pheromones? Every time you two are in the same room for more than a few seconds, I think everyone gets a little amped up on what you both put out there. It's seriously seductive, man. Like chocolate and peanut butter, cookies and milk, grape jelly and hot dogs, you two just fit."

Toinetta grimaced. "Grape jelly and hot dogs? Shew, you had me up to that one." She turned and looked at Archer. "Listen, shugah, you've been mourning Liz for a long time now and ignoring a lot of important things, like the need for human contact. Sure you have Trick, and me, but only because we're familiar. You dove with both feet into the Moonlight Mission with Trick and your studies with me. Now, everything is about getting this store of the ground. It's all to allow you to stay insulated, at arm's length. I'm not saying that's necessarily a bad thing; you've become a fair herbalist, improved your spell craft greatly, and have become much stronger psychically. You've just spent so much time trying to see into and understand other worlds, you kind of forgot about this one for a while. That's a far cry from where you were when we first met, but you were married and happy to be rooted right where you should have been."

"So, I've been so other-worldly minded I'm no earthly good, is that it?"

"Hush your mouth and open your ears Archer Sweet! All I'm saying is you're out of practice with some normal things. And the attraction between two people is the most normal natural thing there is in this life. Wake up and smell the pheromones, child."

"Alright, enough already. My balls are officially busted. I'll worry about her come dinner time, right now let's get back to the more important thing. How much of what we heard today is true and how much sunshine is Luca piping up our asses?" His vision blurred slightly and he swayed, catching himself on the back of his chair.

"We can debate that another time, Archer," chimed in Trick. "You sho'nuff took some pretty good licks from Luca when you broke him down. Luca's whole aura was pretty much leakin' like a sieve. Hell, if psychic energy was blood, he'd be Carrie on prom night. All the nicks and dings you took have you leakin' a mite, too. We need to slap some psychic bandages on ya buddy."

"Yes. Excellent idea." Toinetta said crisply clearing the long table and taking her cardigan from her shoulders. She folded it into a pillow, then patted the table top. "Shugah, you come on and lie down here, rest your head on my sweater. Tellico, would you please go into the other room and collect all of the crystals from the sales rack and bring them to me? Trick, if you would be so kind as to go and lock up, it would be better if we weren't disturbed." Trick and Tell left wordlessly and Toinetta took Archer's hand, ignoring his protests, gently helping him to lay down on the flat surface of the table, adjusting the makeshift pillow as he settled.

"So what's the treatment, doc? Will I be able to play golf next weekend?"

"I am going to heal the minor wounds to your aura and open your charkas with Reiki; the crystals will accelerate the healing and set you back in balance. It should take about twenty minutes for the crystals, longer for the Reiki. As for your golf weekend, as long as you feel like it, sure why not?"

"Damn. I hate golf." Archer chortled as he let his hands rest on the table, trying to relax.

"Uh-oh, you're even worse off than I thought. Now relax. Reiki works best on a calm, pliable person. Unfortunately, it does nothing for an awful sense of humor."

Tell returned with the crystals cradled softly in his massive hands. "What now, Ms. Toinetta?"

Trick came back in and answered because he knew Toinetta was already deep in concentration, gathering her energy to help augment Archer's own. "Separate them by color podna, R, O, Y, G, B, I, V."

"Who's he?"

"Junior high science class. You must have been absent that day."

Tell smiled, "I was home schooled. Momma had more important things to teach me."

"Red, orange, yellow, green, blue, indigo, violet. The colors of the spectrum in the order of refraction from high to low," Trick said, separating seven crystals. He walked over to where Archer was laying and set the rose quartz crystal at his feet, the orange by his ankle, yellow by his knee, green near his waist, blue at his elbow, indigo by his shoulder and violet at the top of his head. "Now you do th' same pattern up th' other side, same pattern except you don't need th' red or violet."

"That's good, since we don't have another amethyst crystal."

"What?" Archer asked, his head coming up slightly off the table. "Did we sell one? Wait, I could have sworn I saw both of them... Ah shit! She had me looking at an amber necklace while she boosted a different one. Son of a bitch!"

"Archer Sweet, you lie down, hush, and let it go. You need to relax and focus or we're all just wasting our time. Can you grasp that concept?"

Archer let his head fall with a muffled thunk onto the table and mumbled,

"The concept is understood, it's the execution that's suspect."

Concentrating on stilling himself, he tried emptying his mind. He allowed the void to grow steadily, becoming more vast, feeling his base consciousness drain slowly away until he was tranquil and could feel the tattered portions of his higher awareness. Every small ripple of oozing energy dripping from his psyche became suddenly quite frightening, real, and more than a bit painful. He was amazed at the way his etheric and spiritual body could compartmentalize such a savage attack, leaving his physical body feeling as if he was only in need of some ibuprofen and a nap.

Tell placed the last of the crystals and stepped away, watching Toinetta move her shoulders, arms, and hands in fluid motions across Archer's body, beginning with his crown charka, the one at the top of the head.

"The body's energy cycles once about every five minutes," Trick said under his breath to Tell, who stood, watching the process with interest. She's focusing on feeling the crystals' energy flowing into and through Archer."

"Trick, shugah?" Toinetta called in a low sing song voice.

"Yeah? What can I do for you?"

"You can hush up so I can concentrate. Tell if you're curious I'll explain later, Shugah. For now, y'all shush."

Trick nodded and guided Tell away leaving her in peace. Toinetta cupped her hands and placed them over Archer's eyes, almost but not quite touching him. She held them still, explaining that she was opening his Third Eye chakra and balancing the left and right side of his brain.

Archer felt restless, uncomfortable at the energy that flowed from Toinetta's hand, but Toinetta bade him be still and remain silent.

She moved her hands over his cheeks next, her little fingers resting just behind the ears. Next, she lifted Archer's head and held him in her cupped hands, one hand resting on either side of his occipital ridge. Finally, she lowered his head back to the table, placed her hands so they hovered just below Archer's throat and collar bones, then placed her hands on either side of his heart.

Toinetta continued her healing, moving to his right side and treating his solar plexus, the center of his abdomen, and either side of his groin, above his pelvic area to heal the root chakra, there above his knees, alternating one knee with the opposite ankle twice, and finally the bottom of his feet. At each position she spent five minutes until she felt his body's energies begin to shift and cycle themselves. When she had finished, she slumped weakly into Archer's plush office chair, directing Trick to collect the crystals by moving widdershins, or counter-clockwise around Archer's body.

She felt so spent. Ordinarily, an exchange of energies after a Reiki session would leave her feeling energized, exuberant. It was possible, she decided, that she was either getting too old to be doing such extensive work, or the energy drain Archer had experienced could be transferred. She looked at Archer, deciding not to think about it. His eyes were closed, a serene mask with the vaguest hint of a smile. His pitch-dark tresses had been unbound so he could lay flat, and his hair had fanned across the table top, adding to the sense of serenity with an ebony hue that seemed to undulate gently as Archer breathed slowly, deeply; snoring like a rusty chain saw.

Archer felt the sensation of the rigid table on his back, his neck becoming sore from the insufficient pillow. His body ached worse now that he was supine and could let his mind zone in on what was hurting. Toinetta was silent but he could feel her hands. Rather, he could feel the energy from her hands as they hovered above his body, helping to rejuvenate his psychic self. The shop was quiet and gradually Archer no longer noticed the solidity of his makeshift bed. He felt enshrouded in a thick veil of cottony softness as colors swirled about him to drift comfortably.

He smelled a familiar aroma of vanilla and strawberries, one that he had awakened to everyday of his brief but happy marriage, and felt gentle fingers running through his hair. Archer sat up, obviously dreaming, as his former wife, Elizabeth stood beside him, smiling and radiant, her ash blond hair catching the light around her and glowing nearly as bright as her broad smile. They met for a gentle lingering kiss as Archer brushed his coarse fingers slowly through her shoulder length silken tresses.

Archer broke contact first and pushed away until he could see her face, sitting for a moment, drinking in her beauty.

"I've missed you Lizard. You could visit more."

"I know Sweetdream, but if I did, you'd never move forward with your life, and it is certainly about time you did so." She sat by him and stared deeply into his dark eyes for a moment. "You're worried that finding an interest in someone else will diminish your feelings about me."

Archer dropped his eyes, feeling guilty and naked before her knowing expression. "Ah, Lizard, not you too. I have been moving on. I've got the store, new things in my life, and a sense of purpose again."

"But your feelings about Daniella Andrej frighten you?"

"God, yes. What if I let her get too close? What if I…"

"Baby-doll, our vows were 'til death parts us'. Newsflash, Sweetdream, the cosmos has parted us, but good. Besides, she's a beautiful woman and you're not destined to be celibate. Even if things don't work out with her, there's a whole lifetime ahead of you. Don't punish yourself if the right woman comes along, unless you've gained a kink I don't know about." She giggled playfully, "I have always been curious about other women; maybe when we reunite, you can introduce me."

Archer laughed, felt his lips turn upward in his sleep. "You were the right woman, Lizard. You always will be. What happens when we're reunited and I haven't found someone else? Will you be disappointed?"

"Of course not. I'll still have you. Don't worry about tonight, everything works out for a reason. You of all people know there is no coincidence in this life." She hugged him tightly then stood up and moved away. "You'll be fine Archer. It's just dinner, after all."

"But she's a thief and she lied to me. Not the best way to start out, ya know?"

"Give her tonight to make a clean breast of things. If she doesn't return the crystal, so be it. Do what you feel is right."

"I'll always love you Liz. You know that?"

Elizabeth Sweet was fading slowly before his eyes, but he was sure he heard her voice in the air, "Always, Sweetdream, and I you."

She was gone and with it the sense of peace and contentment he had enjoyed. Archer opened his eyes and found Toinetta sitting in his chair and Trick collecting the crystals from around his body. He felt refreshed, as if he had enjoyed a long undisturbed sleep, and sat up when Trick was finished gathering the crystals.

"How ya feel there, Archer," Trick asked as he sorted the colored quartz onto different fingers.

"Can't remember when I felt better, actually. Thank you." He turned to Toinetta and thought she looked ashen, exhausted. He hopped off the table and crouched by her side. "Toinetta? What's the matter? Did I drain you too much? Can I get you anything?"

Toinetta looked up at Archer and managed a feeble smile. "Shugah, I'm just old. Give me some time and I'll bounce back. Don't you go worrying about me. A glass of cold sweet tea would be nice,m though."

Archer stood up. "You've got it Toinetta. I'll be right back." He turned to find Tell scanning a copy of The *Times-Picayune*. "Hey Tell? Thanks for your help, too. Could you do me another favor and come keep Toinetta company for a few minutes while I fetch her some sweet tea? Thanks."

After Archer was gone, Toinetta began to cough, reaching for her handkerchief, bringing it slowly to her mouth and nose. The deep wracking spasms subsided as Archer returned with the tea and Tell saw her sleight of hand as she slid the cloth into her lap, noticing the once white cloth was how speckled with bright red blossoms. She sipped the tea gratefully, thanking Archer, then shooed him away when he asked about her cough.

"Shugah, it's all good, now don't you have things to do and a date to prepare for?"

Archer gave her shoulder a fond squeeze and walked out to find Trick. Tell moved back closer to her and asked gently, "How long do they give you?"

"Ah, baby, those doctors don't know what they're about. One says a year, one says two years, less if I don't take their poisons, but I'm not going anywhere until I'm good and ready. Now you hush about what you saw and get along. I'll be fine."

CHAPTER 20

Olivia's serves some of the finest Creole fare in The Quarter at unbelievably reasonable rates. One of the many reasons why Archer enjoyed it as frequently as possible. It was also relatively close to his shop in case the situation with the vampires took an uglier turn and he was needed, but the best feature to the restaurant tonight was its public area. It was going to help him remember to be polite and keep his temper in check. With luck, the forum would keep Daniella from making a scene when he confronted her about the missing necklace.

Archer stood outside for only a moment before he sensed Daniella approaching. Sensed was perhaps wrong, the wind shifted slightly and he scented her. Shaking his head, he smiled to himself as she neared, realizing in that moment what had been so openly expressed to him by all of his friends; she was something undeniably special to his every instinct.

The evening seemed to overpower even the street lamps, its darkness carrying a shallow nip of damp coolness blowing in from the Gulf. The sky was clear, a deep indigo, comforting and inviting in its depth. The rich near-fullness of the moon, along with thousands of stars and satellites, speckling the early evening sky with their brilliance, augered well the promise of a beautiful night to come.

Daniella looked stunning. She wore black slacks that clung provocatively to her dangerously curvaceous hips and a blood-red silk blouse with a delicate strand of pearls. A black pashmina scarf draped over her shoulders completed the devastating ensemble. Archer felt slovenly in his pressed blue Tigger golf shirt, chinos, and spit shined Rockports, as he stood gaping like a boated fish.

Unconsciously, Archer brought his shields to full strength for fear of losing his thin veneer of attitude and control. "You look utterly fantastic," he managed to say with no tremor in his voice, his stomach contorting to slap at the butterflies that had suddenly hatched in his gut.

Daniella stopped short, taking the time to look him up and down, clearly liking what she saw as she hit him with a full smile. "You're looking kind of wow yourself, Shopkeeper." Stepping forward, she took his arm and turned them both to face the picture window, where their reflection over-shadowed the ghostly images of the diners inside.

Archer felt his knees weaken as he saw how well they matched one another physically, their contrasts serving to reveal the beauty of dichotomy. Shielded as he was, he could feel her restraint as well. She felt delicate and absolute on his arm, the weight of a kindred spirit, a like soul with an unlike temperament, a balance that he recognized now was sorely missing from his life.

Holding the door for her Archer followed the intoxicating aroma of fine cuisine embracing them like an old friend. Inside was bustling with active servers and filled with the lively noise accompanied by a gregarious buzz of people in quiet conversation, imbibing their gastronomic desires.

Daniella and Archer were shown to a small table near the window and ordered a bottle of Smoking Loon Cabernet. After the waiter had gone and they were both settled in, Archer said, "This is one of the better tables in the house. They usually reserve it for beautiful women and whatever they drag in with them. It helps bring in business when they have a hottie to advertise that only the best is to be found here."

"I suppose I should be flattered. Your knowledge of this place is better than mine. Bring lots of 'hotties' here for dinner?"

"Usually I'm tucked off in a corner somewhere, eating by myself. I notice things, though."

"I haven't had dinner with anyone in quite some time. Many offers, but none to my taste."

"Speaking of taste, I've got a question I have been dying to ask you since this afternoon."

Daniella leaned forward slightly in anticipation, but sat back as the waiter returned with their wine, water, and basket of warm flaky bread. Archer watched the decanting, tasted the wine and, with a self-indulgent smile, nodded to the wine steward to pour the glasses. After the waiter came by and took their order, Daniella said, "You began to ask me something before we were interrupted."

Archer sat back, looking into the vermilion varietal, twirling the stem of the wine glass gently between his fingers.

"I'll come back to that. First answer me this: Why do you choose to dine alone so often?"

"You first, Archer, nothing is for free."

"Okay, I dine alone because I'm a widower. My wife, Elizabeth was murdered two years ago this past summer. She died in the arms of my best friend and former partner right outside of Saint Louis Cathedral. I came to New Orleans from Kenner, Louisiana to make a fresh start in my life." He took a sip of wine, watching his counterpart's face over the rim of his glass. "Your turn," he said when he set the glass down.

"What can I say? I am very selective with my time and with whom I spend it." She went for a taste of her own wine, but Archer's intense gaze never left her. "Okay, I made the rule, nothing is for free, and I will abide. I lament the passing of your wife, Archer, I really do. My story is not nearly so sad. I have never been married, or seriously involved with anyone. I move frequently, so it is difficult to grow close enough to anyone for something so intimate as that. Besides, I have not been convinced that any suitor for my hand could keep up with me."

"Fair enough," replied Archer nodding his head. "I didn't mean to shock you or make you feel sorry for my situation. I've grieved and I'm beginning to live again. Time will tell if you can keep up with me, Daniella. Keeping with your rule and knowing you'll just turn the next question around on me, I'm adopted and was raised by a pair of lovely people, wonderful parents, here in Louisiana. They still live nearby in Jefferson Parish"

"My father raised me, but I was born in blood. My first moments in this world were my mother's last. There were complications that the doctors could not have foreseen. Thankfully, my father did not resent me for killing his wife with my birth, and raised me all over the world."

"Your accent, is it Spanish? Italian? Greek perhaps?"

"No. It is Romanian. The Romanian language has remained unchanged for countless hundreds of generations. It is the closest thing to pure conversational Latin that you are likely to hear anymore."

"So you were born in Romania? Like Dracula, gypsies, and werewolves? That's cool. You said your father took you all over the world?"

Daniella looked nervously at the table-top. "My mother was from the Wallachia region, near where Vlad Tepes held one of his strongholds centuries ago. My father was a diplomat, an ambassador from Hungary. They met at a state reception. She was serving drinks and he got shit-faced trying to keep her close at hand. The next morning he awoke sick as a dog but tracked her down. They married within months."

"Kind of like my wife and me, except she was sick for even contemplating matrimony to me, much less going through with it. How long were your parents married Daniella?"

"Only a couple of years. They had come back to my mother's village for a visit and were picnicking in the low mountains about a few hours journey from the village where she was born. The reason they had returned was to give the news to my grandmother that they were expecting me. The whole village was ecstatic; since my mother had married such a prestigious man, my birth would bring pride to everyone."

"So what happened, or am I being to intrusive?"

"Not at all. It was long ago, it is not as if I remember it. She was attacked by an animal, a behemoth of a mountain wolf. They are common in that region, but are not usually so aggressive unless cornered, starving, or rabid.

"Papa was off collecting water from a nearby spring when the animal beset her. She hid behind their horses and screamed for my papa, but the beast tore through the frightened animals and had just sprung upon my mother's fleeing back as my father returned."

"Your mother was pretty spry for a pregnant woman, fortunately for you," Archer said in amazement.

"She was only four months along at the time, but I am certain, I was a burden." She paused to take a drink of her wine. "Papa carried a pistol for personal protection in case he needed to defend himself from any ardent political dissenters. He emptied his pistol at the beast and frightened it away. The villagers later tracked the blood trails and paw prints until both simply disappeared in the mountainous terrain. Mama was hurt badly, but refused to be moved from her grandmother's house to a hospital. She was, after all, a peasant girl and believed in her grandmother's folk remedies and magics."

"Would she have survived if she had received modern care?"

"No. She lapsed into a delirium kind of a fugue shortly after papa brought her back to the village. She had only random moments of lucidity after that. She lingered, in great pain for another month, went into labor, and everyone thought I would be born still. I defied the odds, and came, pink, normal and a fair birth weight. My gestation was accelerated somehow. My grandmother swore that I was full term weight and height, as she shook her head to acknowledge the impossible. My mother died just as I began to cry."

"That's a really fantastic and sad story. I've seen enough strange things to know that anything is possible, but there's a lot that's still new to me."

Daniella nodded slowly, as if Archer's response was what she had hoped or expected. "After mama's funeral, my papa had to leave the village with me quickly. Word had spread about what had happened and they believed my birth to be cursed. I've never been back there to see my relatives. Maybe one day I will go and play tourist, but tourists are a rare thing in that village."

"I'm sorry for your loss so early in life. I never knew who my real parents were, so I don't know if I have a mysterious background like yours, but I was raised by a couple who were everything a child could want." He took up a piece of bread, tore it in two and set the larger piece on his plate. "So where did you grow up if not in your village?"

"Everywhere and nowhere. Papa was a diplomat, remember? I lived in another Romanian village with a nanny until I was old enough to travel with Papa. We were all over the Balkans, the United Kingdom, Paris, Australia, South America, the United States, of course, and Canada. My favorite was New York City, with Buenos Aires a close second. Oh, The Big Apple! What a beautifully decadent, down-to-earth city! I spent far too many late nights at The Slaughtered Lamb Pub. My least favorite places? The snottiness of the French was the worst. Their furtiveness and the way they hid themselves behind facades of insufferable arrogance tainted every unique and beautiful thing I saw there. The architecture and countrysides were stunning, the people were not. Quebec was better, though not by much. It is clean and thriving, but the politics are mind numbing. The stodginess of most of Europe, especially before Communism failed, was confusing to me, until I understood the quiet pride in which they tried to eke out a living under oppressive regimes.

Papa taught me how to find the beauty in all things, but in the citizenry of French speaking areas, there was no beauty in the people."

She shook her head. "I must be careful not to paint with such a broad brush. Papa died five years ago, and I have been so many places in the U.S. ever since. This is my second time in New Orleans, and though it has deep French roots, I find it rapidly becoming my new favorite. I met Tell and some of his friends the last time I was here. I was so happy to see him again working at your store of all places."

"He just started with me a couple of days ago, but I can tell he's good people. How long were you in New Orleans the first time?"

"I lived on Bourbon Street last time and partied myself silly for about six months. Tell was a doorman who helped me out of a scrape with a drunk one night and remained in my life for the remainder of my stay. A big brother sort of figure, you know. You're right, he is an exceptionally good one."

Archer smiled. "He thinks the world of you. He wouldn't have trusted the store to just anyone, and we have a serious ongoing problem I thought he may be helpful in resolving. Thanks for minding the place, by the way."

Archer stopped and watched Daniella as their food arrived, the aroma of his catfish creole and Daniella's shrimp and taso pasta distracting him momentarily.

"Mmm. By Bacchus' bushy beard this food is utterly fantastic," she exclaimed, rolling her eyes heavenward with the first bite.

"Glad you like it. The taso sausage and I have a love hate relationship. I love it, but it doesn't much care for me. Now and then, I'll try and get away with ordering it." He had been looking for a segue into the topic all evening and decided this was as good a time as any, so he plowed forward. "Speaking of getting away with it, did the amethyst quartz help you find what you were looking for?"

Daniella's eyes widened as she tried to choke down the ample bite she had just taken. Coughing violently her eyes rolled briefly showing the whites, she snatched her napkin from lap to mouth in a fluid motion. Reaching for her glass of water with a shaky hand she sipped greedily from it until it was dry.

Archer was on his feet ready to help her when she sat back perfectly still, napkin hanging loosely in her hand as she looked up at the cracked plaster ceiling. Archer sat back down and waited a moment. "I doubt you'll find the answer up there Daniella. I can wait all night. Obviously, since I kept our date, I'm not terribly upset about it. I just want to know why."

She coughed once more gently and drew a ragged breath. "I didn't think you'd buy that lame story." Looking into his eyes, shame lined her exquisite features. "I am sorry for the deception, and I will bring the quartz back to you tomorrow and pay for borrowing it. I was curious to see how it went with an outfit I have and—"

"You must like the company of dim-witted men. If you think I'm that gullible, that obtuse, why even bother with this charade? Is tonight just another lie? Another way to get whatever it is you want? Why don't you just tell me? I hate being lied to, Daniella, and if I can help you I will. I like you and my gut tells me that we have more than a just chemistry, but I refuse to be a pawn in someone's game. Your choice right now; candor or the front door. We'll start with an easy one; what were you scrying for?"

"You know about scrying?"

"Don't deflect the question," Archer said heatedly. "I own an esoteric supply shop, of course I know what it is and the different ways it can be done. Do I know how to do it? No, but I know the basic components necessary for the various methods. The map and the crystal were pretty solid indicators. The million dollar question is what were you trying to find?"

"I was looking for something that cannot be seen. Once I find it, I hope to make sure that no one else finds it, or that it finds no one else."

Archer gripped his wine glass and gulped down the last large sip, steeling himself. "You're trying to find what's been killing people here in the city, aren't you?" Icy fingers walked up and down his spine as she met his eyes and nodded once. "Do you have any idea how big a mouthful you're looking to bite off? I have it on good authority that what you're looking for should not be sought. A lot of people who thought they were prepared for what they would find are cooling their heels in the morgue as we speak."

"That's why I'm looking. This nightmare must end. I can stop it."

"Really." Archer asked sardonically, remembering his brush with the creatures days before. "And just how exactly do you propose to do that?"

"Please, Archer, I promised I would not lie to you again. Please. Do not make me answer that question."

Archer bit back the sharp reply, closed his eyes and softened. "Okay. Assuming, just assuming you can stop what's been happening, maybe it would be better if you teamed up with Tell and me. We have been tracking this too, with my friends Trick and Toinetta. Maybe between us all, we can all lay our cards on the table we can solve the puzzle."

Daniella laughed, an eruption she quickly stifled with the back of her hand. "How did you ever graduate high school with such poor use of metaphors? Okay. I will throw in my two cents after I hear what your little cabal has learned."

"Thank you, Daniella. We'll all be at my shop at nine tomorrow morning."

Nodding, she then lowered her head back to her plate, suddenly ravenous. To avert more conversation, Archer, motored through his meal, hardly noticing much less appreciating the superb food he practically inhaled.

Between them, they polished off the bottle of wine and everything on their plates in record time. Archer called for the check, paid, and they left. Walking briskly up Decatur they cut across St. Ann Street, and came across a city employee pushing a big blue plastic sanitation cart full of trash bags. He was languidly sweeping the slate banquette with a nearly straw-bare broom. It looked like such a thankless task, but he seemed to take pride in his work. Archer noticed him flip the broom stick upside down and spear a Styrofoam Café du Monde cup with a nail embedded in the handle, neatly dropping the discarded trash into one of the bags in the bin.

Passing Saint Louis Cathedral they turned onto Royal where Jackson Square ended. Daniella surprised Archer by slipping her cool, soft hand into his, snuggling closer for warmth. As if by unspoken agreement they stopped under the gentle light reflecting from the garden of the church, taking the opportunity on the quiet city street to explore each other's eyes more deeply. She nuzzled her nose against his chest, smelling clean skin and musky anticipation. Looking up at him, her desire laid bare in her azure eyes, Archer drew her more closely into his arms. Feeling flushed, captivated, and helplessly giddy, he reveled in the approval glowing in her features. Their lips brushed gently, pleasantly, not really a kiss, but an intimacy that somehow was exactly what they both wanted. Slowly, they kissed, then with a greater urgency as each scented the others pheromones, then something different that barely registered against their new found ardor.

Daniella broke contact first, leaning her head on Archer's shoulder. "Mmm. I was wondering when you were going to do that. I was going to give you one more block before I made the first—"

Her nostrils flared as the scent that had unconsciously caused them to separate insinuated itself again. "Move!" Shoving Archer sideways Daniella ducked quickly as a shape materialized right in front of her, where Archer had been standing.

CHAPTER 21

ARCHER WATCHED IN disbelief as a second hulking humanoid figure emerged behind the first from the gloom of the soft street lamps. He could see through it, but it also seemed to have mass. The vampires! He turned his attention to Daniella and saw her plant a solid front kick in her opponent's mid-section. Archer threw his arms up and waved at them all, "Hey you oversized ticks! Remember me? You mosquito motherfuckers still want a taste? Well bring it, you B movie rejects! C'mon!"

The pair turned toward him, clearly not understanding the insults but recognizing their missed prey and his taunting tone of voice. As one, they wheeled and began pursuing him, much faster than Archer had counted on, fairly gliding in their gracefulness.

He led the two swiftly-closing attackers away from Daniella, praying she would have the good sense to run the other direction as fast as she could. An idea formed in his head, ill-advised, and as desperate as distracting the vampires away from Daniella had been.

Dashing past Saint Louis Cathedral, Archer's eyes roamed the open expanse of empty ground before him. Off in the distance to his left, he heard the low rumble of solid plastic wheels as they trundled unevenly over the slate surface of the banquette. The street cleaner making his way back up the far side of the pedestrian thoroughfare. The snarls of rage were close, adrenaline pushed Archer's legs to pump faster toward the object he sought.

The hapless cleaner heard Archer chugging behind him and turned curiously, his cleaning rod in front of him in a relaxed defensive position. He had been mugged more than once on this job and was wary of attack, but he didn't want to thump a drunken tourist if he didn't have to. Archer took the decision from him literally, grabbing the rod with one hand while shoving the man backward to land dazed inside the large-wheeled trash bin.

Archer snapped the broom head off with his foot, adjusting the pick stick in his hand, then stopped, whirling nimbly to face his pursuers. The three foot long staff with the wicked nail at one end and jagged wood at the other was now a formidable half staff, almost the same heft as the baton he had learned to use expertly when he was an MP in the Army, then later as a cop.

He felt them before he saw them, their psychic presence buzzing heavily against his mind. As they stalked into the light, Archer's heart skipped a beat, the creature's visage terrifying him. Drawing a deep breath to steady himself, he watched the pair of tall murderous creatures emerge from the shadow near a dim street lamp. He hoped that they didn't enter this dimension with full knowledge of how to leech psychic energy, like their cleric brethren. He doubted he would be able to hold off a sustained simultaneous psychic attack and defend his body until help came. What help? he thought to himself. Bringing the dowel up in a deft sharp move from his elbow, he caught the first, more aggressive creature flush across its throat with a satisfying crunch, causing it to stagger past him and fall to its knees, gasping for its next breath.

I ran off and Daniella doesn't know where to find me even if she could find help.

The second vampire approached more warily, its body shimmering like the alien creature in *Predator*, refracting the light around him, presenting Archer with only an outline of body, a space he couldn't see through. The vampire reached out and made an attempt to disarm Archer by merely snatching the rod from his grasp. Thrusting forward, Archer felt the nail penetrate the hand that stretched outward, hearing a cry more of surprise than pain. Backing away quickly, the creature nearly succeeded in tearing Archer's weapon away.

The labored sound of the first vampire had stopped and Archer risked an instant to duck and turn to see where it was. His ears saved his life as the first vampire had been inching forward to take Archer stealthily. With a panicked cry, Archer charged closing the gap between them and taking away the advantage of attack. The creature was unbelievably fast, its lack of solid form making it difficult for Archer to contend with. Ducking under its guard, Archer speared the monster's foot with the nail, then reversed the thrust straight upward, striking it hard on the chin with the splintered end of the stick.

The brutal contact made the dowel vibrate so hard, the sudden shock and stinging sensation in Archer's hand nearly made him drop his weapon. Backing against the stone wall, removing an avenue of attack from the two creatures now facing him as one, he weighed his limited options. Like specific parts of his life flashing before him, Archer saw every one of the many barroom brawls he had broken up or instigated while in the Army, and tried frantically to remember any sequence of moves or tactics that he knew to be effective in taking down more than one man.

His memory failed him as the first tinges of panic set in. He was going to die, just after he had decided to take a chance on living again. Fate could be so very ironic. Flexing his still tingling fingers he smiled, the right side of his mouth turning up, grimly amused in spite of his predicament. With that smile came a moment of clarity, one possible maneuver he could use and maybe take out at least one of the vampires before he was done.

Switching the dowel from a defensive posture against his arm to that of a barbarian, he held the spear aloft, almost like a softball bat. Feigning savagely at the vampire closest to him on his right he shifted his balance to roll left, tucking his weapon as he tumbled behind the second vampire. Lunging upward rapidly, leading with his weapon he rose in a blur of motion and the vampire turned to face him. The force of their combined movements rammed the dowel head, with the nail leading the way, through the vampire's tough but yielding flesh. Relishing the satisfaction of impact, Archer heard bones crack and felt thick ichor-like blood wash over his hands. An unholy shriek erupted from the beast as the dowel burst out through its mid-spine, completely impaling it.

The vampire staggered backward, feebly trying to draw the rod out of itself, succeeding only in sitting down hard on the grassy edge of the park.

Archer pressed forward and kicking the creature ferociously in the face and groin until it was prone, writhing weakly on the ground. Quickly, leaning his weight on the jagged end of the weapon, he shoved the shaft further into the beast until he felt the dowel dig into the soft earth beneath the vampire, pinning it firmly to the ground.

Archer kept moving, casting about frantically for another weapon, anything, and found nothing. Not even a strand of normally ubiquitous gaudy beads to throw at his other opponent.

It came for him in a blur of motion that barely registered before it was on him. Archer crouched low, and when he felt the weight of the vampire strike him, he raised up and pushed his body and arms back, trying to flip the vampire into the brick wall. All he received for his planning was solid blow to the crown of his head, sending him reeling backward. Stumbling, Archer fell next to the downed vampire, who thrashed in agony but tried to grab and hold Archer for its hunting partner. Archer rolled away reflexively, feeling his shoulder strike slate. His brain screamed, "Get up asshole!" but his body was screening its calls. He lay there groggy and foggy for what felt like an eternity, trying not to lose consciousness. His eyes fluttered and he tried at least to sit up to face the inevitable attack and die like a man.

Archer sat and waited for the killing blow but nothing happened. He was aware of the first vampire thrashing on the ground nearby and of a shrill keening cry of pain and fear. Time must be distorting, he thought. *Maybe I'll get to see my life flash before me. How sad is that? Sure wish I could stop screaming though. Very undignified.*

Archer managed gain his feet, swaying like a coconut palm in a stiff Gulf Coast breeze, surprised to find his vision and clarity returning. He wasn't the one screaming, nor was the vampire he had impaled. He kicked the staked vampire hard in the head as he stepped past it, looking for the source of the screaming.

The second vampire was making the unholy noises. It sounded almost frantic as it wrestled with a large wolf, trying to cover itself as the wolf ripped and tore it with its teeth, shredding its skin with elongated razor sharp claws. Under the dim light, Archer could see it was a beautiful creature, a silky jet-black pelt, long and powerfully built. This was no psychic revenant, but a real wolf, and for some reason it had come to Archer's rescue not once, but twice.

The street cleaner watched the first part of the battle in rapt horror and fascination. When the wolf appeared, he decided he was in more danger from a wild animal than a fight between strange men. Reaching for his mobile phone to dial 911, the first tone on the keypad made the wolf hesitate for the scantest of time. The vampire struck, knocking the hesitant beast from his body and standing, legs apart, prepared for the next onslaught. The wolf charged in low, going for the tall creature's hamstring. As the vampire drew its foot back to kick its tormentor, the wolf drew itself up releasing like a coiled spring for the vampire's throat. The vampire recognized the feint and had been prepared for the jump, catching the wolf in mid-air under its forelegs.

Snapping futilely, at the monstrosity, who held it like a naughty puppy at arm's length, the wolf scrabbled for purchase. Obscenely casual, the vampire slammed the wolf to the ground where it landed hard on its side, wind escaping it lungs in an audible woof. Reaching down languidly, the vampire took firm hold of the wolf's right foreleg. With a flick of his wrist the vampire snapped the bone like a dry twig. The wolf howled in pain as the vampire reached for the other foreleg.

Ramming his elbow into the glass store front, causing large pieces of glass to rain heavily onto the banquette, Archer picked up a wickedly jagged shard as he heard the snap of the next bone and the ensuing agonizing yelps.

Sprinting to where the first vampire still lay, struggling weakly, but with increasingly more energy to free itself, he stomped the abomination savagely on the head, solar plexus, and groin. Dropping to his knees onto the broad chest of the thing, he opened his mind. *"Hey, vampire!"* he said silently. *"I know you read thoughts, you were in my head once already. Let the wolf alone or I'll shorten your buddy by a head."*

The razor sharp dagger of glass pressed into the vampire's neck, drawing more of the foul smelling black blood. Feeling the beast go still beneath him, Archer could feel its palpable terror.

Flinging the wolf away, the other vampire started walking with purpose toward Archer. "Ask your boy if I'm kidding. You leave the wolf and me alone and you can have him alive. One more step and you'll be a lonely vampire. There'll be another time, another place. I guarantee it. Think fast!"

Archer heard the sonorous voice erupt in his head, mocking, "You should kill him now. If not he will repay you pain for pain before slaking himself with you." When Archer didn't react, the voice continued, more subdued, "You leave him with me and I suffer that vile hellhound to live? We have an accord, human. You are correct, there will be a reckoning, and you shall not fare so well."

Standing with the glass shard, Archer paced to the far side of the street, letting the vampire approach his companion. The vampire did not deign to look at Archer, reaching gently down drawing the other up with a slurping, wet pop, leaving the stake in the ground, and placing his groaning brethren over his shoulder.

The vampire glanced up the street at the sound of sirens echoing from approaching police cruisers racing toward him. Gathering himself he leapt vertically clearing the wall of the store Archer had broken into, landing easily on its flat roof, and disappearing quickly from sight.

Gaping as the pair made their escape, Archer turned and ran to his fallen ally. Sprinting past the wolf's struggling, whimpering form, Archer took the large-wheeled bin from the stunned street-cleaner. After dumping the refuse bags out beside the man, Archer pushed the cart toward the wolf. "Don't tell the police which way I went. Just tell them what you saw and how those things got away. We copasetic?"

Stunned, the man nodded. "After this, if the cops don't lock me up for being drunk on the job, I'm going back to the day shift. Goddamn, but I've had enough."

He stopped the bin in front of the yelping wolf as it tried to drag itself away on ruined legs. Archer stooped over and said in soothing tones, "Don't you worry now, I'll take good care of you. I don't know why you've been shadowing me, but thanks to you I'm safe and I'll make sure you get the best care around. I'm going to pick you up to get you in the cart. It's going to hurt like hell, but it's got to be done."

Scooping up the whining animal much the same way the vampire had, Archer noted that, as he did, the legs dangled uselessly but did not flop, indicating they were most likely clean breaks. The whimpering wolf snapped feebly at him, more from pain than fear or aggression as he gently lowered the raven-toned wolf into the wide bin. It was a beautiful animal, and easily over six feet tall on its hind legs, more like a Great Dane than wolf.

"Sorry, it doesn't smell the greatest, especially with your sensitive nose, but it's only a short trip back to my store. We have to go before the cops see us. You might get put to sleep if we get caught."

The wolf delicately licked its painful legs then fixed Archer with an extraordinarily lucid and human stare. Shivering slightly as he looked away from its blue eyes, Archer started pushing the cart around the block past the Cathedral. *Glad the thing can't talk*, he thought, his head aching like Andy Roddick had played five tie break sets with it instead of tennis balls. *Guess it doesn't care for my sense of humor.*

CHAPTER 22

ARCHER, HIS HEAD reeling, vision blurry, wheeled his savior as gently as possible up the darkened streets to his store. Trold and Berg were nowhere in sight as he unlocked the doors, pushing them open, and flipping on the overhead lights. The cart wasn't narrow enough to navigate the displays and shelves on the sales floor so he gently reached down and hoisted the wolf up. Trying to carry it like a one hundred plus pound infant, its legs dangling grotesquely, useless, its eyes glazed from shock, pain, and helplessness, Archer walked through the store, careful not to jostle the brave animal. Setting his charge gently on the table where he himself had lain only hours before, he had to pause a moment until the rolling waves of nausea and dizzy feelings receded.

Moving as fast as his muddled senses allowed, Archer stumbled up to his apartment for supplies. Returning he found the two trolls gathered by the table, their small arms out touching the wolf gently with inquisitive fingers, curious expressions showing on their faces. The wolf had rolled over onto its side, its broken legs dangling grotesquely without support.

Archer approached the trolls, his arms full of blankets, planting spikes and handkerchiefs to splint the legs, and two coated aspirin slathered in peanut butter. Trold and Berg looked back at him gibbering to themselves quietly for a moment, then put their hands on the animal's torso sliding the wolf back onto the firm edge of the table. Archer gently shooed his former door stops away as he set his implements down.

Archer moved to the wolf's head and gazing into its deep blue eyes. This was no ordinary wolf, he knew. Intelligence shown in those eyes, and something more. The wolf reached up to lick Archer's cheek and he knew; it was trust. Offering the peanut butter coated pain killers to the wolf, it sniffed tentatively, whined appreciatively, then licked his fingers clean.

Wiping his greasy, saliva soaked hand on the tail of his shirt he reached for the splints, knowing this would be a difficult task. At best, the bones would heal if the wolf could stay off of them, if not, it would end up crippled and need to be put down, despite his best effort.

Reaching for the first thick plant stake he walked around the back of the wolf, noting as he looked for further injury that he had been incorrectly thinking it to be a he. Archer stood directly before her and showing her what he intended to do. Her tail flopped once weakly as if giving him the okay to proceed.

Archer worked quickly and carefully as possible, being as gentle as he could. Grasping the separate pieces of bones aligning them properly, he set them against the stakes, and bound the stakes as tightly as possible without inhibiting circulation. Moaning, the wolf's flanks were puffing in agony like a blacksmith's bellows, battling its fight or flight desire. When he was finished, the wolf's eyes were closed and her sides were no longer heaving as badly, settling more naturally into a rhythm of sleep born of exhaustion. Trold and Berg had remained close by, watching with interest as Archer worked. They didn't budge as Archer backed away quietly from the still form on the table but shifted their gaze to him.

"Guys?" Archer asked quietly, gazing intently at their pinched emotionless little visages. "Can you do me a big favor and watch over her while I go get something to drink and bring my blankets down? I'm going to sleep down here tonight, if that's alright with you."

The trolls looked at each other, then at the prone form on the table and back to Archer. The slightly larger one, Archer guessed it was Trold, nodded his head and shocking him when he opened his mouth and in a voice that sounded like two pieces of sandstone rubbing together said, "We watch. Go."

Racing across the courtyard, Archer ran up the stairs to his apartment, and began gathering what he would need for his mini-campout. He still couldn't get over that wolf. She could have torn him to ribbons whenever he did anything that caused her pain, yet she was more docile than he would be with two broken arms. Grabbing a water bottle he was heading back downstairs when his mobile phone rang. *Holy shit! I forgot all about Daniella.* Scrambling for the phone clipped to his hip, he saw it was Trick on the caller display.

"Heya Archer, I didn't interrupt ya did I? Jus' wanted to see how things went with that hottie thief a yours."

"Dinner was good, until we had a run in with the vampires. They're almost fully visible now. Daniella and I got separated and I managed to get them to chase me instead of her."

"You alright? Need me ta come over?"

"Nah, I'm okay, just bruised. What else is new? My biscuits were sure in a vice for a while, but that wolf saved me again. She's my guardian angel, I guess."

"You or your fairy god-wolf do any damage or'd they just light out again?"

"I staked one, nearly finished it, the wolf held the other one off until I could get away. I'll tell you the whole story tomorrow, Trick, but I haven't heard from Daniella since we split up, and I have to know she's okay. I'll holler," he said and disconnected.

Quickly, he dialed information resuming his walk downstairs. "Operator? I'm looking for a listing for Daniella or D. Andrej in the French Quarter."

"Hold please for the number," came the bored reply as he walked through the courtyard, and the operator connected the call. The phone rang and rang, until a mechanical voice at the other end instructed him to leave a message. He stepped back into the store as he began to speak, "Daniella, its Archer. I hope the Goddess guided your path safely home. I got away pretty much intact, thanks to some extremely good luck." Retrieving the pillow and blanket, he set them on the office chair and rolled it toward the table, where Trold and Berg kept vigil. "Please call me back or come by the store tomorrow morning and let me know that you're alright. I had a great time getting to know you. I hope you had fun, too. Goodnight."

I hope you had fun? We were nearly killed and you're talking about fun? Nice, Archer. Real smooth.

Returning the phone to his belt, he placed a blanket over the wolf's torso, then plopped into the chair, arranging his pillow and blanket before moving to turn off the lights and kicking off his shoes. Thanking the trolls for their help, he pulled the blanket up around himself.

Had he kept his eyes open for just a moment longer, he would have seen the wolf open her eyes and gaze at him, her tail wagging happily.

CHAPTER 23

D AWN'S BEATEN-COPPER light blazed into Archer's dreamscape as he shifted in the chair, bringing him back into the world of consciousness and terrible pain. His ribs hurt, his body was stiff from sleeping in the chair, and his head was pounding so bad that his vision was swimming. He knew he had suffered a concussion for sure, and his drifting off like that last night without calling someone to watch him was dangerous. Once again, his spirit guardians had taken pity on a fool and let him live, allowing him to retain the hazy memories of the night as they rushed back to him like a slap to the face.

The early joy and late pain of last night thundered back as he rose, a little unsteadily, to check on the wolf. She was gone, the splint stakes and binding were strewn around the table and floor. He checked the entire store, thinking she might have dragged herself off to some place where she would have felt safer, but he could find no sign of her anywhere. He called out, looking for Trold and Berg, but they, too, were conspicuously absent.

Archer's concern for a hurt wolf was compounded by the fact that Daniella had not called him and the store was due to open soon. He expected Toinetta, and probably Trick would be there shortly after he opened for their strategy meeting.

Deciding to risk missing an early customer and making Tell wait to let him in for the day, Archer shambled sluggishly upstairs to his apartment, took four ibuprofen and jumped in the shower for a quick sluicing. The temperamental water heater decided he didn't need a hot shower, which turned out to be a blessing. The cold water helped clear his head but made his entire body ache as he shivered. Freezing, he toweled off quickly and jumped into a gray hoodie that proclaimed 'I'd Rather Pass Out than Tap Out', and donned a pair of grey sweats.

He cleaned out his coffee maker and brewed a fresh steaming pot of Café du Monde blend. The big mug of scalding hot coffee brought him to life as he grabbed a single serving box of Frosted Flakes and went back down to the shop.

Tell was waiting for him, as was Daniella, when he opened the door. Archer ushered them in and latched the doors open, since his door stops were roaming about somewhere in the store. Tell was in his typical earth tones and Lugz, but she was as vibrant as the early morning sun in a yellow sweater, autumnal floral print silk scarf, and denim gauchos with high oxblood leather boots.

"Daniella? I'm so happy to see you're alright." Moving forward to embrace her, to feel her warmth, he felt hesitation, her arms coming up slowly, holding him stiffly. Pulling back and looking at her Archer asked, "What is it? Are you upset that I left you? I was trying to distract the things that jumped us. I would never have left you otherwise."

"No, it's not that, I owe you my life. I'm just not used to that kind of physical activity. I'm a little stiff and sore this morning."

"You know we can call it even. If you hadn't warned me and then kicked the first of them, I'd have been a goner for sure. Where'd you learn to move like that?"

"There is much about me you still do not know. A woman on her own has need on occasion to defend herself. I took some self-defense classes." Reaching into her purse she withdrew the amethyst crystal, letting it dangle by its string. "I nearly forgot to return this, Shopkeeper."

He took the crystal and returned it to the display rack. "Could you stop calling me 'Shopkeeper'? It makes me feel like you're being dismissive, even when I hear the playfulness in your voice."

"I will try, Shopkeeper, if you quit dancing around and admit to me that there are vampires in the city."

Archer's mouth gaped, incredulous for a moment. Turning to look at Tell, who was tidying and squaring the books on their shelves, assiduously ignoring them, he took a deep breath. "Alright. We have reason to believe that there are vampires loose in the city. Actually, we're going to try and find some weapons today to kill them when we manage to hunt them down." He looked at her fixedly, awaiting her reaction with keen interest.

"Thank you Archer. I'm glad our policy of honesty is carrying over from last night." Reaching to rub her arm through her sweater, Archer saw a flash of ugly black and blue blotches on her skin.

She tried to pull away as he reached for her hand, he held her firmly, quickly skinning his other hand up her sleeve exposing a patchwork of mottled flesh. Jerking back quickly, her eyes blazed briefly, until she saw the unvarnished concern on Archer's face. "By the Goddess above, Daniella," he breathed. "Who did this to you?"

"It is nothing, Archer. Nobody did this to me, it was my own carelessness," she answered, backing away as Archer reached for her other sleeve.

"So much for being honest with one another?" Archer's voice was sharp, the question acid on his tongue. "I won't ask again. If you're ever ready to trust me, if you decide I'm more than just an amusing distraction, let me know. I don't play chess, Risk, or head games. I just put some serious faith out there, why is it so hard for you to reciprocate?"

Turning from her he walked over to the register, opening the till and counting out the cash he thought necessary to purchase the weaponry they'd need, studiously ignoring her. She sat down at one of his small reading tables she beckoned to Tell when he came near.

Archer felt a tug on his shoe lace and looked down to see Berg pulling at it with great inquisitiveness. Reaching down he took the lace gently from the young troll and re-tied his shoe, smiling at the small creature's interest. "Wolf," Berg grunted.

"No little guy," he replied with a drawn smile. "That's a shoelace. It might still have the wolf's smell from last night."

Berg looked annoyed as he shook his head. "Wolf here," he continued, and pointed up emphatically.

Archer frowned and stood back up, and found himself face to face with a tearful Daniella.

"The little guy is very smart, or you are quite dense, Archer Sweet," she said as a single tear escaped the corner of her left eye and ran down her fine cheekbone.

Archer felt a gamut of different emotions surge through him; anger, betrayal, gratitude, wonder, awe, tenderness, shock, and more. Reaching out he gently wiped the tear away from her cheek as he felt a warm affinity for her deepen within himself. "You're the wonderful creature who saved my worthless hide twice in less than a week?" Smiling, he let his thumb continue to caress her cheek. "Thank you doesn't begin to cover it, does it?"

A sob escaped her as she took his hand in hers, nuzzling it. "It is I who owe you an apology. I should know that a man who makes my heart sing as you do, who bartered for an animal's life, my life, from a cruel and merciless enemy, could be trusted with my secret. Can we sit down and talk? I'm still exhausted from last night, and I know you are because you sat up most of the night with me."

Archer took a twenty out of the register and walked over to Tell. "You eat breakfast yet?"

"Nah, I overslept. Didn't have time."

"Could you do me a solid? Go to Café du Monde and get yourself some breakfast. Take your time, enjoy yourself; just bring back a dozen for Daniella and me and four large café au laits."

"Hey, sure thing Archer, thanks. I'm glad you two are getting along. She always seemed, I don't know, tormented to me. Maybe you can help her."

"Ya never know," Archer replied as Tell clapped him on the shoulder and left the store to go get breakfast.

Archer walked back over to the counter and took Daniella gently by the hand, leading her to the table, seating her in his padded office chair before sitting next to her on one of the plain hard high back chairs. "I don't figure this needs to be a face to face," he murmured in her ear. "Besides, I want to be able to hold you if you need me."

CHAPTER 24

"It is a long, awful story, Archer, why would you want to hear it? You already know what I am. What does it matter?" Daniella whispered, her head hanging.

"It's important to me. I care for you in a way I don't quite understand and I want to know. Secrets are an incredible weight. Maybe telling me will lighten it for you."

"You have no idea. It's why I move around so much. Can you imagine what it is like to be the only female werewolf ever to be born that way?"

"I can't begin to imagine your life, but I do understand the loneliness you must endure. Acquaintances, but few real friends. People you want to care about, to reach out to, but who can be *au fait* with your situation?"

"Sometimes I've wanted to just blurt it out, tell the world my secret, get it out in the open. Then I visualize being paraded around in a cage like the freak I am, or killed by a scared mob, or becoming an ongoing experiment in a research lab. I honestly don't know which fate would be the worst, but I never stop thinking about it."

"Sometimes, do you ever feel there's is anyone you can trust? Is there anyone to whom you have told your secret?

"No one but you, but there are others who have learned my secret and pursue me. They're werewolves too, and they want me for breeding." Daniella's eyes filled with tears, shivering once violently, before looking at him. "It feels right that you should know. It's just that sometimes, sometimes..."

"Sometimes. Yeah. I've found sometimes to be a real bitch," Archer replied sadly.

"I'm so sorry to drag you into the hell that is my life. I feel something for you I can't explain, but that doesn't mean I'm not utterly, entirely, terrified about what you'll do or say now that you know."

Archer reached his arm over her shoulder and drew her gently against him. "That," he said, tenderly kissing her tears away, "is what I'm going to do." She turned and nestled into his arms, her body heaving with sobs of relief. "What I'm going to say is nothing. It's my honor to keep your secret and it's my desire to know you and be whatever you need me to be. You saved my life twice, gave of yourself freely first physically and now by entrusting me with your deepest confidence. I'm not going anywhere."

Daniella sighed, pushing away from Archer a relieved smile blossoming across her exquisite, delicate features, her cheeks flushed with tears and joy. "Thank you Archer. We will have time. I have a feeling I'll stick around for a while. We'll be able to learn about each other at a regular pace." She looked up at the door. "Right now, it looks like you have a priest here."

Archer's head jerked up so fast he nearly knocked Daniella in the jaw. Standing in the doorway was Father Luca.

Archer stood, his hand still resting gently on Daniella's shoulder. "Padre. You're early. Come in and take a look around. The others will be here shortly." Archer turned and looked back at Daniella. "It may be better if you weren't here when everyone else arrives. Even though you have as much at stake in this as anyone else, I can't justify your presence without arousing suspicions."

Nodding her head, dabbing gently at her cheeks with her sweater sleeve she stood, keeping her gaze at the floor she rooted through her purse, then handed Archer a card. "Call me when you are finished, if I can be of assistance."

Hugging her close, mindful of her wounds that were still healing, he whispered "I will. Promise. We're definitely going to need you. I'm going to need you."

She gave him her mobile phone number. "I'm going to go back to my

flat and crash. I may have healed but I'm still sore and weak. Call me."
Reaching up she brushed her nose across his, then kissed him gently on the
mouth. The movement was so intimate, Archer was left speechless as she
breezed by Luca and left the store.

Luca was dressed in jeans and a cable kit sweater, only his collar and
black shirt beneath the sweater belied his identity as a clergyman, as if he
were trying to go incognito. Archer waited, unmoving, forcing Luca to come
to him, "You're early," he drawled, repeating himself, trying to set Luca on
edge. "Why?"

Smiling, Luca tried to deflect the question, "She's a lovely woman
Archer. You are a lucky man indeed" Archer's eyes bored into him and he
abandoned the small talk. "My apologies, I could not wait. I wanted to speak
to you about your friends, Trick and Tellico."

Archer gazed at him, impassive, stoic.

"Um, yes. It seemed to me yesterday that they bore much more
animosity toward my kind than anyone else in the group. Do I need to fear
for my personal safety?"

"Luca, I think Tell was just shaken, and he didn't see what you can do.
Trick is a different story. His moral structure is much more rigid than mine.
I try to remain impartial. I was a cop, I know there are at least two sides to
every story, but Trick hasn't learned about how wide gray areas can be. For
him, things are either right or wrong."

"You didn't answer my question, Mr. Sweet."

"When are you due to return to The Vatican?" Archer smiled, his
meaning crystal clear, the issue closed.

Luca nodded and turned to study the display of pendants and necklaces
in Archer's display counter. He jumped, startled, as Tell returned with a large
bag of beignets and a small cardboard carrier of café au laits. Tell glared at
Luca as he set the bag and carrier down on the table.

"What's the leech doing here? I feel my appetite slipping away."

"It is nice to see you again, too, Mr. Trufant. Name calling is
unnecessary."

"Well, you ain't human; you prey on humans, and you display an
arrogance that sickens me. S'cuse me if I'm not in a welcoming way this
morning."

Luca smiled, "Humility is what we all strive for, pride is a deadly sin.

It is my frailty to be prideful, and I acknowledge that readily. Some people evoke my arrogance more easily than others. You are one to point fingers. You're not entirely human yourself, are you Mr. Trufant?"

"Half is better than none. Trolls are peaceful sorts. We don't treat folk like chattels or cattle for that matter."

"Whatever gets you through the day, but I have never been to prison, Troll."

Archer stepped between the two, reaching for one of the cups of coffee. "It's early, I'm tired, and it's my place. If you two want to snipe at each other, there's the door. If you want to eat, park your ass." He plopped down on his padded chair, grabbed his café au lait and took a long sip of the sweet caramel colored brew.

Tell took a beignet from the bag and walked around the table, putting his back to the wall so he could see the store. He sucked some powdered sugar from his thumb and asked, "You and Daniella cool, Archer?"

"We're good, Tell, thanks. I was going to bring her in on this, but what she doesn't know is probably better for her."

"You'd be surprised at what she can handle," replied Tell as he tore into his beignet.

Archer sipped his coffee, nodding in agreement. "You're right." Turning to the priest he held the bag up, "Luca have a beignet. I have something to tell you, and you can tell me if it changes anything."

"If I can."

"The vampires are coalescing, becoming visible. What happens when they are completely solid?"

"They will become more subject to the laws of this dimension. They are tall, angular by nature, but this dimension's gravity will compress them to a height and breadth that makes them appear more human. They will adapt their look by glamour and once the acclimation is complete, it will be nearly impossible to differentiate them from human. Their strength and speed will be predicated on the quantity of blood and frequency of consumption."

"How much time until that happens? When I saw them last night, they were all shimmery, a tall outline, but definitely visible and solid."

"Tell me. What did you see?"

Archer recounted the events of the previous evening as Tell and Luca listened rapt. When he had finished, Luca snorted contemptuously. "You traded the life of a wolf for a chance to eradicate one of the vampires? Foolish. They would never show you such charity."

"You wouldn't understand charity, Luca. That's a human trait." Tell said, his voice tinged with excitement. "Archer proved they can bleed. If they can bleed, we can kill 'em."

"Archer has illustrated that he is a skilled and cunning opponent. The *Invictus Morte* are fast and powerful and he held his own against two of them. More important, he has given us a timetable. They must be destroyed in the next two days or their transformation will be complete."

"Two days, eh? Well, I guess we'd better haul balls," Trick said as he walked through the door. He hit speed dial on his cell phone and connected to Toinetta, letting her know not to drop by until later. He disconnected and dropped his phone into the pocket of his jacket and jumped into the conversation. "I've got a friend on Chartres that specializes in antique weapons. We can get all kinds of sharp pointy shit to take care 'a business." He sat down at the table close to Luca and reached for the bag of beignets. He closed the waxed, white bag and shook it vigorously, then opened it and took out the one with the most powdered sugar on it. Tossing the bag back on the table with a white poof, he bit deeply into the sweet ball of dough.

Luca reached for the beignets, disgusted at Trick's manners, muttering, "Heathen."

Trick grabbed Luca's arm, arresting its motion before he touched the bag. "No, Padre, I'm a pagan. Let's get it right!" He took a deep breath and blew on his beignet, sending a flurry of white powder directly into Luca's face.

Luca sat back, stunned, blinking sugar from his face. Tell spewed coffee all over the table in a burst of laughter. Archer stood up, handed Luca a napkin, and loomed over Trick.

"The fuck you doing Trick? I don't like it anymore than you, but until this is over, we need Luca and he needs us. Once we take care of business, you can do what ever the hell you want. I'm not your keeper. If you can't be civil, then there's the door. Don't let it hit you where the good Lord split you. The same goes for you too, Tell."

"I don't need this Archer. You ain't my poppa and I ain't no damn baby that needs you to spank my hand." He stood up, glaring at Archer then turned and fired the rest of his beignet across the room like a powdered baseball. Disgusted, he turned back to Archer pointing at Luca. "That thing is a two-legged mosquito, feeding off the unwilling. He's an abomination, and you want me to work with him? I'll be here for you, Archer, but more to watch your back, so ya don't get bit. You're far too trusting, bro."

"Yeah, yeah. Now go get that ball of dough off my sales floor, alright?" He turned and looked back at the table. "Enough said here? Tell? Luca?"

Tell nodded slowly as he wiped his spewed coffee from the table. Luca was already at the farm sink at the edge of the courtyard, rinsing off his face. He waved his hand once in acknowledgement. "I'll turn the other cheek," he answered before reaching in to splash his face.

Trick was in the sales area searching for the half eaten beignet when he heard a scuttling sound behind him and one of the trolls, he wasn't sure which, ran past him clutching the discarded ball of dough in his small hands. Squealing with unrestrained glee, he disappeared around a corner of the book shelves. Trick chuckled, his dark mood broken as he walked back into the office, joined shortly by Luca, still dabbing at spots on his sweater.

"Alright," said Archer briskly, "let's take a walk. Tell, normally I'd ask you to stay here, but I want your opinion on your choice of weapon. Let me lock up and we'll walk over. I could stand to blow off some steam and walk off breakfast."

CHAPTER 25

"ALRIGHT. ONCE AGAIN Tellico. James was the twin brother of Jesus, and James became one the true followers, known as the Essenes, a sect that exists still today in the deserts of Iraq. Jesus did not actually die on the cross, nor was his son, Jesus Barabbas pardoned by Pilate. The pardoning of one man at Passover by the Romans is a myth; they didn't care one way or the other about Judaic law. After the crucifixion, he was taken to the tomb of his friend Lazarus and laid out to recover from the stab wound in his side. It was likely the same tomb from which Lazarus was 'raised from the dead'. Tombs, you see, were as expensive in that time as they are now. The soldier who speared Jesus on the cross was a follower and made sure the wound was non-lethal, but messy. Jesus went on to sire a family with Mary Magdalene, a line that ruled in Europe for centuries."

"Sorry, Luca, how do you expect me to buy that? There were so many different families that rose and fell. It's just not possible."

"Ah, you are missing my point, Tellico. They did not necessarily sit on the throne in France, England, Spain, or any other country, but they held sway over all of the courts. They were the *Rex Deus*, or Kings of God. They still exist today, though their control and much of their influence in the twentieth century was curtailed. With the advent of Internet and satellite communications, the world has become so much closer knit; anyone can monitor everyone. Power bases have become more fluid to survive. Global consolidation of power is nearly impossible, unless you control media outlets, or run the largest religious organization in the world. The *Rex Deus* has become antiquated while the church survives."

Trick stopped and opened the door to the antique shop and looked up at Tell as they all filed in. "Why th' hell are you listenin' to this, Tell? You know it's all hog's wallow, anyhow."

"I'm just curious, Trick."

"Yes, Trick, if it is merely supposition, why does it bother you so," Luca asked, ducking into the shop to avoid Trick's baleful glare.

Trick was not about to let the topic be, storming into the store behind Luca. "Your kind has filled th' world with lies and propaganda for millennia, an' you're askin' me why I'm bothered?"

"The Bible is merely the history book of the age, the stories told and spun from the perspective of the winner. There is no other text recognized as legitimate."

"Yeah. Everything your kind didn't like or thought was too revealing was hidden, suppressed, or destroyed. Th' Bible is all that's left."

"Yet you believe everything that you read? How convenient," Luca replied smugly.

Stepping close to Luca he smiled, "I'll believe your obituary when I read it. I'll take it for gospel," replied Trick loud enough that only Luca could hear.

"Trick? Luca? Could we?" Archer asked in exasperation, arms outstretched, pointing to the walls of the shop. The walk to the store had been like leading an elementary school field trip. He couldn't wait to get this task over with and get home. He planned on leaving Tell in charge and going up to rest his thudding head.

The store was a converted shotgun shack with a narrow walkway, the floor made of aged, scarred cypress boards. Dust, in a heavy protective layer, gathered over everything like a shroud. Items for sale were all either encased in the long streaky glass counters that ran the length of the store, hung on the walls by display hooks, or sat in a filthy clutter on various shelves behind the counter. The owner of the store was in need of a bit of repair himself. He approached them slowly, leaning heavily on an ornate cane. His eyes were rheumy and pale blue, the whites looking jaundiced in the diffuse, dusty light, his features indistinct, lost in a thick matted white beard.

Trick stepped forward and grasped the man's hand in greeting, then turned and introduced everyone to the proprietor, Willie Gunn.

"Used to have me a sign outside what said 'Gunn's Antique Weapons' but I kept gittin' to many undesirables lookin' for firearms, so me, I jus' don't bother wid' advertisin' no more. What can I do yer for you today?"

"We need some good long bladed weapons. They have to be in top shape and able to take and hold an edge. Can you help us?" Trick asked.

"'Course I can. What'cha ya see all aroun' yer? Why the finest collection of antique and olde timey blades you're likely to see 'less ya goes to a museum." Gunn limped behind the counter and took a set of keys from his pockets. "You jus' lemme know when you sees something what tickles yer fancy and I'll bring it up for yer."

Over the course of the next two hours, they rummaged through the majority of Willie Gunn's inventory, sorting the scrap from the rusty garbage. Finally, when the dust had settled they had two Civil War era confederate cavalryman's sabers and a World War I French bayonet with a solid brass rifle fitting and a single blood track on each side of its three foot long blade.

Tell was looking around, digging in corners and found a long spear with an elongated, spade-shaped blade. "Hey, Mr. Gunn, what's the story with this thing," he asked holding the shaft of the spear aloft.

Gunn looked up from a discussion he was having with Luca about an ornate walking stick with a silver handle and fine filigreed brass rings at intervals up and down the shaft of the wood. "My great-great-great-grand pappy served in the British Army and the story goes he took that from a Zulu tribesman he killed. I don't know for sure if that's true; my papa used to like to stretch the truth like he was pullin' taffy, and I never much bothered with hunting down its provenance. I like other people's history, not my own. Make me an offer, if you want it."

"We do need a skewer, something to keep them pinned from a distance. It'll make the job easier," replied Archer. "We'll take it too."

Gunn went to the back and found the scabbards for each weapon and a long box to carry everything but the spear. He wrapped the head of the spear in brown paper and rang everything up. Archer paid Gunn and collected the box under one arm, Tell taking the spear. Trick led them out and they began to walk back home when they heard the door open and close again and saw Luca emerge from the shop sporting the walking cane.

"Planning on taking up limping," Archer asked mildly as Luca approached them, the brass tip clacking rhythmically on the slate banquette.

"No, I have a colleague who would value this very much," replied Luca, leaning slightly on it as the rest of them examined it in the bright late morning day light.

"That's sho'nuff a handsome stick. How much did it set you back?" Trick eyed the silver head of the cane closely.

"Why, Trick, that kind man is a devout and caring Catholic. After I promised to remember his children in my prayers, it didn't cost me a penny." Luca laughed, "Don't you know priests take an optional vow of poverty?"

Archer caught Luca by the shoulder and spun him around so they were eye to eye, inches separating them. "Don't even tell me you rolled his mind to steal that cane."

"Okay, I won't." Luca smiled benignly at them both. "He gave it to me of his own free will and volition. Priests do not steal."

Trick snorted derisively and glared menacingly at Luca as they all resumed walking back to the store in silence.

CHAPTER 26

THE GROUP RETURNED to the store and discovered someone waiting on the low granite stoop. Archer set the box of weapons down as he dug into his pocket for the keys, intentionally kneeing the man away from the front of the door when he didn't move.

"That's simple assault on a police officer, Sweet. A felony," Detective Tommy Corgan said acidly as he stood, rubbing his shoulder where Archer's shoe had struck home. "I could run your ass in right now for that, you know."

"You're right, it was simple. Stick around and maybe I'll show you how complex I really am. You're trespassing and impeding my ability to conduct commerce. You won't be taking me anywhere. Why don't you go back to the donut shop and quit trying to piss in my soup?"

Corgan followed Archer inside, glaring as Trick walked by picking up the box, and flipping him off with his free hand, then Luca slunk past, his face blank. Stepping in front of Tell as he tried to gain entrance, Corgan asked "What cha got there convict?"

Tell froze and Corgan snatched the wrapping paper from the head of the spear. Corgan pulled out his cuffs, bracing a shocked Tell roughly against the doorway, patting him down after the cuffs were cruelly biting into the big man's thick wrists.

"What the fuck are you doing, shitwad? That man is my employee and has done nothing illegal," Archer yelled as he charged Corgan, murder in his eye.

"Wrong Sweet!" Corgan brandished the spear, "He was carrying a concealed weapon which is a violation of the terms and conditions of his parole. He's carrying a one way ticket to finish out the rest of his jolt in Angola, instead of living the 'Sweet life'."

Archer was dumbfounded as Tell pleaded with his eyes. "You've got sand Corgan, I'll give you that. Tell me, how on God's green are you going to justify a six foot long spear as a concealed weapon? I'd love to be a fly on the wall when you try and sell that to the D.A."

"The blade was wrapped up, therefore, concealed from view. Period and point blank." Corgan gave Tellico a rough shove that barely moved the giant of a man. "C'mon big man, we're going for a ride." Tellico turned his head back to look at Archer.

"He was carrying that for me as my employee at my request. One call to his parole officer and your chief, he'll be kicked loose before you even get to the precinct. You know that as well as I do," said Archer quietly. "You've got nothing. Now what are you really doing here? C'mon Corgan, don't take your impotence out on him when it's my ass you want to tack to the side of the shed."

Corgan stopped trying to push Tell forward and leaned on the door frame as he turned to face Archer. "You've got more stories than hooker's got johns. Someday, you're going to run out of luck."

Trick had put away the box of weapons and walked past Archer to take the spear out of Corgan's hand. "Nobody here saw Tell holdin' this thing, and we got a priest who'll vouch for him, won't you Father Luca?"

Luca nodded nervously, clutching his cane closer to himself.

Corgan glared at them each in turn, then his expression softening, he nodded. "Alright maybe I took the wrong tack here. Since trying to get a straight answer from you is like trying to nail jelly to a wall, I'll play nice, start over, and hopefully have a mutually beneficial conversation."

That'll be the day, Archer thought, nodding as he felt his mobile phone vibrate against his hip; a text message. He looked down and was shocked to see it was from his old partner, Wendell Pierce. The message was simple and cryptic: *I've got your back.*

"Like I said, what are you doing here?"

"A report came across my desk this morning about an altercation last night near St. Ann Street. Witnesses place someone who matches your description to a tee at the scene."

Archer looked puzzled. "Someone who looks like me got into some kind of fight last night and you're rousting my employee and me about it. Do I look like I was in a fight?"

"No you don't, but this wasn't your everyday brawl, was it? Seems the person in question was fighting two others, though the descriptions of the assailants were a little hazy. Our witness said you stabbed one of them and pinned him to the ground. If that's not odd enough, there was also a report of a large dog or wolf involved in the fray. I started thinking, who could get themselves in that kind of a jam, and has a past link with wolves?"

"Brilliant, Corgan, you must have spent, what, a good fifteen seconds or so formulating that hypothesis. What if I was to tell you that I was on a date last night and have the receipt and lady's number to prove it?"

"You didn't ask when the fight occurred, Sweet, so maybe that receipt, and your love life is worth a steaming, fat pile to me. Anyway, the officers who responded found a shit load of oxidized blood, and followed a vertical trail of it up onto a rooftop on Decatur. The witness also says you ran off with his sanitation cart, toting a wolf in it. There's also the matter of the vandalism our witness reported, a smashed window on a store front."

"So what are you saying? I killed someone? I'm keeping a wolf here? I committed a smash and grab? What kind of fish are you hoping to hook on this expedition, Corgan?"

"A real big one with a smart mouth. I'm going to tear your little shop of horrors apart and if I find any blood, fur, city owned property, or even a wolf, I'm going to send you to Angola to how your attitude plays there."

"You're searching exactly shit without a warrant, Corgan. This is a private business and residence, and I'm refusing you in front of witnesses. You have no probable cause, and nothing solid to go on. Bring me back the judge's autograph authorizing you to look for a wolf in a residence and place of business, and I'll let you rip everything to pieces. Fact is, you'd get laughed out of the office if you tried. That's why Willig isn't here with you. You don't have a warrant, and you're hoping to get lucky and see something for probable cause or scare me into cooperating by rousting Tell. You're a piece of work, Corgan. Just remember, bad karma always comes back to bite you in the ass. Now unhook my employee and get the fuck out of my store."

Suddenly, Corgan's eyes got huge as pie plates as he looked at Tell's feet. "There's my probable cause right there!" He pointed at Trold and Berg who were toddling around Tell's legs, nuzzling their faces against the coarse denim of his jeans. "You've got exotic animals in here and no license for them. I'm going to. . ." His tirade was interrupted as he reached for one of the trolls who backed away from him and lumbered up the aisle away from him. As soon as Corgan turned to pursue the trolls, Pierce stepped through the door with a stun gun held high, giving the detective a charge high on the nape of his exposed neck.

Corgan whimpered his eyes widening before rolling up into his head before he collapsed to the floor in a twitching moaning heap. "Hi' ya Archer," said Pierce gesturing with the stun gun. "Thought it was about time I stepped in." He reached down and popped Corgan again in his ample abdomen.

"Good timing, Wendell, but now what? When he comes to I'm hosed."

"Aw, don't you go worrying about him." Pierce shrugged. "I figure I still owe the bastard a turn or two for all the stupid questions and bullshit he put me through when Liz died." He looked meaningfully at Archer and said, "He had no cause to come after either of us the way he did. I figure this is my next step to getting my life back."

"What was the first?"

"Two and a half days sober and counting, one day at a time. I want to make a difference again, Archer, and to do that, I need to crawl out of the bottle and try to earn back some of my life. That begins with respecting myself."

Archer nodded, slowly. "So now what? Can you uncuff Tellico?"

"Oh, no need Archer," said Tell as he flexed his shoulders. A metallic screeching ensued and the shackles fell to the floor behind him, his arms coming free. He rubbed his chafed wrists and smiled. "I wasn't about to let that cop hurt the trollkins."

Pierce smiled and Archer looked suitably impressed. Trick was cackling softly as he kept an eye on Corgan's twitching form. Luca was wide eyed, not understanding at all the events that had just unfolded. Pierce slipped on a pair of latex crime scene gloves and said, Okay, I need someone to drive my car while I take Corgan and his away from here."

Tell scooped the inert cop off the floor and said, "Lead the way."

Archer looked at Pierce, "Do I want to know?"

"Plausible deniability my friend. He was never here and once I'm through with him, he shouldn't be bothering you for a long while. Problem is, when he comes back, he's gonna hate ya even more."

Trick laughed as he walked away from Archer and into the back room. "I'm going to unpack our haul and put an edge on everything."

"I'll be in to help in a minute or two. I'm going to get rid of the trash cart that's in the courtyard."

Archer turned to Luca and took him by the arm as he headed for the door. "Is there anything else we can do to attract the vampires to a specific spot where we can kill them? Someplace maybe away from witnesses?"

"It is a long shot, but now that they are becoming part of this world, maybe they will be more willing to return to the church to discuss their future, or to get another free snack."

"Okay, when you get back, see what you can do, and call me. If you strike out, we'll still plan on linking up with you at the church at 8:00 p.m."

Luca nodded without a word and went to help sharpen the weapons. Archer headed back to the courtyard through the front door of his house and dismantled the large plastic-wheeled trash bin. Carrying the pieces out one by one, he dropped them into the Fahy's Pub dumpster across the street in their alleyway access.

CHAPTER 27

DETECTIVE TOMMY CORGAN awoke to a burning sensation in his fingers and toes, and a tapping noise by his head. Pulling his head up he was blinded by the sunlight through the windshield of his unmarked car. He had been slumped over the steering wheel and a long rope of brownish colored drool connected to his mouth from the worn wheel cover. The tapping continued and he turned his head to see a New Orleans Motorcycle Patrolman thumping on the glass of his still running car.

Something definitely ain't right, Corgan thought, his mouth tasting like he had spent a long night in a roadhouse. Urgently, he tried to remember how he came to be sitting in his car in the middle of the day. He smelled alcohol and felt his stomach twist with panic. He could taste bourbon on his breath. Hell, he reeked of it, he realized, as he sniffed at his sports coat. It was then he noticed the mostly empty bottle of Wild Turkey on the seat beside him, uncapped and threatening to tipple out the rest of its contents.

Without raising his head from the steering wheel, he hit the button on the console and the window powered down. The policeman backed up from the odor, and ordered Corgan to step out of the vehicle, hands in front of him.

Corgan had little choice but to comply. He awkwardly stepped from his car and felt as muddled as he appeared to be. Desperately, he tried to recall his last memory prior to waking. *Son of a bitch, I'm gonna kill that shithead Sweet,* he swore as his memory came flooding back. He wasn't feeling hung over and didn't remember taking anything from Sweet that would have knocked him out. Someone must have snuck up from behind and decked, no, tasered him; repeatedly, judging by how groggy and muzzy-headed he was feeling.

The motorcycle patrolman braced Corgan against his own car drawing his weapon lightning fast, pressing it to Corgan's neck when he felt the presence of Corgan's service weapon. "You've got some 'splainin' to do Lucy," said the patrolman as he reached for his cuffs and snapped the first bracelet on Corgan's wrist.

"I'm a Detective, Eighth District. Check my wallet. Badge and identification are there, back pocket," Corgan yelped as the second cuff bit into his plump wrist, immediately cutting off circulation.

The patrolman backed away from Corgan, speaking quietly but forcefully into the shoulder-mounted microphone, requesting backup before closing on Corgan for the identification search.

"I've found and removed your primary weapon, Detective. I am now going to search you for additional weapons and contraband. Do you have anything on your person that is sharp or will cut me when I reach in your pockets?"

Corgan shook his head, taking a moment to look around, gathering his bearings trying to clear the cobwebs, and realized his car had been parked by the Claibourne Street underpass leading to Highway 10. Shit, this was going to take days, maybe weeks to clear up.

The patrolman had retrieved Corgan's identification and was eyeballing it closely. "Where were you plannin' ta go before your drunk self passed out? Gotta at least give ya props for decidin' not to get on th' highway. Maybe that'll save your ass when you come up for your internal review and inquiry board."

Corgan knew better than to talk to the badge and just let himself get taken to the cop shop before calling for his union representative. The kick in the ass, the burr that sat like a razor sharp needle in his brain was, he had been stupid enough to go see Archer Sweet while he was Code 20, off the clock. Had he let Willig or anyone else from the Task Force know he was following up on a lead, he would have a much stronger leg to stand on. As he saw it, he would be lucky to get off with probation and mandatory counseling. Unless someone believed his story, he would be pulled from the Task Force for sure and probably given a desk to ride until he completed his counseling.

Corgan was shaking in cold fury as the patrolman placed him in the black and white unit that had arrived to take him away. Somehow, someway, he would get even with Archer Sweet. This stunt had gone way beyond personal.

CHAPTER 28

WENDELL PIERCE RETURNED to Archer's shop half an hour later, smelling vaguely of Bourbon. "Don't worry Archer. I touched a bottle, but didn't have a drop." He removed the crime scene latex gloves, pitching them in the trash, forestalling Archer's questions. "Corgan is out of play for a few days, at least."

"Whatever you did Wen, I hope you didn't put either your job or his in jeopardy, but thank you."

"So am I in? Can I be included in whatever Corgan was rousting you over? I know it has to do with his involvement in that Task Force for the serial killer, and you were talking some kind of bullshit with vampires. The M.O. would fit, so I guess you have the problem sorted out."

"No joke, Wen, it's vampires, but not exactly the way you might think."

"What's to think about? They kill people and it needs to stop."

"Easier said than done," came Luca's voice as he emerged from the back room with Tellico.

"I'm Wendell Pierce," he said as he extended his hand first to Tell then to Luca, nodding cordially as they introduced themselves. He shivered slightly as he touched Luca, his eyes glazing, his face growing momentarily slack. He snapped quickly out of the mini-trance state looking at the smaller man as Archer grabbed Luca, slamming him in the mouth with a back-handed blow, then grabbing his sweater roughly in both hands, holding him, shaking him like a mongoose on a snake.

"What did I tell you about feeding on anyone in my presence? I let you slide at the store because I didn't see it, but I see something like that again, or sense you mind jacking someone, and I will break you down, permanently."

Luca pried Archer's hands from his sweater easily, surprising Archer with his physical strength. "A bee has to buzz and a bird has to fly, Archer." Straightening his sweater, he tried without success to smooth out the wrinkles, wiping away small trickle of blood from his split lower lip. "This one's mind is oozing pain. Delicious, guilty pain. I could not resist."

"Try harder."

"What the hell just happened to me?"

"How do you feel," queried Tellico

"I feel unusual. I don't understand how or why, but I feel lighter somehow." Pierce gazed at Luca, comprehension dawning on his face. "You do that?"

Luca nodded and Archer explained. "Luca is a priest, and a vampire. Instead of blood, he feeds off emotion, but that won't happen again, will it Luca?"

Pierce moved nearer to Luca, scrutinizing him closely. "All priests are like you?"

"Most, but not all."

"And you feed the way you just did on me?"

"Yes. However, in a Mass setting, the effect is much less noticeable. We feed from the many, so only a little is taken from each. What you just experienced was the effect similar to going to confession but more intense. You were unburdened, cleansed, and my hunger is slaked."

"That explains why confession was so popular for so long," Archer said caustically. "You addicted people."

Luca shook his head. "You misunderstand again, Archer. My species has a symbiotic relationship with yours. We mean no harm."

"No, but you readily cause it by mind raping humans. If your kind came forward and admitted what you did, and people still came to you, that would be symbiosis. You're nothing but a thief."

"I know I'd go back," said Wendell, "I feel better than I have since before..."

"Some of it may be his doing," Archer replied gently, "but you were already beginning the process of forgiving yourself. With that, comes a great lightening of spirit."

"Yeah, but that feeling of self-loathing, the one that makes me want to crawl inside a bottle feels smaller now. When I came in, the smell of the Bourbon on my gloves was driving me insane. I wanted a drink so bad I would have slapped my mother around for a single drop, but I don't feel that now."

"Regrettably, what you are feeling is only temporary, and such a cleansing can be performed by fewer and fewer of my kind as time passes. Now that you know who and what I am," Luca looked meaningfully at Archer, "you are free to come to the church and visit me or another of my colleagues. The priests in Orleans parish are quite ... gifted."

Archer shook his head and turned away, wincing from the pain of the motion. Watching his friend gladly trade his obsession with alcohol for something equally addicting—and no less dangerous—was difficult. At least, he thought as they all walked back into his office where Trick was sharpening one of the sabers, he won't suffer from this. Unless he begins to loathe himself again for his weakness to have this type of religious fulfillment, his inability to feel good about himself without psychic substantiation.

Tell draped a large arm over Archer's shoulder, sensing his friend's discomfort. "There are a lot of shitty things in this world Archer, but in the greater scheme, for now, your buddy is better off. He can function with a degree of peace in his life, so long as he can accept that the peace he feels is fleeting and not of his own volition."

"Yeah, I was just thinking pretty much the same thing. I guess I'm transferring my disgust of Luca onto Wendell. Who knows, maybe he can even reconcile with his wife and bring his kids back home."

"There's always an upside, Archer, always. Sometimes you just have to look harder for it."

"Well, howdy there stranger," Trick said, extending his hand to grip Pierce's tightly. "Good to see you again. I know Archer doesn't wanna know what you did to Corgan, but I sure as hell do. Can't wait to hear." He turned to Archer. "I've got a great edge on th' bayonet and on th' first saber. This second one isn't taking an edge so well, lots of small pits in th' steel, but I think it's gonna work out jus' fine if I keep workin' it."

Luca and Pierce sat down at the table with Archer and Tell joining them. It didn't take as long to bring Wendell up to speed as Archer had thought, thanks in part, he guessed, to Pierce's direct experience with Luca and the police report he'd read.

"So you fought them last night? Both of them?" Pierce asked. "Why am I not surprised you did something that stupid on your own?"

"Yeah, just like when we were partners, eh, Wen? You know I didn't have much choice in the matter. If I hadn't distracted them, they might have taken advantage of my date. Besides, we discovered they aren't solitary; one bargained for the safety of the other. We also know that decapitation really may be the only way to kill them."

"I'm surprised you didn't try to burn them so long as you are experimenting," Luca said sarcastically.

"There's always tonight, don't you worry none, Padre," replied Trick casually, as the whet stone rasped across the blade. "Or have you forgotten you're supposed to be helpin' us?"

"I have not forgotten. They are dangerous and need to be stopped. But don't think I am pleased by being a party to their destruction."

"Nobody thought you would be," said Archer trying to get the conversation back on track. "Just do as you promised, Luca."

They discussed their plan to hunt that evening, hoping the vampires would be more active then, and Luca's sensitivity would be more attuned to them. The church was still the most sensible location they could think of, since it would be empty, precluding the chance of innocents getting caught in the middle. Archer watched Luca during the planning. The priest was absently spinning the cane he had obtained while listening, responding at appropriate times but seemingly distracted. Pierce was paying minute attention, like he used to when he and Archer had been partners. He asked questions to clarify things that were new to him. He had a machete he used when he went into the bayou so they had an extra blade, and he volunteered to be the decoy. Interrupting, Archer said, "Sorry Wendell, that job falls to me. They've had two run-ins with me already and both times they took the worst of it. It's only logical to believe they'll be wanting a bigger piece of me than any of you. We have to be sure that they'll heed Luca's call to the church. I think I can make that happen."

Wendell nodded. "Yeah, if I got whupped on twice and believed that it was a matter of revenge or honor, I'd make you a priority, too."

Archer's head was still pounding. It had been bad all morning but had grown progressively worse as their strategy session continued. He was losing his concentration, his vision blurring slightly. *Maybe a quick lie down would help.*

"Hey Tell? Could you stay until closing tonight? I feel like my head is going to explode."

"No problem Archer, it's been dead here except for that dumb-ass cop. I can handle it."

"Yeah Archer, go get some rest, and maybe an ice pack on that melon and leave the rest to us. We'll be ready," Trick added.

Archer nodded his thanks and began to shuffle out through the courtyard and up the stairs to his bed. As he was exiting the store, he hear Trick's raised and sharp toned voice, "Luca, you'd better not have nothing to do with his headache." A pause, a muffled reply, and then, "You know, I'm gonna want to test the sharpness of these here blades, so for your sake you'd best not be lyin' to me.

CHAPTER 29

Archer was just crawling into bed when his mobile phone chirped. Looking at the caller identification through his pained and blurry vision, he saw that it was Daniella. Groaning, he pulled the phone to his ear and hit the talk button. "Did you get the weapons? Did you find everything you were looking for," she asked

"Yeah," he replied, his voice nearly a whisper more like a death rattle, "We found what we need."

"Archer? What's the matter," she asked, worry seeping into her rich, husky, voice.

"My head. It feels like my brain has outgrown my skull. I swear, the pressure is making my eyes bulge. Gods, I feel like I'm dying."

"Go upstairs and lie down, I'll be right over."

"Already upstairs," he slurred as he sat on the edge of his bed, kicking off his sneakers. "The guys are all in the shop; it wouldn't look good for you to just come up here."

"Poor sweet baby," she cooed gently into his ear. "In all of your pain, you worry about my reputation. Can you get downstairs to leave your apartment door open? I can come in and no one will see. I want to be there for you, like you were for me. Besides, this headache has me concerned, considering the beating you took last night."

"'K. I'll go unlock my door. See you when you get here," he said then hung up. He managed to make it down the stairs and turn the deadbolt.

No sooner had he turned to trek back upstairs then Daniella was there, helping him, half carrying him up the stairs. It felt to him like he was suddenly weightless as she helped bear his mass. He felt the bed's reassuring surface under his body as he moaned in pain and gratitude.

Abruptly, he was blinded as Daniella shined a pen light in each eye, the light lancing through his brain, threatening to make his brain seep through his ears. She was talking to him, something about his pupils being dilated, but he wasn't hearing her over the hideous hammering pain in his head. He didn't, couldn't, protest when he felt Daniella push a pill onto his tongue, tilted a glass of water to his mouth, then guided him gently to lay back. Even the goose down pillow felt like a sack of concrete to his splitting head. Mercifully, in moments, he passed out.

He awoke to darkness outside and a warm furry body lying stretched out languidly beside him. There was a knocking on the door, sharp and insistent. The noise, he realized, was what had woken him. The wolf slipped silently off the bed and padded wraith-like into the bathroom, her claws clicking gently on the hardwood where the sectional rug ended. He watched her nudge the door closed with her nose and wondered if he was hallucinating before his recall returned. Archer sat up and realized his headache was nearly gone. Mostly he felt hungover, kind of weak and shaky, the pain in his head a receding memory.

Staggering to the door he opened it to find Trick standing there, a fretful, worried expression on his face. "You okay bro? I tried calling up here first, but you musta shut off your phone. I've been knockin' and hollerin' to beat th' band for th' last five minutes. I was gettin' ready to call Tell up here to smash down th' door." He looked past Archer's shoulder into the murkiness of the room. "Did I hear somethin' clickin' on the floor? Did one of them trolls get up here?"

"I'm alright, just feel like a bar towel; wrung out, nasty, and in need of a good washing. Don't recall hearing any sounds as I got up, except your pounding. Maybe something outside. What's the haps?"

"It's nearly time to go huntin', Archer, sho'nuff. Are you going to be able to go, or are you a game time scratch? It won't be easy without ya, but

Tell, Pierce, and I can go get 'em."

"Luca would probably withdraw his help entirely and lock y'all out if I'm not there to prod him," Archer replied feeling a little bit of vitality seeping into his body. "He knows you want him dead, and thinks Tell could go either way. He's got his hooks into Wendell pretty deep so don't count on him to support your *jihad*."

"Least we all know where we stand on matters. Luca ain't to be trusted, and he won't get any leeway with me. I just may kill him if I have the chance to get away clean."

Archer was shocked by Trick's statement of premeditation and the depth of anger and odium he felt radiating from his friend. "Why is it so personal with you? What bothers you so much to think, much less say, something like that? I've got your back, Trick, unless you kill him. You do that without being in defense of your life, you're worse than he is."

"Th' fuck do you mean?" Trick yelled vehemently. "You're sayin' you got no truck with what his kind did without your knowledge to you an' your family or th' hundreds of billions of other families throughout history? That's cool with you? Th' way I see it, what they've been doing to humans for so long, is nothing short of a covert race war. You kill th' enemy in war, Archer."

Archer's head began to pound again as the naked emotion and volume of his friend's voice grew. He put his hands up to his ears backing away. Trick was by his side in an instant, helping him to the battered lounger Archer had in front of the television set, flipping on a reading lamp. "Archer? Archer! Are you alright? What's th' matter man?"

Archer could see again, the pounding receding like the tide as Trick's anger ebbed with concern for his friend. "I'm okay, I'm okay," Archer replied. "I finally get the picture. Even though your mother wasn't Christian, she integrated and invoked Jesus as part of her personal Pantheon of worship. You believe she was a victim too.

"Ungh. I think that knock to the head last night did something strange to me." He looked up at Trick, the Trick he knew, not the raging xenophobe he'd seen not a moment ago. "You don't understand do you, Trick? Luca and all of his kind are repugnant to me, but what they've done and will continue to do to us can't be reversed by murdering one priest. If it did, if I could make the difference by killing one non-human for the sake of humanity,

I'd tear him to pieces with my bare hands, jump rope with his entrails and dance an Irish fucking jig in his skin. But we're talking about an entire race of beings living beneath the shroud of perfect cover. No one would want to believe us, even if we could convince them."

"Yeah, but Archer, it's not about all of that."

"Yes, it is. That's all it is. It's the nature of a species to do what its instincts dictate, and if Wendell is an example, human nature lends itself to willingly, maybe actively seeking out guidance. As a result, we're often exploited by those who understand that."

"I do see it, Archer, and I understand, better than you may think. I just don't cotton to th' notion of waking up one morning to discover I'm one rung lower on th' evolutionary and food chains. Look at your bible. In Genesis 2:20 it says 'And Adam gave names to all cattle and to th' fowl in th' air and to every beast in th' field'. Does that mean that Adam was a vampire and we were th' beasts? If so, what'd they really do to lose Eden? Does God even care about us?"

Archer was quiet for a moment before looking at Trick. "Just remember what Confucius said about vengeance, 'when seeking it, one should dig two graves'."

Trick stopped his nervous pacing and looked his friend in the eye. "We'll all be waiting for you in your office. Try not to be too long." Trick left the apartment and went down the back stairs, opening the door to go through the courtyard.

CHAPTER 30

A SHAFT OF light appeared behind Archer as Daniella came out of the bathroom, her hair radiant in the halo of false back lighting. She was buttoning a pair of low rise boy cut jeans over an immaculately flat stomach. A lacy blue demi-bra complimented her cerulean eyes flawlessly. Utterly unselfconscious, she walked over to the bed and picked up her sweater; skinning it over her head and pulling her arms simultaneously into the sleeves, not a wasted motion.

Archer felt his passions rise as he watched her glide about the room, the image of her entrance etched pleasantly in the caveman portion of his brain. She brought him a pair of small white pills and a cold glass of water from the bathroom. "What are you feeding me here?"

"What I gave you this afternoon was Vicoden, you were in too much pain to sleep. It took the edge off. These are simply aspirin."

Archer knocked them back then sat heavily on the edge of the bed gazing at nothing, trying to collect his thoughts. Settling herself down behind him Daniella began to rub his neck and shoulders with an exquisite firmness. "What is the matter? Your trepidation is palpable, even if I could not feel it beneath my fingers."

"What's the matter? Oh, not much. I'm worried my best friend is going to get himself arrested or killed trying to satisfy his guilt over his mother, and his anger toward what's being done to the people around him. My old partner finally seems to be trying to get his act straight, but damned if I don't invite him into the spider's parlor and introduce him to a predator as bad or worse than booze. Finally, and perhaps the most ironic is the dichotomy; there's a wonderful, dangerously beautiful, woman touching me as no one has for so very long, but all I can think about was waking to find a wolf in my bed. I'm at a loss."

"Archer, you cannot worry about your friends right now. They will look to you for guidance. Whether they admit it or not, they need your strength not your doubts." She gave one last caress and released him, coming to kneel before him on the floor between his legs, hands resting on his knees. "You can not and need not worry about me. I am still someone you do not know, regardless of the instinctive attraction we feel."

Archer reached out and put his arms around her neck, resting them on her shoulders drawing her closer so he could see her eyes. "My whole world is visceral, gut reactions and trusting my senses. My senses tell me you are going to be the ship in the night, but I just can't accept that. The words you say, the tone in which you say them, makes me think otherwise. Please. Tell me I'm wrong?" Her eyes betrayed her and Archer sighed as she looked away, unsure how to respond. "Why did you take wolf form when you were in my bed? Were you trying to avoid me getting frisky? Hoping for a belly rub, an ear scratch, maybe a rousing game of fetch when I woke?"

She tried but failed to veil the hurt in her eyes at Archer's words but she knew the attempt was fruitless. As she saw her pain etched in his vision, she knew that he wasn't trying to hurt her, but to distance himself. For a change, she was the one being rejected, but for reasons she couldn't explain, she wasn't ready to withdraw from this contest just yet.

"I chose my form because in your pathetic state, you couldn't have repelled a nightmare, much less a physical attack. Obviously, I have certain advantages as a wolf."

"Like the ability to lick yourself or shed on my bed?"

"I do not shed," she replied with mock indignity.

"Yeah?" Archer said as he brought her close to him in a vice-like embrace. "Well I don't care if you do shed, so long as you don't lick my face to wake me, or hog the bed. As for licking yourself in bed..."

Daniella was a little confused. The stable, sensible man she had watched for weeks, the one who seemed to have one mood: mellow; the person who had calmly and coolly fought against monstrosities that would leave normal men gibbering in panicked fright was nuzzling her with his face within moments of trying to distance himself from her. Not that she minded, she had the urge to do the same thing, to reassure him that things would be...

"Archer, how do you feel right now? How is your head?"

"Mmm-hmm-hmm, it feels fine, thanks to you."

"You're not worried about tonight? No concern for Trick or this ex-partner of yours, or even Tellico?"

"Nope. I wonder why that is? Seems like I was all tense about it a few minutes ago," he smiled.

"Your friend, Toinetta, could you give me her phone number? I need to speak to her urgently."

"Okay." He rattled off the number and she repeated it back, memorizing it. "Now you've got to do me a favor."

"What?"

"Be there tonight at the church. I'd like you there as a secret back up, an ace in the hole. Trick and Tell know a wolf has been involved in both of the vampire's attacks on me and it, you, are on our side; Luca doesn't. I have the feeling I might need a surprise reserve."

"Sure. Archer, I'll go there after I speak to Toinetta, and find a good spot in the shadows. You give a shout when you need me, just don't call me by name. And for the love of the Goddess, don't whistle or clap for me."

Archer laughed, sobering quickly as his head pounded with the residual of his mirth. "Yeah, I suppose that would blow your cover or make Trick and Tell think I'm obsessed with you, naming 'the wolf' for you. I'll just call for help, and if you're really good, I'll hook you up with some Milkbones."

"Okay," she laughed. "But for the record, Milkbones are good for the teeth, but I prefer Snausages. Now get out of here and call me when you want me at the church."

"One more question, I promise," he said, not wanting to burst the bubble, relinquishing the closeness they shared.

"You're stalling, Shopkeeper. What is it?"

"I thought werewolves only turned during a full moon and were mindless slavering killers when their beast overtook them."

She pushed him away playfully. "So where is the question?"

"I made you wait for calling me Shopkeeper again. How do you do it? How do you control when you change?"

"How much of your vampire lore did you have correct, you goof? It seems your lycanthrope lexicon is inadequate, as well. Truth to tell, newly turned weres can only change on the monthly anniversary date of their bite, and full moon phases. As we grow into our power we can control more easily when and how often we change. It's easier for some than for others."

"But since you were born a lycanthrope, how was it different for you?"

"I didn't experience my first change until I hit puberty. Papa, God bless him, sought out the most powerful shamans, root workers, witches, and practitioners in the world to try to cure me. When he discovered that to be impossible, he decided to make my life as an outcast as bearable as his money and influence permitted. Over the course of a years of multi-discipline study, the specialists who couldn't cure me, helped mold me. They taught me to control my change through meditation, minor spells, and potions until I could control myself. Once I had and maintained control, I concentrated on changing when I wanted to change, doing it quickly, and being able to change more than once a day, if need be."

"I don't want to make light of it, but you make it sound like you were training for a triathlon." Archer said, stroking her glorious tresses gently. "I know what it means to make that kind of commitment to yourself. First in the military, then as a cop, and now studying with Toinetta, trying to understand my powers and grow into them."

Daniella nodded. "The training was much more mental initially, but transforming takes a lot out of you physically. To my knowledge, there is not another lycanthrope that can make multiple changes." Shrugging away from him she stroked his chin, the caress of her fingernails across his stubble sounded like paper being torn. "You are still learning Archer, and I think, soon, you may be in line for a new lesson. Remember to call me when you need me."

Archer watched Daniella disappear down the front stairs and heard the door click shut as she locked it behind herself.

CHAPTER 31

Archer came down the stairs and through the courtyard entrance to the store, not noticing Trold and Berg following along behind him, little arms and legs churning in exaggerated exuberance as they played their own version of follow the leader, mimicking him as he strode into the office.

Trick and Wendell were sitting at the table, talking quietly, Trick gesturing sharply for emphasis as Wendell nodded in agreement. Tell was sitting slightly away, facing the courtyard, the spear in his massive paws, honing the spade-shaped blade to a keen edge with a whetstone. Flipping the spear over he began working the blade across the stone without breaking rhythm.

"Hi Archer, how ya feeling?"

"I'm good to go Tell, thanks."

"Ready ta kick some ass Archer?" Trick asked, guardedly.

Archer could feel the trepidation in the room, they were all looking at him for guidance. Why did that irritate him so much all the sudden? "I'm ready to do what needs to be done. I just want to make sure that nobody here feels like they should be somewhere else. We're about to bite off a sizable hunk of shit. Anyone who has any doubt about the danger, the real possibility that there won't be a tomorrow for some or all of us, speak now. No judgments, no hard feelings if anyone wants to sit this one out. Uncertainty or indecision equals an ugly death tonight."

"I'm in," said Trick standing up, grasping one of the cavalry sabers, giving it a few slashes and feints, getting the feel of its balance and heft. "Lookin' forward to th' challenge, sho'nuff."

"I ain't not as excited as Trick, but I know what needs to be done," replied Tell as he went back to work on the spear head. "I don't want anyone I know ending up being a to-go order for one of these butchers."

"I'm up for whatever, Archer, you know me. The real me, not the pickled one," replied Wendell quietly

"Thanks Wendell, thank you all. Let's make sure we keep each other from winding up a midnight snack. I figure we can work in pairs, one sword each, one spear or bayonet each. If one of the swordsmen manages to skewer a vampire, the spearman can get a good position and pin it solidly. Then the sword comes out and the head comes off, as quickly as possible."

"I agree. Get all Red Queen on 'em...off with their heads, chop-chop," replied Trick with a smirk.

"There are two problems I see beyond the basics of the plan," Archer said, ignoring Trick for the moment. "First and most important, there's no guarantee that we get to choose the battleground. One thing I've learned in hand to hand situations is that nothing is a given except the unknown. Be prepared for the fight to be fluid and move. Whether it's just the battle flowing or them breaking away and us having to chase them, be prepared. Try and think a few moves ahead. Do your best to keep your opponent confined to where you want him, and don't get separated from your partner."

"Let's go th' 'what if' route. My partner falls, then what?" Trick wanted to know. "I got no intention of dukin' it out with these things on their terms. We need ta move, not be stuck with dead weight."

"So, you're saying you'd abandon your partner, your team? No offense, but I don't want you as my partner," Tell said, disappointment clear in his voice.

"Dead is dead, dude. If one of us falls, what chance ya think ya got of gettin' back up? If you're wounded, I suggest ya try 'n' keep up."

"The point is moot, guys. I'm going to partner up with Trick," Archer said. "Now, the other thing we need to consider is the interior of the church. The floor and walls are marble. Those aren't conducive surfaces for pinning them down. We can't rely on maneuvering them toward a pew or confessional either."

"Now wait just a damn minute! You're buddyin' up with me to keep me in check in case I decide ta go after Luca, aren't you? I can't believe this!" Trick roared in naked fury.

"I was thinking maybe we should try to lure them outside closer to Lourdes Grotto." Archer said, ignoring the angry outburst. There's not as much open space for the spears, but it will curtail their ability to move and give us more places and surfaces to secure them to so a *coup de grace* can be delivered."

"Oh, that's great! Now you're gonna fuckin' ignore me, like I'm some child tossin' a fit? Man, oh man, Archer! When'd your nuts fall off, huh? Maybe you *should* sit this one out. Sure as hell, I ain't partnerin' up with someone who's gonna hold me back!"

"Me. I. Listen to yourself. Get over it already; this isn't about you Trick!" Archer said, slamming his hand down on the table top, the other saber rattling as the table shuddered. "Can any of us trust you to have our back right now? You're raving. You're so focused on killing that you don't have a thought to spare about the living, do you?" Archer glared at Trick for a moment, seeing the chasm gaping between them as Trick matched heat for heat, fury for fury. "Maybe," Archer said softly, his eyes riveted to Trick's, "for the sake of all concerned, we'd better bag this safari, and trust that the Church will take care of its own."

"You're outta your fuckin' mind Archer, totally off your bird! These bastard's are mine. I'm goin' for 'em, with or without any of y'all."

Archer turned away, throwing up his hands in frustration, showing his back to Trick's vitriol. He would never have believed what happened next. Uttering an inarticulate cry, Trick lunged forward, saber raised, poised to strike down his friend. The blade began its long arc downward. Archer heard the hiss of air as Wendell watched in disbelief. Whirling, Archer was in time to see the blade shrieking toward him, deflected at the last moment by a clanging intervention of the spear in Tell's strong hands. Tell stood up, his body between the two men. Archer stepped back in shock, Trick stood stock still, breathing heavily, livid with manic obsession.

Slowly, Trick lowered his hand, the blade dropping to the floor with a cacophonous clatter. He slumped to the chair, his head in his hands. He was still for a moment, then his body began to convulse with sobs, spasms shaking his body.

"In the name of the Goddess, what is going on here?" thundered a stunned, angry voice from the front of the shop. Archer, Tellico, and Wendell all turned to see Toinetta standing in the threshold of the back room, mouth agape, her incredulity at what had nearly happened frozen on her timeless features.

Archer watched as Tell set the spear down gently and went to Toinetta, leading her out of earshot. He leaned down and murmured something in her ear. Frowning, she nodded and patted Tell on the hand, then the pair came back into the room.

Toinetta stopped with the table between herself and Archer and took a deep breath. "The air in here," she stopped and shivered, but not from the temperature, which was stifling. "Tell be a dear and prop the door to the garden open."

Trick scrambled to his feet and trailed after Tellico, not wanting to face his old family friend and mentor just then. What could he say? He wasn't even sure he knew what had happened.

Toinetta came to stand close to Archer, took his cheeks in her hand and lowered his head so she could see into his eyes. Her gaze was so intent, Archer began to feel uncomfortable, like something in the back of his head was itching, trying to claw its way out to avoid her scrutiny.

"A woman named Daniella called me and told me she thought you might be in some trouble, Archer. She sure nailed it, boy." She let him go and sat down, gesturing for him to sit as well.

"What's happening Toinetta? It's like I'm amplifying the emotions of everyone around me and reacting to them, badly. I didn't realize it before, but I could feel Trick's hate, see the ember of loathing in his heart and I intentionally stoked it, fed it, until it blazed out of control."

"You're starting to question. Archer, that's a good thing. You realize there is something different afoot. Think back, when did it first start to happen? Try and pinpoint what may have triggered this new development in your psyche."

Archer closed his eyes and replayed the day, the skull crushing headache. What had caused that? "My dust up with the vampires last night. I took a hard blow to the head. I think I got a concussion. I guess adrenaline kept the pain of it subdued until I woke up this morning, feeling lousy. Things have been in the crapper ever since."

"Alright, we have a place to start. Now, try and remember, during the fight, did the vampires try to get inside your head, like that priest did?"

"No, I mean I don't think so. I don't remember anything other than the physical combat. They could have. I remember being worried about that before we fought. Maybe my shields were to strong. I could sense their psychic powers were weaker than Luca's, kind of guttering like a candle in the wind. Maybe their psychic capabilities grow beyond telepathy as they become more attuned to this dimension. What do you think?"

"I don't know, shugah, but something has opened within you. Where you used to be clairsentient, you are now much more receptive, dangerously open to others, empathic to the point of projecting what someone is feeling back on them. With this receptiveness, it's possible you are reflecting other's thoughts and feelings, turning them back to the sender, amplified to such a degree that it creates a kind of mental feedback. You or they lose themselves in their emotion. Daniella told me you were upset, distraught one moment, and the next, playful and flirtatious. She started to feel that way too, and she felt like you were feeding off each other's energy."

"Oh Gods! Am I becoming like those creatures then, some kind of psychic leech?"

Toinetta shook her head and took Archer's hand in hers. "I doubt it, shugah. You've been 'becoming' for a long time now. It could be that intimate contact with a more highly evolved telepathic being has caused your growth, your evolution to speed up. Like Monopoly, when you get one of them cards telling you to move ahead a couple of spaces. It's where you're supposed to land, you just get from Point A to Point B a little ahead of schedule."

"I'm scared, Toinetta. What if I keep doing this to everyone around me? What if I can't control it?"

"Its not happening now, is it Archer? Look at us, just two people having a conversation. We simply need to put the pieces of the puzzle together and look at what it shows us. Then you can worry about control. Lawdy, who knows where you can go from there?"

"What if I can't reign it in Toinetta? It'll be chaos wherever I go. I'll have to become a hermit or something."

"Don't worry about the future. We're in the now, and the danger to you now is very real, more so than for others."

"What kind of danger is he in," Wendell asked from his seat at the opposite end of the table. He had been immobile with shock when Trick had snapped, and had been quietly debating the merits of diving head long back into a bottle as he absorbed what he had heard. "What can we do to help him?"

"The danger is that Archer might overload, mentally. I don't know what would happen, but it's a sure bet the outcome would be bad."

"Well that brightens my day. Thanks, Toinetta," replied Archer glibly. "What can I do to dampen this new 'gift' so I don't go Chernobyl at an inconvenient time?"

"Is there really a good time?" Toinetta chuckled at her own joke, sobering quickly when she noticed Archer didn't share in her mirth. "Well, shugah, you're always telling me to lighten up; guess I gotta work on my timing." She cleared her throat. "Let's see what we can do."

"Keep working on it," he replied sadly. "We'll make someone laugh, yet."

"Forget it, shugah. We need to ground and shield you. I know you can do it, but we're going to try something a little different. I'm going to lend my energy to yours to strengthen you. It's so simple, it's barely even a ritual."

"Alright. I trust you, Toinetta. There aren't any surprises at the end of this road? Anything I should know about?"

Toinetta patted Archer's hand. "Honestly, I don't know. My guess is the boost in your shielding should keep you and those around you safe. Tomorrow we'll start trying to figure out the parameters of what's going on in that head of yours and work on harnessing it. You need to control it, shugah, not the other way around."

"What are we waiting for? Let's do this. Wendell? Can you excuse us for a while?"

"Sure, Arch, whatever you need. I'll go out and check on Trick and Tell, let 'em know what's going on."

When Wendell had gone, Archer said, "It's your show. Tell me what to do."

Toinetta pulled her chair up so she sat directly across from Archer. "It would be best to have a third person, someone sensitive or even gifted in magic. We can work with two, but next time we should have a third. A trinity is best." She gazed intently into Archer's face, studying every inch of his young but care-worn face until she met his eyes. "Archer, the best magic usually comes from ritual work. The rhythm of the routine, the familiarity it breeds for the spell caster. I've never worked that way with you. Do you know why?"

Archer kept his eyes riveted to Toinetta. "Never gave it much thought. Even if I did, I bet I'd be wrong."

"Don't sell yourself short, shugah. Be confident. When in doubt, do something, even if it's wrong. You can always fix mistakes. You can never turn back the clock on lost opportunity. Believe in yourself. There are really two reasons why I never taught you much in the way of ritual. First, ritual tends to remove the self-assurance of the practitioner. They rely on ceremony and sacrament so heavily that they often become convinced the only way to get things done is the way they have always done it. Magic doesn't have to work that way. Magic, real magic, comes from our ability to utilize the forces around us, to meld with them, or sometimes bend them briefly to our will. You have an innate ability to wrangle the natural and supernatural in ways I've never seen."

Archer wasn't sure what to say. "It's always just come to me, what I need, when I need it. If nothing happens, I figure that's the way the universe wants things. What's the second reason?"

"You're a man, Archer Sweet, that means you're lazy and not supposed to be so readily pre-dispositioned to magic. I don't mean lazy in the conventional sense, but when it comes to study and discipline in your mystical training, you avoid it like a gator with a mouthful of sore teeth avoids dinner. If something didn't work for you the first time, you'd probably quit trying. Typical human, but mostly male response. Trying to teach you by rote would only deaden what comes to you naturally. Maybe someday, you'll take things less lightly and understand what you can do, and why. For now, it seems irresponsible of me, but the best way for you to learn is for someone to point you in the right direction, spoon feed you, and let you wing it."

"Thanks a pant load, Toinetta." Archer tried to pull himself away from Toinetta's grip, but she held fast. "You tell me I'm lazy and undisciplined, then expect me to go out and 'wing it'? How is that helpful?"

"Because realizing your shortcomings, accepting the things you can't change and having the humility and courage to improve yourself is the next step in your evolution." She squeezed his hands tightly, her rings digging into his flesh, making him squirm slightly as she held his gaze. "Like it or not, you are changing Archer. Your encounter with a new supernatural entity has triggered some evolutionary marker in your brain. You need to be *au fait* with that, and allow yourself to acknowledge that you're growing, changing. Otherwise you're just spinning your wheels and I can't be any more help to you." She released his hands, thrusting them away from her as she broke eye contact.

He sat there, gazing blankly into space, wringing his sore fingers, cogitating.

"I'll be back in a few minutes, Archer. Ground, center, and shield on your own. When I return, we'll do it together and bind you for the time being." Toinetta turned and walked to the tiny employee washroom by the entrance to the courtyard and closed the door behind her. Archer could hear the ventilation fan clunk and clatter to life as the light came on.

She was right; Archer knew it. It was one of the things he despised most about himself, the real reason he didn't delve as deeply into his studies. It all fascinated him as much as it frightened him. He wanted to know all there was about everything he could get his hands on, but self-doubt hung over him like a dark cloud. He had not been able to defend himself psychically against the power of the psychic revenant once he had destroyed its physical form and dispersed its energy. Only intervention, literally divine, had saved him from the hellish abyss into which he had been drawn. He had mastered the simpler things, like improving his shields to keep the dead from disturbing him when he walked through The Quarter and while he slept; honing his intuition to a fine edge. But what if his next test was too big, too much for him to tackle? He didn't want to fail, so he refused to advance himself in order to avoid having to try. Fear of success was what his high school counselor had accused Archer of when he was called into the man's office to discuss his lack of grades despite his intelligence and placement testing. Denying that had become an art form, a way of life until he had met Trick and Toinetta. Archer realized that there are varying degrees of self-confidence and achievement. He was scared to be great; he never believed he could be.

He shook himself and stood up, feeling a slight head rush as he rose too quickly. Toinetta was right. If he was to ever discover his place in the world, he was going to have to surrender himself completely to who and what he was. If it meant living in the ether more than he was comfortable with, so be it. He would expand his comfort zone.

The ventilation fan was still clattering in the wash room when Archer's phone chirped. He didn't recognize the number scrolling across the screen, but he flipped the phone open and listened.

"Archer? Are you there? Hello? It's Luca."

"What is it Luca?" Archer sighed, annoyance creeping into his voice. A phone call from an enemy was a lousy way to top a personal epiphany.

"I-I need your help. I've been trying to reach out to the vampires and summon them to me as we discussed, but either they are beyond my ability to commune with them, or they sense a trap. Could you come to the church earlier than we agreed? Maybe between the both of us, we can entice them to come."

"They're not the only ones who smell a rat, Luca. What's your game now, vampire?"

"I could give you my pledge of ignorance, but would you believe me?"

"Probably not, but I'll be there anyway. Twenty minutes by Lourdes Grotto?"

"Excellent. I'll meet you there."

Archer hung up the phone and walked over to the table where the second cavalry sword rested, its blade glittering in the false lighting of the store, a fresh coat of oil gave the newly sharpened blade a vaguely menacing sheen. Picking it up, he tested its heft and balance, then sheathed it in the scabbard. The swivels on the belt chain rocked silently as the blade housed itself with a metallic sliding sound and a satisfying click as the guard caught the end of the sheath. He went to the register and grabbed a piece of scrap paper and pen, jotting a quick note that he had gone ahead. He told the others to meet him at the church as soon as they could, set it on the table top by the bayonet, and left the store.

Flipping his cell phone open, he dialed Daniella. "I'm leaving early for the church. Can you be there in ten?"

"I'm on my way. I'll be around. If you need me, call. And Archer? Watch yourself."

He disconnected with a brusque, "Yeah." There was just one stop to make before he went to meet Luca. If he had been paying attention, he could have tapped the resources of his own store, but doing that now would mean running in to the people he was trying to protect. They wouldn't allow him to steal away alone.

He slipped in and out of Esoterica, the only other store that competed with him for fine magical supply and occult goods, separating the appropriate bags into different pockets as he walked.

It was time to see if he was any good or had learned anything from Toinetta during his studies. More importantly, it was time to stop the bloodshed in his town.

CHAPTER 32

TRICK CAME BACK inside with Tellico and Wendell, his whole body shaking, eyes red and slightly swollen from the unabashed primal bout of crying he had experienced after Tellico dragged him away from Archer. How could he have become that angry with his best friend? Worse, if Tell hadn't had been there to intervene, Trick would have most certainly cleaved his unarmed friend from shoulder to groin, from behind, something he wouldn't have done to his worst enemy. Not being able to excuse behavior like that in others, how in the world would he ever make things right with Archer or his own conscience again?

He slid into the chair closest to the discarded saber and kicked at the weapon in an impotent war of emotions. The blade caught air and arced for a moment before landing against the frame of the wash room, clanging against the iron hardware that held the door's wooden slats in place. The door opened and Toinetta emerged, stepping carefully over the offending weapon. She looked around the room. "Where is Archer?"

"I probably chased him away, sho'nuff. Pushed him right outta his own store and away from his friends. Guess he's got no cause for thinking I still got his back, since I nearly put a sword into it."

"Nonsense Patrick! Listen to me, all of you. Archer is not stable right now. I don't mean he's gone mental, more like he's mentally gone. Without trying, he can elicit the basest emotions in people and somehow amplify them beyond the control of the person being affected. In other words, Trick, you were angry, but you would never in a million years dream of attacking anyone, much less someone as close to you as Archer. His mind augmented your emotions to such an uncontrollable, insensate state that you reacted the only way his mind would permit. He's aware of this now, and I fear he may be off to do something rash."

Tell goggled, grabbing up the spear. "Like going after those vampire things by himself?"

Toinetta nodded sadly. "Exactly, something rash."

Trick ran over and scooped up the saber from the floor and rushed for the door. "We've got to stop him, y'all. This is all my fault. We can't let him go alone."

Wendell picked up the long bayonet, staring at the note, then set it down for everyone to see. He walked toward the door, blade in hand. "Guess this'll do instead of my machete. I've got your back, Trick. Let's go finish this."

Toinetta gazed at Tell, a questioning look on her face. He nodded and joined the pair at the door. Only Toinetta understood what Tell knew, with his troll blood, he was not susceptible to Archer's transference and emotional instability. He would have to be the voice of reason, the dampener, when they all reunited.

Archer arrived at the wrought iron church gates five minutes early, finding them barred against after hour visitors. Making a quick recon circuit around the perimeter of the church, he let his senses precede him, peering deeply into shadows, listening for sounds that didn't belong, smelling for anything that was distinctively out of place from the miasma of odors in the poor section of The Quarter. The overpowering intoxicating aroma of the incense that emanated from the inside of the venerable church made him feel psychically full and sated, almost groggy, but he was still able to locate the delicate musk of Daniella, lurking someplace nearby. He nearly missed the rustle of dead leaves tumbling along the concrete near Lourdes Grotto, the dry, husky sound of autumn's end pushed along by a gentle breeze, or a soft careful footfall.

"Luca?" Archer asked as he stood before the front of the church once again, and let his hand slip casually to the hilt of the saber. "If that's you, better let me know now, or you might wind up short about a head."

A shadow detached itself from the rounded mass of The Grotto, the white robes of Father Luca separating themselves from the white-washed mass. "I am glad you came, Mr. Sweet. I wasn't sure you would trust me."

"Consider it divine intervention. What's the situation?"

"Where are your friends? I would have thought they would have been close by your side."

"Don't you worry about them, they're right where I want them to be. Now enough stalling. What's going on?"

"After I spoke with you, the *Invictus Morte* seemed to respond better. They are close. I was worried that they would arrive first, but I promised to meet you here."

Luca scurried to the gate and produced a big barreled skeleton key from his robes, and inserted it into an ancient lock around the chain on the gate. The door opened with a small squeak of protest and Archer slipped inside. Luca reached to re-lock the gate, but Archer grabbed his hand. "Let's keep it open for now. It's either good guys or bad walking through here tonight. What say we give them an even chance?"

Nodding in agreement, Luca handed the key to Archer. "Alright, you be the gatekeeper if it makes you feel any easier." Archer was reaching for the key when Luca fumbled it, the heavy metal clattering onto the concrete at Archer's feet. "My apologies. It's unlike me to be so clumsy."

As Archer leaned down to retrieve the key, his hand digging and plunging through the dry leaves made enough noise to mask the soft snick of the tumblers as Luca re-locked the gate.

Luca led Archer through Lourdes Grotto along the narrow pathway. The Grotto was eerie at night with electric candles on timers, flickering weakly beside guttering votives. The glow they emitted cast a soft radiance from the bronze plaques, creating odd shadows and spots of brighter light. The priest picked up a votive flame left behind by a devotee and motioned for Archer to follow him through the Grotto and across the narrow alleyway toward the church.

Archer again extended his senses out in front of him, like a form of radar, trying to anticipate where the trap would be sprung, feeling the buzz of psychic probing in his brain, stronger than before, but not as focused or worrisome. They reached the door of the church without incident; Archer didn't expect the attack to occur in the open. He let Luca pull open the heavy door and slid silently behind him, using both the man and the door as a shield, knowing the vampires were extremely close.

"Inside, quickly," Luca urged Archer. "I don't know if you are as in tune to them as I am, but they are near and they are most definitely not happy to be summoned."

"Lead the way holy man. Believe it or not, I feel exactly what you feel," Archer lied, not understanding what he was feeling. He knew that Luca was leading him into a trap and that with or without his cooperation, the result would be the same. It was better for Archer to try and contain the situation than let it spill out into the public.

"You really can sense them, Archer? That is amazing. I myself was unable to detect them until they allowed me to feel their presence." The door closed, leaving only the low ambient street light streaming through the windows and the votive candle that Luca extinguished once he was past the niche containing the saints.

"Oh, yeah," Archer replied acidly, realization dawning. "I feel them, you prick. You've been a bad, bad clergyman. Letting uninvited guests join the party."

"But they are invited Archer. You wanted the *Invictus Morte* here so you could dispatch them. They are here, the ones those giggling co-ed fools accidentally summoned, and the ones I called before I returned the parchment to The Vatican. And I believe they are all in accord. They do not wish to be killed. The pair who have been here the longest have let them try your people's blood and they found it is much sweeter than the alternate life of psychic feeding that waits for them under His Holiness. No, I think you have some, how do you Americans say it, 'unresolved issues' before you." Luca laughed maliciously, "In your vernacular, I'd say you are galactically fucked."

Archer froze by the door as a loud howl sounded as from a distance through the oak door. No wonder he was able to feel them so easily, to taste, the betrayal of Luca like a bolus of ipecac forcing its way down his throat splashing heavily into his stomach, churning and causing his gorge to rise. He realized the epic mistake he'd made in underestimating Luca's lust for power.

Twenty vampires began to close on his position, teasing him as he imagined a pack of cats would play with a really stupid mouse. They were all in his visual range, either focal or psychic, all in various stages of visibility; his inner eye allowing him to see the truth clearly. Luca had created a formidable army.

As Archer's saber cleared its sheath with a rasp, he again heard a not so distant howl from an angry wolf and felt the cool marble against his back. Toinetta was wrong. There would be no growth and development for him. Not for the first time that day, he was happy to be alone, and he was grateful beyond measure that he had left the others behind. Reaching into the pouch of ingredients he had purchased at Esoterica with his free hand, he kept the saber in front of him in as much of a guard position as an untrained swordsman might. *Baton, saber, what's the dif?* he thought as he brought the hand with ingredients to his mouth. *Baton's got better moves, but it can't cut off heads.*

CHAPTER 33

Daniella prowled outside, impotent in her fury. She had allowed
Archer and the priest to walk right past her, the priest never noticing the
mortal peril just feet away as he opened the door to the church.

The stink of the vampires, her race's ancient adversary, had washed over
her like a deadly tide and she rushed for the door, but was too late to squeeze
her lithe body through the heavy, rapidly closing, oak door. She bayed once
in utter frustration. Her sworn enemies were regaining a foothold in her
world, in obscene numbers based on their stench, and she was out in the cold,
literally. It would take her at least two minutes at her fastest to transform her
paw back into a hand to open the door, and at least that long again to regain
her lupine form. It would weaken her greatly, but what choice did she have?
Archer was inside, alone. Nobody should die alone, and if she had any say in
the matter, he wasn't going to die tonight.

She prepared for the transmogrification, anticipating the excruciating
pain of her long muscular foreleg transforming into a hand or at least a
heavy claw when she heard motion both from inside the church, near its
gate. Her eyes caught movement at the public gate and she stopped, backing
away, melting again into the shadow. She would still be there, but they would
not be alone.

CHAPTER 34

Trick WAS GRUMBLING the entire way to the church. Tell knew it was the man's guilt more than anger at Archer for leaving them behind. Who could blame Archer for wanting to keep his friends out of harm's way? Tellico was concerned but not surprised that their plan, nebulous at best, had fallen apart so quickly. Wendell alone seemed nonplussed by Archer's cowboy action. As his former partner, he knew Archer's behavior best, Tell supposed. Wendell's demeanor was helping him feel more at ease, but no less anxious about the coming showdown. All of them knew Archer was hip deep in the hurt locker, but it was comforting somehow to see that someone who knew him so well seemed unworried by the predicament. Trick alone was as jumpy as a sack of bull frogs, and Tell knew he only wanted to redeem himself.

Reaching the public entrance of the church, Trick pushed at the gate, rattling it in frustration when it didn't open. Tell put his hand firmly on Trick's shoulder and pried him away from the fence.

"My man, we've gotta keep our shit together. Archer's outta sight and if he's already inside, letting Jesus and everyone else around the block know we're here isn't gonna do him any good."

"Yeah, or he might wanna know th' cavalry's here. Now, can you do anythin' 'bout gettin' this fuckin' gate open?"

Tell set his spear aside and grasped the lock for a second, giving it a test tug. "Mmm." He nodded, then said to Trick casually, "Only one thing wrong with this particular type of old lock." He gave it a sharp twist, working the bolts against the hasp until the two separated with a satisfying groan of metal. "Can't take excessive amounts of torque." The pieces of the lock fell to the pavement with a clatter, as Trick pushed the gate open. Tell jumped to catch the spear before it hit the ground, then stood to let Wendell pass. "You're welcome," he muttered to himself slipping behind his companions.

"I don't see him," Trick hissed. "He's either inside the church or next door. Do you feel any connection with that priest, Wendell?"

"Mm-hmm," replied Wendell dreamily. "He's in the church and he's not alone."

Trick glanced at Pierce, muttering low to Tellico, "Sho'nuff that boy's gone on 'round th' bend. At least we know where Archer is."

Nodding wordlessly, Tell ambled to the entrance to Lourdes Grotto, studying it intently. Was it darker than it should have been in there? He couldn't remember ever noticing it on his nocturnal walks, when life got too busy in his head.

"Could be. Somethin' jus' don't taste right to me. There's somethin' in the wind that's just...wrong."

"Hell, I coulda told you that Spooky!" Trick hissed at him, "There's a pair of mental hijackers and their handler that need to be shortened by a head."

"No," replied Tell anxiously, "There's something else. Can't you feel it? An almost palpable energy, oppressive, like trying to catch your breath through a thick wool blanket after running a hard mile."

"Oh, I don't know," replied Wendell, "I'd say it feels kind of placid, you know, serene. Like now that we're on holy ground, nothing can touch us."

Tell was about to reply when he heard a heavy thump against the side door that opened near the Grotto. "All right boys, let's move this party inside. One at a time through the Grotto. Me first with the spear, then Trick, then Wendell. Nobody goes in until the man before him is on the other side, cool?"

Trick nodded and Wendell smiled, making Tellico reconsider the order of procession. Maybe the head case or the basket case should be the fodder. *Nah,* he decided, *if I'm the only one thinking straight now, I need to watch out for these yahoos, not serve 'em up on a platter. Sure wish Archer hadn'ta bolted.*

Taking a deep breath, Tell brought his spear to bear, and ducked his massive body through the gaping aperture into the Grotto. He didn't stop to look around, figuring he probably couldn't see something partially invisible anyway, but he noticed most of the electric votives were out, which seemed unusual for so early in the evening.

When he emerged, on the other side, he motioned for Trick to come through as he turned to face the walkway toward the church. Another hollow thump sounded from the big wooden doorway as Trick emerged from the Grotto. Brushing past Tell, Trick brandished his saber and bolted for the church door leaving the big man torn between covering Trick's reckless behind or providing safe passage for the last in line. Wendell unsheathed the bayonet, and pointed toward the church, "Go. That wild young buck's gonna get his ass handed to him. I'm the cautious cop. I'll be close behind you."

Turning, Tell chased Trick the short distance to the side door, where the smaller man was bending himself nearly in half trying to lever the heavy oaken portal open. An unearthly howl emanated from within, then the muffled thwack of steel striking flesh, and a loud curse. Pushing Trick from the door, Tell grabbed one handle in each hand, flexed his fingers and tore the doors free with a vicious jerk. Iron work and hinges sheared with great protest, and Trick was instantly inside, a battle cry in his throat, steel bared to the night air.

Tell was one step inside the building, carried in Trick's manic wake, when he saw something; big, tall, and uglier than a mule's butt, hoist Trick up from behind, his saber flailing uselessly as he tried in vain to strike his attacker. Grabbing the thing from behind, Tell wrenched it to its knees, struggling against the monster's raw power. Trick was free in an instant and glued his back to the wall, saber in front of him. "Wha' the' fuck? Where is it Tell?"

Tell, too occupied with the brute strength of the thing he now held in a head lock, didn't answer. Slowly, he slid his arm up as the thrashing beast hissed impotently in his grasp, until he had one hand on its broad sloping forehead and the other around its elongated neck, near the shoulder. With a wrenching contra-lateral motion, Tell heaved, nearly tearing the ghastly head from its body in a satisfying snap of bone and cartilage. The body sank motionless to the floor in a heap of ungainly limbs. Tell wasn't sure if it was dead or incapacitated, but one down was one less to worry about.

"Can you see them? Can you see them?" Trick asked Tell in a long string of panicked words. "We should be able to see them. Why can't we see them?"

"Sure can," Tell replied as calmly as he could. "Can't you?"

"Fuck no. Ya think I'd have been taken that easy if I could see 'em? Thanks for unjammin' me, by the way"

"Damn! Looks like we got us a problem Trick. There are a lot more than two vampires in here," replied Tell. "If you can't see, then what good are ya? Just another vulnerability to defend. Give me your saber, take my spear and go keep Wendell from coming in. I'll go and fetch Archer. He's just up yonder. You two keep our exit route clear, hear?"

Trick strangled an inarticulate cry, trading the big man sword for spearm then backed quickly of the church. Wendell was peering in the doorway as Trick emerged. "Looks like we've got mop-up. There's more than just th' two of them in there. Luca summoned some back-up. Guess we get th' one's we can see and hope none of the invisible ones notice us out here." He motioned to Wendell, "Get to my back and stay alert. We can handle anything we can see. One of us goes airborne, th' other's gotta be there, you feelin' me?"

"I heard that," Wendell replied, confusion clouding his face, "but why would Father Luca let anything happen to us?"

"Oh, man your brain really is catawampus! He ain't a friend. You're just amusement for him." Trick shook his head, frustrated. "Man, I think I liked you better when you were hittin' th' sauce instead of th' religion."

Wendell smiled, bayonet firmly in one hand, Glock cocked and ready in the other. "Don't worry," he said, in the tone of utter faith and serenity. "I think we're going to pull through this okay."

"Jesus, Mary, and Joseph," replied the Agnostic.

Tell wasn't surprised by his ability to see the creatures before him thanks, to his half troll heritage. He was amazed at how easily they fled before his presence and scything blade. They probably were unused to their food giving more than token resistance.

"Archer! We're here," he called, pressing forward to where he could see his boss, back flattened to the marble wall, battling with two vampires, their outlines glowing with otherworldly energy. "I'm comin'. Watch your head!"

Archer crouched quickly as two vampires attacked simultaneously. Remembering how easily the vampires had scaled the side of the building's concrete facade during their last encounter, he risked a glance away from the pair of reaching vampires he was battling in front of him to look up. To his horror, he saw three more scaling the smooth marble wall above him, their talons digging into the pristine marble, moving easily to drop on him and overwhelm his position.

None of his attackers seemed intent on incapacitating him, just getting him into position to feed from him. Giving a strangled shout of renewed fury, pirouetting away from his position, blade whistling before him in a lethally protective arc, he hoped he could avoid the onslaught until Tell could reach him.

As Archer tried to close the gap between Tell and himself, he realized the same thing Tell had noticed; these newer vampires seemed unnerved by the fact that their victims were fighting back. Archer slashed one shimmering vampire in the gut, causing it to scream in unearthly torment. As it doubled over, Archer swung down with all of his might, wrists jarring as the sharp blade slammed into the creature's exposed neck, severing the spine from its head. He jumped over the quivering body and landed next to Tell as his fellow warrior separated the head from another vampire. "Alright Tell, let's beat feet. These things may be hungry, but they don't seem to have the belly for prey that bites back."

"I've got your back," Tell replied slicing the head cleanly off a charging vampire. "That makes three for me, how many'd you get?"

"Killed two, wounded two, but let's count the bodies later and skedaddle," Archer replied as they put their backs together and started moving toward the side door.

"I have Trick and Pierce watching our escape route. They can't see what we see, so I think they're safer in the rear."

"Good man," Archer replied ducking under a flailing vampire's slashing claws and bringing his saber across the creature's exposed back, missing a killing blow. "Have you seen Luca or the two solid vamps we were after, originally?"

Tell's blade glittered in the candlelight as it whistled through the air, taking another head clean off its shoulders, blood arcing behind, the body continuing forward for a few macabre steps as momentum gave it the illusion of life. "No joy there, I was kind of hoping you had that matter taken care of." With the last kill, the other vampires had backed away slightly, forming a fluid half moon around the men, none brave enough to face the prospect of death the sharp steel promised.

"My guess is they're gone. I didn't see them after the vampires attacked, but these don't seem possessed of the confidence the original two have. Let's get to stepping."

Tell nodded, saber held high, feigning at the creatures around them if one become bold enough to come closer. Back to back in a slowly revolving circle so a lateral attack would be detected, the pair made their way back to the set of heavy doors. As they neared the reprieve of the exit, Archer suddenly broke away from Tell and sprang forward to the door of the church, saber raised. Hearing a sickening thump, like an overly ripe melon smashing open on the street. Tell chanced a look over his shoulder at the exit.

A vampire, barely visible even to Tell's sensitive sight was lying prone; arms splayed wide, its head cleaved neatly in half down to its lower jaw. Tell kicked the doors closed and took the spear that had fallen from Trick and ran its shaft through the iron pull handles, momentarily barring pursuit. Archer's stood slack, staring blankly at the ground. Tell followed his unfixed gaze and felt his blood suddenly cool. Trick and Wendell were lying motionless on the concrete near the spot he had killed the last vampire.

Shaking his head in disbelief, Archer howled wordlessly. *Luca is going to pay for his lies and betrayal,* he thought blackly, as he sprinted to the rectory door, a good idea of where they would be waiting for him.

Tell knelt checking Wendell's pulse, feeling it weak and fluttery, like a caged butterfly beneath his fingers. He was out but other than a blow to the head, seemed unhurt. Stepping over Wendell's body to look at Trick, he saw the damage was far worse. Trick's shirt was torn and four bloody bone-deep gashes blossomed blood renewing their freshness with every beat of the heart that was miraculously spared. Archer was nowhere to be seen.

As Tell tore off his own shirt, creating a makeshift bandage for Trick's chest, he could hear sirens wailing in the night, their shrieks drawing nearer and nearer. Tell was compressing the wounds and trying with blood slick fingers to tie off the wounds when Trick began moaning and thrashing weakly. Tell looked up again hoping to spy Archer, and to make sure there were no more enemies sneaking up on him. All he saw was the blue and red pin-balling strobes of emergency vehicle lights and what looked like a large dog disappearing into an open door leading to the rectory.

A snarl from behind warned Tellico belatedly as a vampire, flushed out by the light and noise of the cavalcade of vehicles, jumped on his broad back wrapping one of its long slender arms under the big man's jaw. Trying frantically to snatch the beast from his back made the vampire's hold sink deeper. Tell tried to flip it over his shoulder, then ramming backward to smash it against the wall of the church. The creature's grip was relentless. Before he realized it, Tell's knees were hitting the sidewalk with a jarring thud and his vision began to swim. Thrashing feebly, each effort growing weaker, he felt the darkness of unconsciousness mingle with a sharp stabbing pain on his neck and back. With a sigh that his fading mind found revolting, Tellico Trufant pitched forward face down on the sidewalk, his world going black.

CHAPTER 35

WENDELL PIERCE CAME to his senses, the sharp smell of blood in his nostrils. Groggily, he sat up absently patting at his own body. Other than a ringing in his ears and a dull hammer blow headache, he felt alright. *I've had worse hangovers,* he thought as he looked around. His bayonet and Glock were lying next to his hand and the sight of it brought back the situation in a rush of panic. Trick was down, but someone seemed to have at least started to patch him up. The big guy, Tell was down too his body shivering spasmodically. What the..., he thought as he realized there was a shimmering form lying on top of Tell's quivering form.

Lurching to his feet, bayonet in hand, he stumbled over to Tellico's body and drove the bayonet's twenty-four inch length laterally through the body lying atop Tellico, impaling the creature's lungs, heart and other vitals without damage to the prone victim. The creatures wet, satisfying, slurping sounds turned instantly into keening gasps and bubbly screams as it struggled to disengage itself from Tell and remove the source of its sudden agony. *I can see this one,* Wendell thought dispassionately as he kicked the beast in the head with all of his might, launching it off Tell's body to land in a thrashing heap of red smear against the church wall. Reaching for Tell's saber, Wendell advanced carefully, knowing wounded animals were always the most dangerous. *Maybe it's the blow to the head that did it,* he thought. Wendell studied the pathetic semi-transparent creature for a moment; watching its feeble struggle to remove the bayonet from its body, as he leveled the saber blade like a baseball player stepping into the batter's box, taking a practice swing. *Guess it doesn't matter. At least I finally know what we were up against.*

The saber bit deep and the vampire's head bounced away from the body like a gutter ball in a bowling alley. The ringing in Pierce's head wasn't really a ringing anymore so much as it was a constant siren. The walkway to the church was beginning to glow with blue and red lights as well as the constant harsh glare of spot lights.

Wendell knew the lights well and welcomed them. He didn't relinquish the dripping saber, as he staggered over to make sure Trick was still breathing beneath what he guessed was the tattered makeshift bandage of Tell's shirt. Wendell turned and tottered over to the big man. No point in trying to find a pulse on the man's wrist or neck, small amounts of blood surged from the puncture wounds on his upper back at regular intervals. Somehow, to varying degrees, they were all alive.

Relieved, Wendell sank down next to Tell, suddenly very tired and not at all sure he could stand without assistance. He held onto the saber, its point digging into the sidewalk, his arms resting on the pommel just about eye level. Closing his eyes as he heard the first sets of pounding foot steps enter the church courtyard and walkways, Wendell smiled. "Mind the vampires," he mumbled as he slumped forward, balanced against the upright brace of the sword.

Detective Al Willig and Detective Tommy Corgan were the first to arrive on the scene. Corgan had been trying to explain the earlier events of the day to a man whose give-a-shit was on mute when the call had come from dispatch.

Willig popped his magnetic roof top light on the car and they had arrived as the first uniforms were pulling up. "Secure the perimeter of the church," Willig commanded, "I want this place locked down tighter than a nun's—I don't want anyone getting out without our stamp of approval on their ass. Until we figure out what the hell is going on, that order includes the priests in the rectory. Are we clear?"

The uniforms fanned out and the two detectives joined the paramedics as they pushed through the front gates. The first thing Willig noticed, beside the twisted padlock and the askew gate doors, was about five distinctive blood trails leading away from the church into the gloom. Collaring the lead paramedic Willig ordered him to follow up on the trails immediately, but make sure his men had a patrolman along at all times.

Willig and Corgan came into the alleyway where Pierce sat unconscious resting against a saber, and saw Trick Boulieux lying in a pool of fresh and congealing blood, making small movements and moaning as awareness gradually returned to him. A huge ebony-hued man stood propped by the side door to the church, sluicing an upturned jug of holy water over his head, letting the rivulets of water wash away blood and dirt from his bare, chiseled torso. A spear barred the church door, its length resting inside the iron pull handles in easy reach, and Willig noticed his partner draw his pistol.

"Trufant!" Corgan bellowed as he leveled his weapon at the large man's chest. "Care to tell us just what the fuck you're doing? It'd better be the best story you've ever told or I'm driving your ass back to Angola myself, tonight. Ya hear me boy?"

The paramedics were examining Trick's chest wound, peeling the shirt gently from it before adding their own bandages to it for the ride to the hospital. "This one's not too serious. Needs some stitching up and probably a unit or two of blood, but he should be good to go in a few days."

"I don't like the look of this guy here," replied another paramedic who had removed the sword from Pierce's grasp and helped him to slump gently to the concrete. "His right pupil is dilated, there may be some inter-cranial bleeding that needs attention STAT. His vitals are strong, but that don't mean shit if he gets shocky on us." Reaching down to his belt and grabbing his radio, the paramedic requested two gurneys.

Tell listened intently to the assessments. "I found them both on the ground, out cold. Trick was bleeding pretty bad but the other dude was just out. I was binding Trick's chest when something hit me from behind. All I remember until just before you got here is grapplin' with the motherfucker, and losin'. I musta blacked out and the damned thing, the thing took a bite outta me for dinner, 'scuse my language."

"So what about this guy?" Willig motioned to Wendell, as the paramedics eased him down to the ground, noting with annoyance that Corgan still had his gun on the big man like he was a violent perp, responsible for everything that happened here. "How'd he end up looking like the last samurai?"

"Don't rightly know. If'n I hadda guess, I'd say he came to as the vampire was bleeding me and killed it, then collapsed again."

"Vampire? Where is this alleged vampire, Trufant? All I see is you breaking the terms of your parole, again, and two people badly wounded. Where's the vampire?"

Tell looked at Corgan for a moment, shaking his head before he fixed his eyes at the man's feet. "Take a step to your right and give the air in front of ya a good kick. The body's lying right in front of you, or can you not tell which pool of blood came from which body, Detective?"

Willig nudged his toe forward, and then grabbed Corgan's gun hand by the wrist. "Stow your weapon. I can't see it, but something is definitely there, and it's still leaking." Corgan looked down at Willig's toe, pushing against something that yielded to the pressure of his foot, but he didn't lower his gun.

"I don't know why you're so soft on this son of a bitch, Al. I really don't. If you want to approach someone as dangerous as Tellico Trufant unarmed, it's your call, but I'm keeping a lead barrier between me and the scum whenever I can."

Tell looked at Willig and shrugged as if to say, what can you do with an asshole, except follow it around with a pooper scoop? Suddenly Tell's eyes widened slightly and he reached blindly behind him for the spear.

"Freeze asshole!" Corgan roared as he flipped the safety off his gun, shifting the point of his aim to Tellico's bullet-shaped head.

Tell was a blur of movement as he snatched the spear ducking away as Corgan's first shot parted the air where he had just been standing. The big man bowled Corgan and Willig over as he raised the spear high, driving it into something mere inches away from a paramedic who had just entered the alleyway with a gurney.

Corgan sat up, re-sighted and squeezed the trigger as Willig's hand flew upward in a chopping motion to strike the weapon away, then punched the flabbergasted detective in the mouth, yanking the weapon from the stunned cop. Corgan whirled on Willig, ready to square off with the man until he saw Willig training the weapon at the wall of the church. Heavy streams of blood ran in two separate rivulets down the wall between where Tell had driven the spear. A ghastly howling emanated from nowhere they could see and, Tell seemed to be meeting some stiff resistance at the business end of the spear.

"If it ain't too much trouble, officers, could one of ya to hand me that saber? Its gotta die now, tonight, or all Hell's gonna break loose."

The two cops stood agape as the paramedic he had saved reached into the puddle of gore and handed Tell the blood-slicked implement. Using his body to steady whatever was pinioned to the plaster wall; Tell hefted the saber and in one deft move, removed the head of the beast. The tension against the spear immediately went limp and an arc of blood blossomed higher on the wall. Something rolled onto Corgan's foot and he yelped.

"Maybe," said Willig quietly, "we should go inside and talk."

Shaking his head, Tell returned the spear through the pull rings of the door. "Inside wouldn't be good right now. If I was you, I'd order everybody outta here quick as you can. We managed to kill six, well seven including that bastard, but there's at least two times that many left, some of 'em wounded all of them hungry."

Willig got on the radio as Trick and Wendell were strapped to gurneys and wheeled out to the waiting ambulances at the front of the church. "This is Willig. I want all non-essential personnel cleared from church grounds immediately. Copy that? Give me your twenty en route and hot foot back to your cars immediately. I'll explain later. Out."

The crackling silence from the radio was deafening as Willig again tried to recall his men. "How many men responded to this call, Detective?" Tell asked gently.

"I've got eight patrols of two men each and four paramedics for Christ's sake. I know most of the meds are gone, they took the wounded out in front of us, but someone should be responding." He tried again, nothing.

"Look, detectives, I know this is a real bad scene for you, but you might have to accept that all of those men are dead. Archer and I discovered a priest has summoned more'n just the two vampires we thought were responsible for all the deaths. Looks like he brought over about two dozen or so."

"Speak of the devil, where is Archer?" Corgan asked, his mocking disbelief, despite the shock of what had just transpired evident on his face.

"Troot be told, I don't know. My advice is to leave now, wait until sunlight and come back for your dead. I've gotta go find Archer. Maybe he can tell y'all why he and I can see these things and what we can do about that."

Willig was nodding his head slowly, seeing some logic in Tell's words but Corgan was having none of it. "We leave you alone so you can do what? Go butcher innocent folks in the rectory or church? Maybe Willig's fuckin' radio is broken and nobody heard him. Maybe Archer's got the drop on 'em somewhere and keeping them quiet. Whatcha think about that boy? I'll bet I could walk into that church now and—"

"No!" shouted Tell and Willig together as Corgan wrenched open the side door to the church and took a half step inside.

Tell lunged forward and savagely sliced the saber through the air at Corgan's ear. In point of fact, it was so close that part of Corgan's left earlobe was whisked off cleanly. The spatter of blood that nearly blinded him as it struck his face was not his own. Corgan fell away howling like a stuck pig and crazily wiping at his eyes with his free hand.

"Goddamn it! You saw that Willig, the bastard cut me on purpose. He's going away tonight and I'll add aggravated assault on a police officer, assault with a deadly weapon, resisting arrest, and any other charge I can think of to make sure this piece of shit rots under Angola."

Tell secured the door again and he backed quickly past the two officers, sword out in front of him, but not menacing the cops.

"Detective Willig, I gotta go find Archer. Please! He may be in more trouble than any of us."

Willig nodded and Tellico set off at a trot around the church away from the two men. "Call me and let me know what happened and how we can help clean this up, hear?"

Tell nodded, waved over his good shoulder, and was gone. Corgan was livid, one hand pressed to his ear, the other pointing maniacally at his partner. "Are you out of your ever loving mind Willig? You let that piece of shit get away, armed no less, after he assaulted me! Why do I get stuck with the wingnuts and incompetents?"

Willig surprised his partner with a left cross that made him stagger into the wall, tripping over the invisible head of one of the corpses. "You're just sharp as a bowling ball, aren't you son? That man saved your life twice tonight, God knows why. I'm leaving now because there are just some things sometimes that we as cops or human beings just can't handle or explain. I know that what I saw—or worse yet—what I didn't see, was something way out of my depth. You want to stay here? Fine. I really could care less. You're an albatross around the neck of anyone you work with you fuckin' Yankee retard. Stay here, go back to New Jersey, or go fuck yourself, whatever makes you happy."

Raising the portable radio to his lips he repeated the order to withdraw. He turned back to his partner. "I'll tell you what's the what Corgan. I plan on getting my retirement, not widow fund benefits for my wife and kids. Trufant can see what going on. Until we can too, he and Sweet are the best hope we've got of putting a stop to all of these homicides. Now get your sorry ass outta my way, fuckwad."

Willig turned on his heel and strode away, weapon drawn and ready in case something grabbed him as he walked to the patrol car. It was eerie, all of the flashing lights but none of the crackle of activity from within, the usual white noise of a crime scene oddly absent. Only the sound of Corgan's rapidly moving hard sole shoes could be heard up and down the block as he raced to catch up with Willig, his only ride out of hell.

CHAPTER 36

ERUPTING THROUGH THE church doors, Archer had found his friends besieged. Adrenaline made his overhead swing with the saber shear through his enemy almost completely. Checking to see that both Wendell and Trick were still breathing, he took off howling up the sidewalk toward the back side of the church where he knew Luca had fled during the pitched battle.

He could sense Luca, and the original two vampires were with him. Plus he could sense something else he hoped they could not. Daniella, in wolf form, was nearby, most likely watching for an opportunity to make her presence known. The vampires he had left alive troubled him, but there was little he could do when only he and Tell could see them. It occurred to Archer once again that there was more to Tellico Trufant than met the eye. Until the vampires gained mass and substance visible to the naked eye, or Archer and Tellico could go hunting, the surviving vampires would get a pass.

A squeaking hinge ahead brought Archer back to his physical senses. In seconds, he reached the door to the rectory, stopping short, looking to see if there was a way to keep the same sound from giving away his pursuit. Daniella appeared suddenly by his side and nudged the door gently with her nose, causing it to squeak with less exuberance. The offending hinge was at the base of the door and Archer bent over it, spitting down the barrel of the bolt. He waited for a moment for the makeshift lubricant to make its way thoroughly through the hinge. Daniella whined quietly at his side, understanding the need for delay but hating it just the same.

"I'll open the door and you slip inside. If it's a trap, bark and I'll come bursting in. If all's quiet, make yourself scarce and let me take up the lead. Do you sense them?"

Daniella nodded her head, one ear twitching. "Me, too, so I don't want you out in front of me once I'm inside. Are you ready?" Daniella licked his hand, the very human eyes disconcerting on her lupine face as she looked meaningfully at Archer.

Archer opened the door slowly, the hinge protesting, but not nearly as much. "Good hunting," he whispered, as the wolf slithered inside the small opening. Waiting for what felt like an eternity, his body ached with the tension, prepared to hurtle his way inside and join the battle should Daniella call. As the seconds ticked away, he relaxed a bit and realized he had been holding his breath.

Archer entered the pitch dark room letting his senses flow outward. He couldn't see the furnishing in the room, but his mind's eye detected nothing out of the ordinary as he groped his way across what appeared to be a small kitchen to a spiraling staircase leading up to the pastor's quarters and common areas.

His foot touched the first wooden stair and Archer tested his weight, hoping they wouldn't screech or make sounds of protest as he ascended. Only a slightly hollow grinding sound from the grit on his shoes gave away his presence and he was soon at the top, staring down a dimly lit hallway, closed doors on both sides. Daniella was ranging back and forth, her nose working each door, seeking their prey.

Archer made his way toward her, his own senses extended. The floor reeked of vampires, and not just the ones he was hunting. Stopping three quarters down the hall, Daniella's hackles went up, her lips drawing back in a silent snarl. Passing her, Archer recognized the room as the one he and Trick had been taken to when they met with Father Finnernan just two days before. Grimacing, Archer recalled how Finnernan had hemmed and hawed around the truth. Would things have been different had he just been honest? No, Archer thought sadly; he couldn't know what Luca was planning. He probably died for discovering the truth.

Archer stepped into the room, taking in the entire scene. Luca sat in one of the high backed chairs, his cane resting on his lap, the two vampires, now entirely visible and utterly human looking, stood behind on either side of the chair, just behind it. Except for above average looks, and overly large incisors they could walk down any street in any country and never be noticed by the world's citizenry. Archer detected one of the newer vampires, still invisible, lurking in the far corner, probably as added security for Luca's peace of mind.

"I don't suppose," Luca said casually as he motioned to a tea service on the table nearby, "that I could interest you in a refreshment?"

"You help yourself, Luca. The condemned should receive a last request." He shook his head at his own naivety. "I kept telling Trick not to kill you. It's a mistake that's cost me dearly. A mistake I intend to correct."

"I am sorry about your associates, especially that delectable one you brought me today, what's his name? Wendell Pierce," he purred. "His pain was pure succulence. Mr. Sweet, and it's all because of you." Luca shifted in his chair, his fingers lingering on the head of his cane "I had hoped that when you arrived tonight, it really would have been alone."

"Well don't go patting yourself on the back just yet, Luca. Everybody is still alive, the paramedics probably have them out of harm's way by now, and the pathetic suckhead you sicced on them went all to pieces when it met my blade. I've already beaten those lap dogs standing behind you without a good weapon." He paused to look at the vampires who seemed to grow in stature as he felt their anger flare. "By the way, how's that chest wound? Musta hurt like a son of a bitch, huh?"

Shaking with mirth, Luca looked first at his minions, then at Archer. "Archer, in a nut shell, you are what is wrong with today's culture. You gave up on blind faith, in your priest as your arbiter, your intermediary with God. Somehow, even though you were baptized, promised to the Church as a Catholic, you lost your way. Maybe it was your priest's fault, or maybe you were just a bad Catholic; all flocks have their black sheep."

"My spirituality is my own. The Creator I believe in doesn't conform to what the Church espouses. My Creator isn't short of money and doesn't require a standing appointment on Sunday with someone to speak on my behalf. I believe, I love, I care, and I try everyday to make sure my actions don't harm others. That is all that can be expected of a man."

"No. What is to be expected of a man is what has been throughout history. You are livestock with free will, nothing more. I, we, the priesthood, are your shepherds and sometimes we must cull a troublesome sheep, such as yourself, from the herd."

Luca motioned to the two vampires and they circled around the chair coming slowly toward Archer from opposite directions. They had learned respect for his skill in battle. Though they were stronger and more agile than their opponent, but he was armed.

Archer brought the saber up to guard position, flicking his eyes from one to the other. The buzzing that preceded a psychic attack erupted in his head. Panic swept through him as he realized the exertion it took to get Luca out of his head the last time he had attacked.

The vampires, sensing his distress moved fluidly to close the gap on their prey. Archer was vaguely aware of the third vampire stalking its way toward him as the cacophony in his head doubled. Archer bellowed wordlessly and dropped to one knee, the hand holding the saber going momentarily slack. Suddenly, the din in his head faded and a howl of rage echoed in his ears. He looked up to see the non-formed vampire lying limp in front of Luca, its throat ripped out and Daniella, hackles up, teeth set in a ferocious snarl advancing on the still seated priest.

He stood, bringing the saber up to guard again moving swiftly to close the distance between himself and Daniella calling out to her as he moved. His warning was too late as one of the solid vampires picked her up by the scruff of the neck, avoiding her snapping maw, trying to turn her around to crush her throat with its other hand. Struggling futilely for purchase, her hind legs kicked and skittered on the wooden floor as the vampire changed its mind, lifting her long, struggling frame effortlessly over his head, savagely slamming her body to the floor with a thunderous crash. With a great whoosh Daniella lost her breath and lay on the hard wood, stunned and momentarily helpless. Smiling, the vampire took his time playing with his food.

Archer was running headlong toward the vampire as it reached for her again. Realizing the saber blade was too long to be useful, he reversed his grip, and driving the hilt of the weapon into the creature's temple sending it in a heap to lie next to Daniella.

Luca screamed furiously and Archer looked up to see the priest staring at the fallen vampire. "You dare strike your betters?" Archer's mind was suddenly ablaze with pain dropping him to his knees, the saber clattering uselessly to the floor. "Do you see now, you walking buffet? Our power goes beyond the ability to feed. You caught me unaware the first time, but now I am ready for you. Taste the pain we can inflict on your simple minds, feel the way your psyche can be stripped from you one exquisitely thin layer at a time. Enjoy your final cogent thoughts, Mr. Sweet. You'll be a drooling vegetable when I call the police and tell them how I found you on the floor downstairs, twitching and mumbling incoherently."

Archer writhed under the attack, struggling to center his thoughts, to round himself up into a cohesive center and fight back. He saw Daniella begin to stir and the remaining vampire closing in on her. Daniella's eyes met his for a moment and he suddenly could feel her inner calm, her indomitable will wash over him. The pain ebbed in him like a tide calming after a storm, and he stood up, glaring at Luca who gaped at him in disbelief.

Turning toward the vampire, Archer thrust out with his mind as he extended his arm, as if to physically push it away from Daniella. The vampire's face registered the surprise Archer was feeling as it was suddenly off its feet and hurtling backward across the room, slamming with timber-shaking force into the far wall, where a row of coat rack hooks were mounted. The thud of the impact was overwhelmed by a keening wail of misery as the vampire slid down the wall a few inches, the hooks digging deeply into its back and shoulders, trapping it.

Luca's attack was two-pronged this time. The buzzing in Archer's brain felt more like a twig poking against his skull and he easily shrugged it aside. It was the silver tipped cane, opened to reveal a concealed thrusting blade whistling forward to impale him that nearly did Archer in.

Ducking awkwardly away, Archer tripped over the still inert form of the vampire he had knocked unconscious. Before he could move, the point of the sword cane was nestled tightly against his throat. "My life, my entire existence to this point has been for but one purpose. To reclaim the right of my people in blood. The days of passive psychic feeding is over. I copied the incantation before I sent it away. I will continue to bring over my pure blood brethren from their dimension and with their strength and my knowledge of this world and its politics, we will once again rise and gorge ourselves at the trough of human frailty and decadence. Pity you won't see that day."

Daniella's snarl came from Luca's back, but his baleful gaze never wavered from Archer. "Even if you jump on me now wolf, this sword will run him through before the first drop of my blood is spilled. If you choose to fight another day, I'll let you leave now. Stay and my brethren will enjoy picking their teeth with your bones."

Archer's eyes absorbed Luca's seething hatred, feeling the gut-turning, bile-washed energy seep into his body. The first time he had channeled his emotions had been a surprise. Now he knew what to do.

The vampire trapped on the wall fell suddenly quiet as it lost its battle with consciousness and Luca's eyes flickered to the silent form for an instant. Archer felt the saber's point dig into his throat as he moved enough to bring his hand across his body. Choking back a cry he slapped the razor sharp blade away, watching with detached interest as a sizeable chunk of his throat's flesh tore away tumbling through the air, warm blood suddenly flooding down his chest. With his other hand Archer pointed at Luca as he channeled every ounce of rage, pain, and anger into him in one massive surge.

Luca screamed and clutched his head, falling to the floor, writhing against the cognitive overload. Archer stood up watching blood fountain away from his neck each time his heart beat. Clamping down on the wound with one open hand he picked up his saber with the other. Lurching toward the unconscious vampire on the floor, he fell to his knees, his strength inexorably leeching from him as surely as if he had been bitten by one of the vampires.

He heard a litany of noises that swirled in his ears like color he could hear, then everything went black as he slumped forward, his last sight was that of Daniella fleeing from a crowd of white robed men who had somehow managed to capture Tell, or was he leading them?

CHAPTER 37

"WE HAVE GOT to stop meeting like this, Sweetdream."

"Liz? Izzat you?"

"Nobody else had better be calling you their Sweetdream."

"So, I'm dead?" He opened his eyes to a blinding white brilliance. "Why can't I see?"

"Because you're not dead, you dumb lug. That light is the doctor checking your pupil reactivity."

"So what happened to me Lizard?"

"You just missed severing your jugular vein with that stunt you pulled on the priest, that's what happened. Lordy, are you a typical man. If you could have waited just a few seconds more, you would have been rescued, no harm, no foul, and we wouldn't be having this conversation."

"I'm always glad to talk to you, Liz, just wish I could see you. I can't always remember what you sound like anymore and your image in my memories is getting fuzzy around the edges. I don't want those things, those parts of you, to go away."

"Oh, baby, they won't. You're just trying to hard. That happens when someone or something new comes into your life. Just let it be and it'll all come back to you. For the record, you did good with Daniella. I mean I approve. She's going to be even more of a handful than I was."

"Why did she run away from me? I saw her as I was—"

"Once again, Archer Sweet: world class conclusion jumper. I swear you could medal in the Olympics if that were a sport."

"But I—"

"Perception and perspective, two things you're missing in this picture and well, pretty much all of your life."

"Hey! I'm damned perceptive. I was an undercover cop, for shit's sake. A damned good one, too."

"Yeah, you were."

"So what do you mean? Why are the dead so enigmatic?"

"Again, perspective. You're not dead, so you don't understand. And you haven't been all that perceptive since you decided to quit being a cop. You're so gung-ho to 'move on' with your life that you overlook the everyday important things that never used to slip by you. You've forgotten how to live in the moment."

"I'll give you the losing moments, but not the everyday things. Name one thing, Lizard, one thing I've let slip by."

"I'll give you three. Your birthday, our anniversary, and your friend Toinetta."

"I always forget my birthday, its ritual for me. And I didn't forget our anniversary, it's— " Panic seized him suddenly. "Oh Lizard, I'm so sorry. I've replaced the happiest day of my life with the worst. I marked the anniversary of your death this year."

"Mmm-hmm. And the last thing?"

"Toinetta? What about her?"

"Look at her the way you used to see things, not with the myopic mindset you have now. You'll see."

Archer could make out a faint shadow moving away from him. "Liz? You have to leave already?"

"That isn't me you see, Sweetdream. Tah for now."

Archer's eyes cracked open and he realized he was lying on a hard mattress in what looked like a very Spartan hospital room, or a priest's cell. He tried to sit up but firm hands forced his shoulders back down.

"Hey now, easy there. Ya wanna tear out the sutures? Don't make me have to go out lookin' for a new job, alright? Just lie still now, Archer. Ol'

Tellico's got your back."

Archer tried to speak but no words came. Tell's gigantic ovoid head appeared upside down in his line of vision. "Don't try talking yet either. They got your throat wound stitched and packed tight with cotton. Jus' breath through your nose and relax. Trick's alive and gonna be good as new, and your buddy Wendell is okay; saved my life, as a matter a fact. As for me, I found out my skin ain't as tough as I thought it was, but I'm good."

Archer sensed motion at his periphery near his feet and saw Toinetta sorting through pants pocket pulling, out the item he had purchased at Esoterica. She handed his hosta leaves to someone and chuckled. "I always hoped that boy was paying attention. Bless his heart, he was." He heard a muffled voice next to her and her reply, "Hosta leaf, shugah. When ingested, it temporarily masks your psychic signature in the spirit realm. Probably why he didn't get killed by those vampires right off, they couldn't see him well enough to put the bite on him."

Archer closed his eyes, wondering why her normally rich café au lait complexion seemed to have more milk than usual.

CHAPTER 38

T HE NEXT TIME HE AWOKE, it was to the unpleasant sensation of someone removing gauze that had knitted to his skin with dried blood from his throat wound. A slight buzz in his head, not probing, just hanging in the periphery, accompanied the voice. "Just a little bit more. Hold still, Mr. Sweet, you're doing fine. Excellent. How does that feel?"

The raspiness of his voice shouldn't have surprised him considering what had happened to him. He felt like he had swallowed a wad of coarse sandpaper. "It would be dandy if you sucked back your psychic antennae for five minutes. I want to ask, and I hope I'm not being rude, but is it ever off? Is there ever a time you don't try and feed on those you can?"

A new voice interrupted, one more authoritative, with greater presence and a distinct Irish brogue. "Mr. Sweet is feeling his oats today. 'Tis a grand sign. Perhaps we might trade some answers. a little *quid pro quo.*"

"I'm amenable to that. You got a name?"

"Father Liam O' Herlihy, recently of Vatican City. I am a Jesuit, not a Dominican, if that makes a difference."

"But you are still a, uh, what is your species politically correct empowered title?"

"We still prefer to be called priests, Mr. Sweet. Though fewer and fewer of you prefer us a'tall with every passing year."

"Amazing what bad press can do to an institution, isn't it Father?"

"'Tis a terrible thing to have one's reputation sullied time and again and so frequently these past few years. Horrible behavior by a lawless few and we all bear the burden of suspicion. Child molestations, embezzlement, adultery with our own parishioners, and a few randy homosexual blow ups, no pun intended, thrown in for good measure. Things like that diminish the Church in everyone's eyes. Regardless of what they believe, they can't believe in the Church anymore. They feel used and foolish for placing their faith so blindly, victims just the same as if something happened to them or one of their own. I've found that if I reversed the positions, I'd probably feel the same."

"Would you rather have those who were abused in any way keep their silence, the pain of betrayal to themselves?"

"Of course not, boy-o!" replied O'Herlihy, his face reddening. "One rotten apple in the barrel will corrupt as surely as the next harvest of apples will be produced. The bad egg must be thrown out, the cancer excised. The Church truly does have the welfare of your soul in our hearts," he said with passionate fervor. "I hope you can believe that?"

Archer glanced at the man. He was mid-fiftyish with thinning straw blond hair tonsured evenly about his head and could mix metaphors with the grace of Yogi Berra. Bifocals and a fair sized belly could make him a ringer for Santa Claus in the proper attire and accoutrements. All in all, he looked benign, but there was an agenda, something that was driving this conversation. "I believe you want the best of what's around, Padre, that keeps your soul cleansing to a minimum, feeding simple, and probably helps it taste better, more satisfying. As for claiming your kind should be custodians of the most sacred thing of all to humans, hope, that's a bit of a stretch to my way of thinking."

O'Herlihy nodded slowly, then faster as his point came to him. "'Tis true, 'tis true, Mr. Sweet. You've seen the absolute worst of our kind doing ghastly things and boasting about the how and why of it. What you don't see is the literal billions of souls who come to us with every problem imaginable. Helping others is where my people shine. Maybe early in our history that wasn't necessarily true, but then again, I think it's safe to say both of our species have evolved over the past thousand plus years."

"Helping others helps yourself, doesn't it? Where is the altruism in that?"

"Bless me, but you're sharp, and you're right. When we do our part to lift a soul's burden, we do feed. We feed and there's no denying it, but the penitent leaves us feeling all the better for it. Whether or not they know the reason why is unimportant."

"I guess I'm more of a black and white kind of guy when it comes to ethics, Padre. I acknowledge the multitudes of grays out there, but it's not where I can be comfortable standing."

"You've a fine moral upbringing Mr. Sweet. Your parents should be proud. But it is that gray area where all religion lives. What we do is neither right nor wrong; it neither balances nor tips the cosmic scale. We celebrate births, baptisms, Holy Communion, weddings, and preside over last rites and funerals. A priest's reason to celebrate is different than your own, but we are part of people's lives, we do serve a greater good, and we do love you all, even the least of you, as dogma has taught us."

Archer was silent a moment, digesting the other side of the story. Liz was right, he had definitely lost a step since he quit the force. "Alright, I'll concede that church is so deeply ingrained in most lives that extraction would create more problems than it would solve, and that you do love us, like shepherds love their flocks. After all, without the flock the shepherd has no purpose. You have tended us and kept us, and in all ways encouraged us to be God's children. But it still comes down to a lie begun nearly two thousand years ago. A lie refined and revised over generations until most everybody believed it. There was wisdom in letting go those who didn't except your teachings, for whatever reason, and credit should be given the Church for not crushing these ideological offshoots." Archer sat up, wincing as the suture drew tighter around his throat, making his voice harsher than he intended. "What I can't countenance is all the blood shed, all of the violence, the needless death and degradation of our race and the corruption of man's religious philosophies for the sake of the Church's gain."

"Mr. Sweet, the gains were worth it. Salvation for the heathen, purpose for the pagan. They were all brought to the Glory of God and were permitted to embrace the path that travels to heaven."

"Your gain was the blood, agony, and hardship for those you 'saved', not to mention the gold it put in your coffers. How do you and yours know that you provide the one true path? How can you guarantee that there is but one paradise? My idea of heaven differs from that of my best friend. When we die, if we both find our way to heaven, will he enjoy it more or less than I? Buddhists, Hindi, Moslem, all have a different ideal and vary in dogma from the Holy Roman Catholic Church. What door prize do you offer that they don't? You can't even use Jesus as your proverbial ace in the hole. All ancient cultures except Judiasm have a version of the virgin birth, and most continue with an innocent death and resurrection. Answer that and you can ask me anything you want. C'mon, I'm waiting."

O'Herlihy was silent for many moments, his eyes closed, chin resting in his hands, fingers pointed up as if praying, a picture of calm reflective repose. Finally, he drew a deep breath and let it out slowly. "Mr. Sweet, there is nothing I can tell you that doesn't hinge greatly on faith. Not just faith in God. It's quite clear to me you possess that in abundance. However, if there is a single path one must take to reach The Almighty, then nothing I can say or do here today will sway you in one direction or the other. The simplest thing I can do is illustrate my point in the here and now with your friend, Wendell Pierce."

"What about Wendell? I was told he survived your storm troopers just fine."

"Please, Mr. Sweet. I have not disparaged you or insulted you in any way. Please do not lump my entire people in with the deplorable deeds perpetrated by a few ambitious outcasts within the walls of this decadent city. The church had a situation that spun out of our hands briefly, but we are remedying things as quick and as best as we can.

"Now, as I was saying, Mr. Pierce is a perfect example of what we can do for the willing. By his own admission, he was a functioning alcoholic, a man who had lost everything in his life except for his thirst for death. Killing himself one drink at a time. True?"

"You have a way with words, but yes, I would agree."

"Was he always in such a state or was he once a purpose-driven person of sound moral and ethical fiber?"

"Wendell was always a stand up guy, until my wife, Liz died."

"He believes in his heart that his poor decision making and improper actions resulted in her death."

"But I've forgiven him, Liz has forgiven him. All I wanted was for him to move forward with his life. Part of his problem is entirely my fault. I refused to let him accept any blame for what happened. To me that would be like asking someone to pull my finger, then blame them for the smell. I never guessed that he needed to bear some of the blame to make up for his survivor's guilt. I forgave him too early and unconditionally, didn't I?"

O'Herlihy's nose wrinkled involuntarily. "Pleasant analogy aside, essentially you're correct. Mr. Pierce needed time to permit himself to grieve and fully experience his sense of loss and culpability before he could forgive himself. You never gave him that chance and it made him resentful and bitter toward everyone and everything in his life. He compared what he had to what you had lost. Instead of being grateful for his blessings, he felt selfish for having them."

"Alright, I get it. I'm partially accountable for Wendell's problems because I dismissed his guilt so easily. How could I have known? I tried to stay in his life. He didn't just shut me out, it was everyone he knew. I tried, but I couldn't be there for him."

"That's right, but the Church can be there for him, to lighten his burden, to siphon off the negative energy that's nearly consumed him and help bring him back to self-respectability. With our help, he might even be able to reconcile with his wife and have a family again."

"So you're saying in your own convoluted way that the good you do far outweighs the bad when it comes to the victimization of our race, and for that I should be grateful to you and never bring it up in polite conversation?"

O'Herlihy laughed and clapped Archer hard on the shoulder. "And you say I'm convoluted, boy-o? That's what I've been trying to say all along. Live and let live, bygones and all that. Do I have your word or must we watch you? Others have learned of our secret before, but they could be intimidated, bribed, or killed for their silence. I get the feeling that none of that would work with you."

"I'm *au fait* with your kind as long as your bad eggs end up in the weasel's tummy. It's my friend, Trick that we may need to talk to, together, when he and I are both feeling up to it. Fair enough?"

O'Herlihy stuck out his hand. "A handshake, the gentleman's agreement has always been enough for me. I'm going to take my leave and let you rest. I'll be back tomorrow and we can talk some more. As far as the weasel's tummy, well, I'll show you soon enough." He stood up to leave then turned back to Archer. "By the by, there's been a pair of detectives looking for you.

Came here to the rectory yesterday when you were indisposed and said they needed to find you as soon as possible. What should I be tellin' them if we meet again?"

"Tell them that as soon I'm healthy enough, they'll find me back in my store and available to answer questions, sign autographs, whatever they need." He turned pensive for a moment. "I suppose there is the matter of about fifteen newly arrived vampires in New Orleans that will need to be taken care of before the body count is off the charts."

"Don't you worry lad, they're all being seen to by the Church. That's as much as I am willing or able to say on the matter. Rest well, boy-o. God knows you deserve it."

CHAPTER 39

ARCHER AWOKE TO the patter of a heavy rain on the roof of his room. He could smell the water, the unique aroma of the French Quarter; the tang of the salt from the Gulf and the earthy bouquet of the Mississippi. He stretched tentatively, his muscles pulling slightly, but not sore. He had to admit he felt pretty good. Sitting up slowly, he was surprised that his head wasn't hurting, and his energy level seemed to be back to normal.

"You look good, shugah," said a voice behind him. "Better than the last time I saw you."

"Toinetta." Turning, he saw her sitting in an austere wooden rocking chair, propelling it gently back and forth, the sound of the rain hiding an almost inaudible squeak every time she rocked back, her arms resting on her lap. "Have you been here long?"

"No, just arrived, really. Probably what woke you." Reaching down she picked up a bundle of clothes and tossed them onto Archer's bed. "I'm guessing the priest that loaned you his pajamas will want them back." She picked up the other item on her lap, a *Times-Picayune* and raised it to her face, blocking Archer from view while he changed.

When he was dressed, he stood slowly, walked over to Toinetta, and took her hand. "Toinetta, how are you feeling? With all that's been going on, I haven't been paying attention to the important things like I should have. Your energy's been down, you look pale, and..." he looked above her head, concentrating for a moment until her aura shimmered into view. Streaks of black shot through her normally brilliant rainbow-colored aura, like crude oil slicking through crystalline waters. "Toinetta, how bad is it?"

His mentor shrugged, the simple gesture reducing her for the first time from a robust, hearty woman in the autumn of life to a frail, tired, elderly lady, more comfortable in that rocking chair than Archer could ever imagine.

"I haven't wanted you to worry Archer, things have been happening with you, living things. You've found someone you can love, you're growing in spirit and power. All that's happening with me is the cycle of the cosmos."

"But you're treating it right? You're going to be alright?"

Toinetta didn't reply, she just rocked in the chair, watching him with a fond smile. "Shugah, you just hush now. When it's my time, it's time. I ain't gonna go pumping toxins and poisons into my body just to buy a few months and feel miserable. I'm treating myself with herbs, meditation, and prayer. That's all I'm willing to do and if it's not enough, then it's my time."

Archer felt a catch in his throat, his eyes stung. "If there's anything I can do to help you, you know I'm here. If you need anything special ordered from Blessed Be, I'll make sure it gets to you faster than you can imagine."

"Enough, shugah, I have everything I need, but I appreciate it. Knowing you'll be there is a great comfort, but let's not go throwing dirt on my grave just yet. I got time and I got faith. There's no end of possibility when you have that."

From the tone of her voice Archer knew better than to pursue the matter. Instead he asked, "Have you been to see Trick? How about Wendell?"

"Wendell is doing just fine; just a concussion near as the doctors can tell. But that charming Father O'Herlihy told me it was worse than that. Luca had drained much more from him than was prudent, and he had to be ministered to by their healers before he awoke."

"And Trick?"

"Shugah, he's fine as spring wine, but he's nursing a real strong hatred of these beings. I can't quite get myself to call them vampires, I've known so many priests down through the years that the only ones I could slap that label on are the ones who drink the blood of our kind, and there are human beings who do that ritually."

"Trick feels like they duped his mother and abused their position over mankind, especially the poor and the homeless. You know how he likes to crusade. I think his anger is misguided, but that doesn't make it any less real or corrosive. I promised O'Herlihy that we would talk to him together."

Archer patted Toinetta's hand, then stood up. He busied himself taking inventory of his pockets as Toinetta rose slowly to her feet. He knew better than to offer a hand, but he inched closer in case she needed him. "Am I correct in assuming we are in the rectory somewhere?" Toinetta nodded. "Then I'll call a cab to get you home and drop in on Blessed Be. O'Herlihy told me Tell is okay. Do you know if he's been minding the store?"

"On a limited basis. He and Daniella have been splitting their time between here and the store. I'm sure he's there now."

"Okay, after your cab arrives, I'll go check on in on him, maybe send him home for a break, The Goddess knows he deserves one. He was amazing, Toinetta. He walked right into a real live Hell and fought his way to my side, then we fought our way out. I can't tell you how many times he saved me that night."

"He hasn't told you, I doubt he ever would, but you should know. He almost died that night, too. When you left him with Trick and Wendell, he was ambushed and in dire straits before Wendell came to and chased a vampire off him."

"Why would he want to hide that from anyone? Just proves he was as vulnerable as any of us. We all have scars from this, why should he be left out?"

"He thought he let you down. He figured he was late getting to you, in the rectory. He met a group of priests at the landing to the second floor and believed he was going to have to fight his way through them, but fortunately, the vicar was able to convince him they were on his side and he led them to where you were battling the vampires and Luca."

"Then I didn't imagine him leading an army in white. Thought maybe I was having visions."

"Nope. He disposed of the vampires and the vicar took charge of Luca. I'm not sure what you did to him, but Tell said he was rolling around on the floor screaming, his hands clawing at his ears."

"I think you were right about my abilities growing due to my contact with a superior psychic being. I was able to form my thoughts into a focused power, once as a physical blow that knocked a vampire into the coat hooks. Then when Luca had me pinned under his psychic attack, somehow I was able to direct his own energy back to him with a little added punch."

"Hmm. You know we have had success in the past with you moving small objects small distances; telekinesis. Sounds like you've acquired a new and stronger spin on that extraordinary gift. We will have to work very hard to make sure you can control this, shugah. We can't have you getting emotional and sending someone into a wall or reducing their intellect to mental jelly."

"You won't hear an argument from me. Now let's get out of here so I can check on things and you can get home and rest. You'll always be a beautiful flower, but right now, you look a tad wilted."

She smacked his arm, but her normal vigor was lacking.

Archer walked from Our Lady of Guadalupe to the store, his throat raw like he had finished two helpings of steel wool sandwiches. Unlocking the outside door to his apartment, he went upstairs to get a cool drink and popped a throat lozenge before heading down through the courtyard and into Blessed Be. He found Tell filling the herb jars and Daniella writing labels on the empty canisters he had been saving in the back. His back-ordered stock must have finally arrived.

Tell turned for the henbane and stopped, a lop-sided grin splitting his sober face. "Archer, how the hell you feelin' man?"

Daniella looked up, set the marker and container on the counter and rushed to envelop him in a tight bear—or was it wolf hug. "Mmm. I'm so happy you're here, Shopkeeper." She released him, pecked his cheek and said, "Now you can label your own jars."

Tell laughed, a kind of high pitched sobbing that set Archer's nerves on edge, and he followed Daniella with a hug of his own.

Archer's breath whooshed out of him and the lozenge skittered across the countertop, then Tell let him go and stood back looking at him critically, like he was a sculpture at an art exhibit. Archer reached for the lozenge, decided the pain in his throat outweighed the germs on the counter glass and popped it back in his mouth. He looked around. "Everything looks good," he rasped, the first word was so uncomfortable he almost decided not to finish the sentence, but it was too important. "Thank you both for keeping her up and running. Tell, could you get me another glass of water from the back?"

"You got it," he replied and was gone.

Archer gathered Daniella into his arms and nuzzled his head under her silky tresses to her ear. "And thank you," he whispered, "For being there to save my ass."

She giggled as his breath tickled her and she pulled away, kissing him lightly on the lips. "Just paying you back for negotiating for my wolfish life and setting my broken bones for me."

"Just payback, huh?" he growled playfully

"Yep. Sorry I had to run when the priests came in. Lycanthropes kind of have a thing about getting caught outnumbered, especially by other supernatural creatures. Plus, there's an open bounty on lycanthropes placed by the Church, centuries old."

"Here's your water, Archer," Tell said as he emerged from the back room. "Oops," he said sheepishly as he set the glass on the counter, "didn't mean to interrupt nothing."

"Don't worry, Tell," Daniella replied as she moved out of Archer's grasp again. "He was just so hoarse I couldn't hear him, so I moved closer."

"Oh, if that's all—" he started.

"C'mon," Archer grumbled good-naturedly coughed. "I didn't come here to be abused; I can get that from Willig and Corgan. I just wanted to drop in and say thanks. I need to head back to the church and meet with Father O'Herlihy about some things, then go see Trick. Can you handle this busy place for a few more hours?"

"That's what you pay me for," replied Tell. "That is, if you ever get around to payin' me. You know, I'm not one to complain, but a man's got expenses. Do I get a 'save Archer's life' bonus?"

"I'll swing by the bank on the way back here with your wages. I didn't intend to spend two and a half days in bed. Sorry about the bonus, but it's store policy. If I gave bonuses everytime someone saved my bacon, I'd have to declare bankruptcy."

"Mmm-hmm. Well, we'll see you when you get back, then," said Tell lightly.

"Not me," replied Daniella blandly. "I'll finish helping Tell with the jars and I'm leaving. I'm not cut out for this 9 to 5 grind. I need to be home, luxuriating."

"Well, thanks again for the help, both of you. Daniella, may I call you for dinner again? Some oysters from Pearl sound pretty darn good for my throat."

"You have my number. I suppose I can't stop you, Shopk...Archer."

As Archer left, he heard Tellico say, "Shopkeeper? Why not call him 'bootblack' or some other type archaic romance novel terminology? Shit Daniella, that's gotta be the most pathetic pet name I've heard since I was in Angola, and most of *those* were just downright nasty."

CHAPTER 40

O'HERLIHY MET ARCHER in the reception area of the rectory, all smiles and glad-hands. "Happy to see you up and about, boy-o. I hope you feel as good as you look. Our doctor said you should be back in the pink in no time, but wasn't sure if your voice would go back to normal. I'll bet that throat of yours is sore. Can I tempt you with a nice glass of ice water?"

Archer nodded gratefully and in moments he was soothing away the rawness by nursing an ice cube, letting it trickle down his ravaged throat.

"We're going to go see your friend, Trick today, but first I wanted to let you see something else. If you'd be so kind as to follow me," he stood and began walking to the stairway that Archer had climbed just a few nights ago under much different circumstances. As he crested the top of the stairs, O'Herlihy turned and said, "Guess you're a wee bit curious about why I'm bringing you back to the scene of the crime, as it were?"

Archer nodded. "I can think of a few places I'd rather be. Even with all of the kindness you've shown, let's just say my trust in the residents here isn't that strong."

"Can't say as I blame you. But I'll lay odds we'll redeem ourselves with this." O'Herlihy reached into his pocket for a skeleton key and fit it into a door with three sets of locks. "I'm the only one with the master. No one is going to disturb this room without my say so anytime soon." Turning the knob, he pushed the door open, motioning for Archer to enter. Archer eyed the priest dubiously. "Okay then. Just trying to be polite."

They stepped into a large room devoid of any furnishing, the windows covered with heavy black out drapes. O'Herlihy ran his hand along the wall until he found the light switch and flipped it on, then closed the door behind them both.

O'Herlihy turned and pointed to a large cylindrical device in the middle of the room, the only other item to be seen was a small inactive gas powered generator beside the coffin-sized contraption. Cords ran from the box to the sockets in the walls and there was a faint whine in the air.

"What am I looking at?" asked Archer, trying to keep his syllables to a minimum.

"One state of the art, double redundant power backed, sensory deprivation chamber, lined with a formidable layer of lead to prevent stray thought waves from penetrating."

"Thought waves? You mean you've got one of your own in that thing? What the hell for?"

O'Herlihy nodded. "Let me back up a minute. I've been in touch with the Vatican over the course of the past few days and this came down from the Pontiff himself. You see, when a priest steps out of line or does something to blacken the eye of the church, he is usually sequestered, cloistered if you will, at some remote location away from prying eyes and loose tongues. Members of our orders who have taken to the bottle, or been accused, guilty or not, of molesting children are removed and intensely scrutinized to see if they may be rehabilitated."

"That sounds fair, though most people would tell you the priest belongs in jail if he is commits improprieties of that magnitude."

"Sure, and 'tis true in many cases, but fewer than you'd think. However, in this instance, The Holy Father did not take kindly to the notion of one of our own trying to usurp the natural order of things by bringing back the darkest and bloodiest time in our shared history, so a special punishment was devised." O'Herlihy walked to the metal tube and slid an outer port door opened, beckoning for Archer to see.

Floating in the chamber, his eyes covered, ears blocked with wax, arms bound to his side was father Alberto Luca Scalese. A narrow tube had been inserted into his mouth and taped fast, his nose plugged with a small plastic clip, he had been catheterized and colostomized, waste collections shunted off somewhere Archer didn't want to see. Luca seemed to sense someone was watching and he turned his head in the direction of the port hole. Archer felt repulsed but somehow gratified to see him in such a helpless state.

"Our kind cannot starve to death even without solid food nourishment. He receives an IV of saline fluid daily that keeps him hydrated and alive. He is suspended in salt water by the way, to help cleanse him of his negativity and darkness."

"A sensory deprivation chamber. Trapped with nothing but his thoughts and inner demons. Are you sure you've thought this through? He was psychotic before you put him in, he'll come out mad as a hatter."

"Or," replied O'Herlihy as he patted the cylinder, "it will give him unlimited time to meditate on why he is being punished, and he will emerge a better soul for the experience. Without no other ambition than being released from the chamber, with no stimuli, no psychic nourishment, he should be broken down and malleable in a matter of weeks. But that is not how I was ordered to handle Luca."

"What is his sentence to be?"

"Ah pay no attention to the man behind the curtain. It is best you leave the little internal matters like housekeeping to the people behind the scenes."

"After everything he's done, I think I'm entitled to know how he's going to pay for it, and I think you let me see this so you'd have an excuse to tell me, despite your orders."

"Like I said before, you're sharp as a tack, boy-o. Here's the deal. His Holiness sentenced Luca to no less than ten years in there under constant supervision. After the first ten, he will be psychically evaluated and allowed to hear again, but only masses from the Vatican will be piped in to the tube, so he might relearn his obligations to humanity. After an aggregate total of twenty years maximum, he will be removed from the chamber and taken before the Archdiocese. Based on his contrition—or lack thereof—and the Diocese's decisions, he will either be re-instated somewhere that he'll be watched closely, or re-introduced to the tube for the remainder of his natural life. Either way, he'll never bother anyone again, and he will never feed wantonly, like he did on your friend Wendell, or cause mental stress and pain like he did you."

Archer shivered. It was a waking-living death in that tube. Sensory deprivation in small doses can induce higher meditative states, even personal revelations. The thought of being imprisoned with only the prospects of death or more time in the tube, if rehabilitation failed, it was just. . . his brain rejected the word barbaric and decided on, appropriate. "Does this happen to many of your kind?"

"Just the ones who decided to recreate the Church in their own image," came O'Herlihy's cold steady reply.

"I've seen enough. I can't decide if it's more or less cruel than our death penalty or worse that human law could do to him."

"It's our law, Mr. Sweet, that your kind has perverted. Hammurabi's Code of an eye for an eye was effective, but for my race it evolved to the same basic tenet we try to force upon humanity, 'Thou shalt not kill'."

"I don't know. As a former cop, I've always been a fan of the death penalty. The crime rate for repeat offenders drops to zero and it doesn't cost the tax payers to feed, clothe, and house the worthless sacks of crap."

O'Herlihy opened his mouth to say something, but seemed to change his mind. "Let's just agree to disagree on that and go visit your friend, Trick. I understand he's back home and resting comfortably. His wounds, thank God, though more than just superficial, were not life threatening. He'll own a nice array of scars to impress the ladies."

Archer chuckled as he thought back to that not so long ago night in John LaFitte's Blacksmith Shop and the splatter of pimento. "Yeah, he can use all the help he can get, I guess."

CHAPTER 41

ARCHER STOPPED BACK in the store long enough to pay Tell with as much of a bonus as he could spare for all of the man's overtime, and helped him lock up for the night. He was uncharacteristically silent and Tell decided not to push. Archer had dealt with a lot and would discuss things if and when he was ready. Tell appreciated Archer's policy on privacy and opted to adopt it as a two way street.

Archer was upstairs, cutting up onions and ham for a sandwich when his mobile phone rang.

"Hi Archer," said Daniella, her voice cheerful but strained. "How was your big day out with the nice vampire?" His silence made her change tack and tone. "What happened?"

"O'Herlihy was alright. It was Trick that soured the milk."

"I'm afraid I don't understand."

"O'Herlihy shared some things with me this morning, Luca's punishment for one, and on the way to see Trick he told us that of the twenty-two vampires were summoned, including the two that started this whole ball of wax, only nine still survive. He was evasive about what is to be done with them, but their tenet of not killing their own kind leads to a plethora of possibilities."

"Okay. Come back to that. Where did things break down with Trick?"

Daniella asked, her voice sounding warm but detached.

"Trick's healing up nicely, the stitches come out tomorrow, but he was itchy and bitchy, completely out of sorts to begin, with since he can't be back at the Mission for a couple more days. He didn't take kindly to me showing up at his door with 'th' enemy.'"

"What did he do? Surely he heard you both out?"

"He did, but I could tell he was boiling because it looked like I was taking sides with the vampires, especially since they've taken such great pains recently to make me Zagat's rated."

"What other choice do you have? It's an unwinnable war, surely he can see that, despite his anger?"

"I told him before this all went down that once we had taken care of the immediate threat, I was going to leave things to the Church. We went round and round because he wants to expose them somehow, let people know what's being done to them, at least let them decide if they want to be victims, like Wendell. He started talking about hunting down the last of the *Invictus Morte* that Luca summoned. Father O'Herlihy chimed in and told Trick that they had corralled the remaining rogues Luca brought over and were evaluating them to determine if any could be saved since they had tasted blood."

"I thought their mantra was never to kill? What if some or none of them can be salvaged? What then?"

"One of the reasons I never liked organized religion is the hypocrisy. Evidently, if the *Invictus Morte* can't conform solely to the psychic feeding, they will be executed by designated priests of a special order, who are in O'Herlihy's words, 'sanctified to evict their souls from this dimension'."

"Well, that must have placated Trick somewhat. No one else will die because of them."

Archer shook his head, then realized she couldn't see him on the phone, "No. He wants the summoning scroll so he can see it destroyed with his own hands. After the history lessons Luca gave us on their people, I can't say I blame him, especially knowing that some of the ones the Church will bring over are bound to go rogue and kill at will until they can be tracked down. O'Herlihy didn't help much. I think he got annoyed that Trick would ask for so much. He said flat out there was no way that parchment would ever leave the Vatican possession again. The bastard as much as dared Trick to try and take it."

"Trick is smarter than that. He just needs some time to cool down and think things through. You'll see, he'll come around."

Archer's breath caught in his throat. "O'Herlihy implied heavily that Trick would not be long for this world if he made a lot of noise or created problems for the Church or Vatican security. Trick doesn't respond well to threats. He sees them as challenges to be met face on."

Daniella was quiet for a moment. "Archer? There's something I'd like you to do for me," she said urgently.

"If I can. What is it?" Archer said, standing up involuntarily at the tone of her voice.

"Could you come and open your door downstairs, it's absolutely freezing out here."

Archer charged down the steps, threw the bolt open and pulled her inside with a surprised yelp. His phone clattered to the floor as he hugged her tightly, then moved his hands to caress her cheeks tenderly, his lips joining hers before she could say anything. Her phone made a squealing sound as the two mobile units landed close enough to cause a feedback loop.

She pulled back and held him at arm's length. "Archer? We were talking about Trick."

"And we will again. Right now this is more important," he replied in a breathy rasp, picking her up and carrying her upstairs where for the second time in less than a week since they had met, she joined him on the bed.

Daniella allowed him to undress her, to let his kisses and feverish touch inflame her senses, but as his hands found her most tender of places, she shuddered and with Herculean will forced him to stop. He looked at her, tenderness, lust, and confusion chasing themselves across his face, questions in his eyes. "I'm sorry Daniella" he said as he moved away from her, to give her space between them. "It's too soon. I didn't mean to push."

"No my Sweetman, it's not too soon. I want this as much as you do; perhaps more so. But there are things we need to discuss before we contemplate being intimate."

Archer nodded then hugged her close, feeling her shiver beneath his touch. He let her go and moved off the bed, letting her dress before saying, "Okay, talk to me."

"You don't waste any time, Archer. Are you that desperate to get into my pants? Let me rephrase that," she laughed nervously as she slid into her jeans and zipped them back up.

"No need. I'm sorry Daniella. It's just when I'm with you, I'm with you. Your next breath, your next and word or movement is crucial to me. I've never felt so completely enraptured by anyone before, so lost in the moment. I guess it makes me more aggressive than I'd usually be."

"It is I who owes you the apology, Archer. I feel swept up in your energy every time you touch me; time has no relevance when I'm near you. My control is no longer absolute when you kiss me, and that frightens me more than you can imagine."

"I've learned that losing control is sometimes a good thing, but I know what you mean. You saw what I did to the vampire when I lost control."

"My fear is very much like that, Archer. If I lose control, lose my inhibition, then my beast may emerge. I don't want you mistaking that for me being wild during our love making, I might literally start changing during the act."

"So I guess doggie style has its merits." Archer queried, trying to lighten the mood.

Daniella smiled mirthlessly. "It's no game Archer, I wish it were. When I was twenty, I fell in love with a boy, Rickard, another consulate brat like me, whom I had known for years. We became serious, intimate, about the time his father decided to run for national office. It doesn't matter which country. Long story short, we were making love in the hotel where his father had stopped for a fund raiser and I, uh, bit Rickard, and started to change. He was infected with the lycanthrope virus because I couldn't control my emotions, my feelings. He became one himself at the next full moon, just as lore and legend say."

"Daniella. You don't need to—" said Archer quietly reaching for her hand.

"No. You need to know the consequences of life in my circle. He freaked out when I changed, when he saw what I started becoming, and naturally wanted nothing more to do with me. Even though I was crushed, and wanted to respect his wishes. I was compelled to warn him of what was likely to happen. He refused my phone calls and any attempts to confront him were rebuffed by his father's security detachment.

"He changed for the first time during his parent's anniversary dinner, killing his step-mother, sister and two servants before he was run off by his father's security team. His father didn't understand what had transpired, and he didn't see his son until after the funerals. While Rickard was trying to explain what had happened and how, his father put a pistol to Rickard's head and pulled the trigger, then turned the weapon on himself." She paused, tears streaming down her cheeks, her eyes more tormented than any he had ever seen.

"I'm sorry Daniella, I had no idea," Archer said quietly. She slipped her hand from his and wiped her eyes and backed away as Archer tried to comfort her.

"There's is a little bit more left to tell. The reason I know Rickard's story so well is that he told me. You see, the movies have lycanthropes pegged better than vampires, it takes silver to kill a lycanthrope and Rickard's father was slightly off in his aim. What would have slain him as human was merely a 'medical miracle'. Rickard told me his story, just before he tried to kill me. He is a wealthy individual, not without connections in his own right now, and he has sworn he will kill me himself. That is one reason why I move around so much, and that is why I cannot risk condemning you to this life with my passions."

"Daniella, I may not be rich or powerful, but I have connections locally that can help you. I'm also not without power of a different nature myself. Then there's Tell, Toinetta, even that thick-skulled jackass, Trick when he comes to his senses. If you trust them with your secret, you won't need to be afraid."

"I am not frightened of Rickard; I have even thought of giving myself to him to pay for what I did to him. My greatest fear is the other lycanthropes out there who can sense me when they are near enough. If one of the werewolf clans were to capture me, the Ulfric would most surely take me as his First. I am the only female werewolf ever to be born with the curse. There is a prophecy from ancient times—Sumerian or Babylonian, I don't know—that mentions me indirectly since I am 'born of wolf'. The Ulfric who is strong enough to dominate me can take and impregnate me. That Ulfric will have as close to a pure-blood heir as there has ever been, for all intents immortal, destined to unite all lycanthropes under one rule, assuming the reigns of every werewolf clan without a direct challenge. It's foretold in the prophecy canticles and verbal history of the race of werewolves. The Garath Counsel will never permit that to happen so they search for me as well."

"Daniella, nobody can force their will or their body on you here. This is America and we have laws. You don't have to worry—"

"Yes I do. And the fact that you are missing the point after all you know, after all you have seen, frightens me. Yes, there is human law, yes there are consequences if international law is violated, but the clans have no law but their own when they meet. The Garaths, have final say, they rule the clans as near royalty, but there is only one for each continent. The local Ulfrics control their packs and answer only to the Garath Counsel."

"Okay, you have my attention to the danger to you and the collateral damage that's possible, but back up a second. What is the Counsel of Garath?

"Garath Counsel. They are the ultimate ruling body for lycanthropes everywhere. Arbiters of local dispute, theirs is the final word. They have ruled that I am not to be touched, but the temptation to have me is too strong for many Ulfrics. It is even said that certain members of the Garath Counsel would like me for themselves."

She turned and began to walk down the stairs. "I learned today that I have been discovered by a local rogue who will no doubt try to claim the bounty on me. The incident with the vampires has drawn too much attention. I'm leaving," she choked back a sob, as she moved toward the door. "Again. At first light. I came to say goodbye, not pour out my soul. I know how to reach you Archer, but it is best if you don't know how to reach me, should anyone come asking. Please tell everyone goodbye for me. If you trust them with my secret, then I trust them, too. You can tell them the truth or make up some story, or just play dumb. They'll understand, they're good people," she smiled "and you're very good at playing dumb."

Archer rushed across the room and grabbed her arm, slinging her around with the force of her motion so she faced him but he was between her and the door. "If you're not leaving until tomorrow morning, please stay with me tonight. We can talk, or not. I just want to be near you until it's no longer possible."

She seemed to deflate, her energy spent on her revelation and tears. She walked over to his bed and dropped her back onto its yielding comfortable surface. "Hold me while I sleep, my Sweetman?"

Archer joined her silently on the bed, wrapped his arms around her and drew her long frame close to him. She sighed and nuzzled into the hollow of his shoulder, closing her eyes. Archer stroked her hair gently as he gazed down at her face. Within moments she was asleep, her breathing steady and quiet. So lost in thought was he, that he never noticed when the sun broke the horizon for the following morning.

CHAPTER 42

DANIELLA HAD AWAKENED and with one final embrace and gentle kiss on his cheek, she was gone. Walking back upstairs zombie-like, Archer went about his quiet morning ritual, cleaning out the coffee maker, then brewing a strong pot. He took a large steaming mug down to the shop with him.

The coffee scalded his lips and tongue and the chilly morning temperature bit into him unmercifully as he crossed the courtyard. Walking through the backroom, crossing the sales floor, he came to the front door and collected his *Times-Picayune*. He had given Tell the day off with his paycheck and decided he might wait awhile before opening; maybe just sit and read the paper, just disconnect his brain briefly before dealing with customers, Trick, and the problems of Daniella.

Opening one French door and reaching for the paper, he saw a pair of black wingtip shoes appear in his sightline. "I was wondering when I'd see you guys," he rasped, as he picked up the paper. "C'mon in," he was still surprised at how his own voice sounded in his ears and hopeful it would one day return to normal. "It's just me today, so I don't have to open until we're finished."

Detectives Al Willig and Tommy Corgan filed inside, and Archer closed and locked the door behind them. "I'd offer y'all some coffee, but all I have on hand is in the mug. I've got a table in the backroom, we can sit back there. If you don't mind waiting, I can go upstairs and bring down the pot."

"Thanks for the hospitality," replied Willig as he and Corgan followed Archer back to the table and took seats. "I'd like to say this will be quick and painless, but I can't make that guarantee."

"Like I said," Archer replied, "I've been waiting for you guys. I'll answer as much as I can."

"No asshole, you're gonna answer everything we ask, 'cause if you don't, we're dragging you to our house to continue the talk."

Archer looked at Corgan, gazing flatly into his eyes until Corgan blinked and looked away. "That threat is idle and you know it. You could drag me to your shop and sweat me, but unless you arrest me for something, I'm free to walk out of there anytime I choose. Are you always so adversarial to start all of your interviews, Corgan? No wonder your conviction rate is so low. I remember the good cop/bad cop routine, but your spin of stupid cop is fresh. I just don't see it as effective."

Corgan didn't reply, seething as Willig pulled out a notebook and pen, and cracked his knuckles. "You ready?" he asked, his voice mild, unassuming.

Archer sipped his coffee, and nodded.

"Let's start out broad and narrow it down as we go. First off, what the hell has been happening in my city for the last couple of weeks?"

Archer's voice was sand paper on coarse-grained wood. "You don't dance Detective. I like that. The long and short of it is what you were told by the survivors at the Moonlight Mission. There were vampires in the city, honest to God night-stalking, blood-drinking vampires."

"Were? You saying they've moved on? The last bodies we found were our patrolmen at Our Lady of Guadalupe the morning after that shit storm we responded to."

"The threat is ended, hopefully for good. Tellico Trufant and I were able to take care of things."

"Should I ask where the bodies are so we have some physical proof they existed, or am I pissing in the wind?"

Corgan interrupted before Archer could reply. "And speak of the devil, where the hell is Trufant, Sweet? That bastard tried to kill me that night. I want his black voodoo ass back in Angola, hard time."

"Yeah, I talked to Tell. He said you were a heartbeat away from not having a heartbeat because you couldn't take him at his word that the church wasn't safe."

"When you were a cop, did you believe everything a con told you? Yeah, you probably did, that's why you ain't a cop anymore."

"I'm going to say this once, not just because my throat is killing me, but because if you don't get it now, you never will. Tellico Trufant is a good man who made a bad decision in his youth and he's paid for it. I'd trust him to watch my back anywhere, anytime. I could never say the same of you Corgan because I don't and can't trust you any further than you could throw Tell. He saved you because he's willing to risk himself for others. Some might say Tell was saving an asset to the police of New Orleans," he sipped his coffee as Corgan gave a half smile. "Personally I think he's off by two letters."

Willig coughed into his jacket sleeve as Corgan colored and started spluttering. "Relax Tommy. Just contemplate the fact that your life was saved by someone you wouldn't cross the street to piss on if he was on fire. What kind of person does that makes you? I'd like to get back on track here. Where are the bodies of these things, Archer?"

"As you can hear, I didn't walk away from this adventure without consequence. I was indisposed for a few days so I don't know what happened to the bodies. Since nobody is tripping over putrid smelling things they can't see, I can only guess. Maybe they go back to where they came from or turn to dust after a time. I'd direct that question to Father Liam O'Herlihy down at Guadalupe. He's a Vatican-trained supernatural specialist. He may have precedent for this."

"How could you and Tell see them? I'm convinced something bizarre, maybe paranormal, occurred that night. I saw the blood splash and felt one of the bodies hit me as it fell, but I was blind."

Archer sighed, deciding a break from the truth was easier than trying to explain things to skeptics. "I think it's simple, really. Tellico believed in them and could see them. After I was attacked at the Mission, I was a believer too. I could see their shape, like a solid shadow. We did some research on the best way to kill them and gave it a try."

"And Trick Boulieux and Wendell Pierce could see them too?"

"You'll have to ask them, but I don't think so, since they were ambushed. I think they thought they could see them and found out too late they couldn't."

Corgan broke in front of Willig. "We did ask them. Boulieux said he'd lawyer up before he answered any questions and Pierce claims he doesn't remember anything after leaving this store until he woke up in the hospital."

"Enough, Detective. We discussed how we were going to conduct this interview, and we already have a statement from Pierce there's no reason to muck things up. I'm not trying to trip anyone up; I want answers. The man suffered a bad concussion, so I believe his story," said Willig re-establishing control of his interview.

"Douche bag's a wet-brain anyway. He was probably tanked, that's why he doesn't remember."

Archer opened his mouth to tell Corgan where he could stick his theories, but Willig beat him to the punch. "Goddamn it Tommy that's it! You haven't added anything to this investigation but dead weight and bad personal hygiene from jump. I want you out of here, now. You just lost any claim you had to this case by disparaging an injured fellow police officer and antagonizing my witness. Go on, and don't let the door hit you where the good Lord split ya." He pointed to the door while Corgan opened and closed his mouth his color reaching a vibrant shade of chartreuse Archer had never seen before. Getting up, kicking a chair out of the way, Corgan stormed off.

"Remember, you break it you buy it, asshole," Archer called scratchily after Corgan. The cop unlocked the door, threw it open and promptly fell on his face as Trold grabbed his feet and pulled them together while Berg jumped up and shoved the man hard.

Corgan didn't even look back, but Willig, who had watched it all turned his gaze back to Archer, his eyebrows raised, a grin lighting his face.

"Where'd you find trolls? They're kind of small. How old do you think they are?"

Archer laughed and looked at Detective Al Willig, reappraising him.

"Ah c'mon Sweet. I've been working this city for nearly twenty years. I've seen a thing or two and learned from it. Why do you think they assigned me head up the Task Force on the vampires? I can suspend my disbelief better than anyone else they've got."

"You're full of surprises, Detective Willig." He stood up walked over to the doors, locked them again, smiling and winking at Trold as he peeked around the corner of the occult book stand. "My coffee is cold, how about we continue this upstairs? I'll brew another pot for us."

"I could use some coffee, sure, and call me Al," replied Willig as he peered closer at Berg who was climbing the exposed brick wall in preparation of a sneak attack on the unsuspecting Trold. "I'd love to hear about these little fellas and maybe just between us," he flipped his notebook closed and pocketed it as he stood, "you can tell me how Corgan ended up cuffed to his car covered in booze. He's up for disciplinary action over that, you know?"

"Honestly Al, wish I knew something about that one. I'd love to hear what happened too. All I can say is it couldn't've happened to a more deserving guy." Archer led the way through the rag curtains out into the courtyard.

"Ya got anything to go with the coffee? I could use a bite," said Willig as Archer ushered him up the stairs.

"That's a phrase that has a much different meaning for me now, Al, but I'll see what I can rustle up," replied Archer with a laugh as he closed the door behind them.

CHAPTER 43

Detective Tommy Corgan stood against the chilly concrete wall of Blessed Be trying to slow his racing heart. He flexed his hands as he pulled on his gloves, barely noticing as he effortlessly jerked his fingers through the cheap leather, the gloves exploding, stopping halfway up his wrist.

He hadn't been this angry in years. The last time he had lost it, really lost it, was the reason he was slogging along in the fetid sewer of The Eighth District for nearly nine years instead of enjoying life back home in Hoboken, New Jersey, Captain of his own house. *Deep breaths Tommy, deep breaths. It don't mean nothing, you got thrown off the case. You got what you came for, and neither that asshole Sweet nor that aw shucks detective Willig you had to buddy up to, is any the wiser.* Corgan's temper began to fade, to slowly change as he reminded himself of the real reason he had volunteered for the half-assed Task Force assignment in the first place. *She* had been there, in that store, recently, too; unless her scent was stronger than your average werewolf. The only question he couldn't answer was whether she had been in the shop as a customer or she had been up close and personal with Sweet.

He had been waiting for years for Daniella Andrej to re-surface in New Orleans, biding his time, hoping that the mystery, allure, and relative anonymity of the French Quarter would draw her back, following any leads that might have a whiff of her about it. Rickard Gideon's private bounty for the woman's capture was so great he could retire in style and comfort anywhere, simply disappear from the stink of humanity and live in the deep forest. Maybe Montana, or Washington, even Maine, he speculated as he walked up the street to find a pay phone, stripping off the torn gloves but not discarding them.

Stopping at the first pay phone he found on Decatur Street, he wadded the scrapped gloves, one around the receiver the other over his finger, after he dropped his change into the coin slot, and dialed the number. He knew it by heart, as did any other of his kind. He wondered fleetingly as the call connected whether he should tell the local Ulfric of his discovery, cut him in on the deal so there wouldn't be any repercussions. *Nah, now I know where someone can find her for me, she's as good as got,* he decided as the phone rang on the other end. He almost giggled.

Not a good sound for a respectable werewolf, but then again, fuck it, I've won the goddamn lycanthrope lottery!

Printed in the United States
R3269700002B/R32697PG79761LVX5B/2}